# *"What Happened Today?"*

*"I heard people talking,"* she answered curtly, some of her earlier suspicions of him returning. *"They were talking about us. Something about a 'sweetheart deal.' They couldn't tell who was conning whom."*

*"Why, those stupid—"* Duke bit off the word. *"Wynn, the way I feel about you, it's a whole other thing from business."*

*"Is it? It won't work. Everyone will be saying we're in cahoots with each other. Nobody will let us be together. This is no good, Duke."*

He looked up at her and said solemnly, *"This is the only good thing that's ever happened to me. And, lady, if you think I'm giving up on you, you'd better think again."*

---

## PAT WALLACE

*is a longtime writer who models all her heroes after her husband. She lives in New York City's Greenwich Village and prefers to "travel" through her reading, since she hates to be away from her husband—or her cats—for long.*

Dear Reader:

Silhouette has always tried to give you exactly what you want. When you asked for increased realism, deeper characterization and greater length, we brought you Silhouette Special Editions. When you asked for increased sensuality, we brought you Silhouette Desire. Now you ask for books with the length and depth of Special Editions, the sensuality of Desire, but with something else besides, something that no one else offers. Now we bring you SILHOUETTE INTIMATE MOMENTS, true romance novels, longer than the usual, with all the depth that length requires. More sensuous than the usual, with characters whose maturity matches that sensuality. Books with the ingredient no one else has tapped: excitement.

There is an electricity between two people in love that makes everything they do magic, larger than life—and this is what we bring you in SILHOUETTE INTIMATE MOMENTS. Look for them wherever you buy books.

These books are for the woman who wants more than she has ever had before. These books are for you. As always, we look forward to your comments and suggestions. You can write to me at the address below:

Karen Solem
Editor-in-Chief
Silhouette Books
P.O. Box 769
New York, N.Y. 10019

# Sweetheart Contract

## Pat Wallace

Silhouette Intimate Moments
Published by Silhouette Books New York
America's Publisher of Contemporary Romance

**Other Silhouette Books by Pat Wallace**

*Silver Fire*
*My Loving Enemy*

SILHOUETTE BOOKS, a Division of Simon & Schuster, Inc.
1230 Avenue of the Americas, New York, N.Y. 10020

ISBN: 0-671-47783-8

First Silhouette Books printing May, 1983

10  9  8  7  6  5  4  3  2

For 237 past and present;
for Delois, Felix and Reggie Key;
and many thanks to Bert Rose

# Chapter 1

Wʏɴɴ Cᴀʀꜱᴏɴ ᴘʀᴇꜱꜱᴇᴅ ʜᴇʀ ꜱɪᴢᴇ-ꜱɪx ꜱʟɪɴɢʙᴀᴄᴋ ᴏɴ the gas pedal of the sporty Fiat. The game little sedan wasn't responding as it should, which was a headache on Manhattan's West Side Highway. Luckily she was near an exit. The engine rhythm was uneven—either spark plug or gas line trouble. Three generations of Carsons had driven everything on wheels; if there was anything she knew, it was an automotive off-sound.

Usually she didn't take the highway uptown, preferring the less relentless pace and the challenge of dodging traffic on Broadway, then Sixth Avenue. But this time she'd been in a hurry, having stayed later at the office than she'd meant to and expecting Howard Bartley at seven. Not that she was thrilled by a date with him; sometimes she thought he was just "too-too," as her father, Big Mike Carson, used to say. Wynn felt a snag in her breath, an ache in her small, slender throat. A whole year, and she still couldn't believe he wasn't there anymore.

She had a suspicion that Howard might have to wait. She slowed for the exit, finding herself on Washington Street, near West Eleventh in Greenwich Village. The Fiat wasn't that sick; she could easily have continued on east past Seventh, Sixth and Fifth avenues to her airy mews apartment near Washington Square. Maybe she wanted to be late tonight. Howard was just so . . . dull. He didn't do a thing for her blood pressure. If anything, he lowered it, she decided, and grinned. She looked around. The only handy parking spot was in front of a diner. Its sign read "Ceebee."

Well, well. The name was short for Citizens' Band, the radio frequency so many truckers tuned into. Wynn was well acquainted with CBs and their genially fanatic users; she'd learned CB esoterica from Big Mike and Marty, her younger brother. That reminder of her departed men warmed her heart, then saddened her. She pushed back a strand of long, honey-colored hair that had curled around her brief nose in the April wind that had whistled past her as she drove with the top down. She pulled up in front of the Ceebee and braked, sitting still for a moment, overwhelmed by memories of her family.

Wynn Carson had adored them all, from her grandfather Bill Carson, dubbed Buffalo Bill by the other truckers for the bucking rhythms of his Depression-weary rig, to her father Big Mike, born and raised on Thompson Street in a flat housing seven people, who had turned a single rig into a small trucking empire. Her brothers Greg and Marty should have been the heirs to Carson Trucking, but Marty had died in Vietnam, and Greg, to everyone's astonishment, had become a classical flutist. Luckier than Marty, he had survived the war, married a woman Wynn was very fond of and produced two beautiful children. That had left Wynn to replace Big Mike after he died following a sudden heart attack. He had had enough time, however, to make arrangements and to tell Wynn she was at the wheel. But not enough time, she reflected gloomily now, to prepare her fully for such an awesome job before she had metaphorically learned to drive. She had worked only in a junior executive position; taking the wheel had been a big step for her.

Big Mike had hoped Wynn would be a boy, but when her mother died in childbirth, he thanked "God and the angels" she wasn't, because she grew up looking just like her mother. For a time Wynn had tried not to be a girl, tried to make up for Marty. But there was no chance now—she'd been told and told—of mistaking Wynn for a boy. Her brother Greg and her sister-in-law Dolores worried about her being alone, asking how someone so stunning had "avoided" marriage for so long. That had a simple, double answer. One part, which her relatives didn't know, was her disillusionment with Don. The other, of which Greg and his wife were probably aware, was that the Carson men were a hard act to follow. The latter was a constant complaint of Howard Bartley, Councilman. Howard's Ivy League good looks, his politician's suavity, left Wynn a bit cold, even if she couldn't help being flattered by his unswerving attention.

Well, she couldn't dream all evening. She had to get out and check the car. Wynn opened the door, looking around. It was a pretty raunchy spot, one she was unfamiliar with after a lifetime in Forest Hills, Queens, then Rye, New York, and lately the prettier parts of Manhattan. This was the west side warehouse district, where truckers picked up and delivered freight. Wynn was consoled by the Ceebee's friendly proximity. She'd heard that some rather strange characters slept in empty trucks after hours.

If this had been a turnpike instead of Washington Street, she thought, the Ceebee would have been a truck stop. Here it was just a diner, she supposed, but evidently a truckers' hangout from the looks of the customers—tough but cleancut workingmen, obviously not drifters. Out of the corner of her eye, she saw some of the men at the counter swivel around on their stools to eye her. The stares were indulgent and admiring, not insolent and threatening, as they would have been in a really rough area.

Wynn was used to all kinds of male stares. She was five-feet-two, but scorned to raise her height with needle heels that would leave her tottering. She stuck to neat medium height heels that added psychologically reassuring inches and let her move with grace, holding her golden head high.

Her waist was negligible, blooming into surprisingly full breasts and soft, narrow hips. Her eyes were hyacinth blue and big as quarters, but no one could mistake their canny expression. That brightness was a plus in the tough spot she occupied at Carson's, where she suffered the handicaps of her sex, youth and size . . . and from being the late boss's daughter. Her first negotiations with the union were coming up. And, though she was armed with Big Mike's notes and reams of information, thinking about it made her palms sweat. Well, she had to forget that now and attend to the Fiat.

She went to the hood and opened it easily, peering in. Nothing grossly wrong was visible. It had to be a loose spark plug wire. She could fix almost anything in a car, but her small fingers couldn't reach under the engine far enough to tighten the wire cap over the spark plug head. It would take longer fingers to do it. Annoyed, she got out a tissue and rubbed at her hands.

Wynn straightened, dimly aware of comments and laughter from her audience in the Ceebee. She ignored them, looking around for a phone to call a Carson mechanic. Triumphant, she spotted a public booth and entered it. She should have known: The booth, like so many isolated city phones, had been vandalized.

Annoyed, she resigned herself to looking for a phone in the Ceebee. It was the only public place on the block, aside from a questionable-looking bar and a closed secondhand goods store. The interested truckers made her feel like a china doll in a bullpen, but she ignored the feeling and kept going.

After all, she thought, I'm a trucker myself and I ought to be used to them by now. Let's get moving, Wynn Carson. She kept her expression pleasantly neutral and stepped into the diner. The only other woman in the place was a middle-aged waitress with dyed red hair, a broad, maternal body and a look of habitual resignation. Everyone else was male. The counter was lined with big, long-legged men. Most of them turned and stared when she came in; a few whistled.

Wynn unconsciously enjoyed a whiff of the air, compounded of smells of iron-strong coffee—it was a cliché that truck stops served the world's best coffee—tobacco, plain cooking and that undeniably pleasant aroma of masculinity, a musky leather-denim-gasoline-crankcase oil odor that had always been Big Mike's and Marty's scent. For some reason it titillated Wynn more than usual today, maybe because she was facing the prospect of Howard's ultra-civilized cologne. She recalled her father's remark about men's "perfume" and the old days when "men were men and women were glad of it."

"Help ya, honey?" the waitress was asking.

Wynn shook off her preoccupation, embarrassed at her sudden absence of mind. Strange that the very smell of the diner had set her off like that. Maybe her friends and family had a point. Maybe she'd been alone too long. "Just coffee, please," she said hastily, returning the woman's smile. "I'm going to use the phone. Okay?"

"Sure. I'll leave your coffee right here." The waitress went to draw the strong, dark brew, and Wynn walked toward the pay phone on the wall at the end of the counter. The whole place seemed to go quiet, and she fervently wished they wouldn't stare at her so hard. But she supposed a grounded Fiat and a midget dressed by the city's choicest boutiques weren't exactly common fare in the Ceebee.

"Oh my, oh my," one of the younger men said in a soulful voice. Another laughed softly. Feeling as if she were on display in some store window, Wynn dipped into the pocket of her well-cut cream blazer and brought out a dime. The men at her end of the counter had turned very quiet, frankly listening. Out of the corner of her eye she made out one in particular. He seemed immensely tall. His long legs rested on the sill below his stool, and he was looking carefully straight ahead, as if he didn't want to be caught eavesdropping. Yet his head seemed to be turned slightly in Wynn's direction. His hair was as black as her Fiat, and he had disgustingly long eyelashes for a man, but there was nothing else soft about him. His head was like that of one of the

Caesars at the Metropolitan Museum, his body strong and slender as a Donatello. He was tanned and tough-looking, yet there was something about him that suggested command, a kind of apartness from the others. Odd. Wynn was dismayed to feel a peculiar flash of heat along her body; the light blazer, even in the cool air, was suddenly too heavy. A faint dew of moisture on her back made her silk shirt feel sticky.

The garage was answering; Wynn gave herself a mental shake. She spoke into the phone, then listened.

"Oh, for heaven's sake, Sam." She'd spoken louder than she'd intended and quickly lowered her voice. "Okay, okay. I'll have a cup of coffee. If one of the men isn't here in fifteen minutes, I'll try to get somebody else. It's all right . . . really. Yes, I'm at the Ceebee, at . . ." She leaned toward the window, straining to see a street sign, feeling stupid because she hadn't checked before.

". . . Eleventh and Washington Street," the dark, quiet giant supplied, unsmiling. He stared into her eyes. For a hot instant Wynn's mind clicked right off, and she stared back into his crow black, penetrating gaze. A word popped into her head, a word she hadn't used for years—*wow*.

She pulled herself together, nodding her thanks to the man, and repeated the location into the phone. Then, feeling her face pinken, she hung up and started back toward her stool.

"Excuse me, little lady." The tall, dark man got up from his stool, towering over her, looking down at her in a protective way. She thought, If I hear "little lady" one more time this year, I'll scream my head off. It made her feel about six inches high, ten years old and just too cute and helpless even to button her own buttons. So did this stunning monster, staring down at her now. "Can I help you?"

His companions were talking among themselves, as if eager not to interfere in the chase, Wynn's cynical judgment said. But she was set off balance by the man's voice. It had an overlay of tough New York, yet he spoke with a lucid quietness, like a man used to public speaking. It galled her not to be able to pigeonhole him.

"No, thank you very much," she said coolly, looking straight up into his eyes without a smile. "It might interest you to know that I can fix a carburetor link with a bobby pin."

The other men were frankly listening. One whistled softly and chuckled. "That's one on you, Duke," he commented.

The smiling giant called Duke took it good-naturedly. "Okay, little lady," he said to Wynn. "Whatever you say. But you were calling a garage, so I figured I could give you a hand."

He had her there. She felt the flush on her cheeks deepen. "No, thanks," she repeated. Some imp in her made her add, "Thanks anyway, beeg mayunnn."

The others caught her comeback and bellowed with laughter. A little regretful, even embarrassed, Wynn walked quickly back to her stool and sat down. She became very intent on sugaring her strong black coffee.

She felt mean—he'd been trying to help, and she'd made fun of him. But then, she reflected, he'd been making fun of her in a way, of that wretched, helpless-looking size that was so deceptive, as many a man had found to his cost. Wynn's own mother, Big Mike had said, had been about big enough to go in his pocket, but when she got her temper up, the whole male household had fled, massive as they were.

The moments crawled by and there was still no sign of a man from the garage. Wynn caught fragments of talk from the dark man Duke and his companions—"fringes . . . triple time . . . low-balling . . . retroactivity . . ." Union talk, after the years with Big Mike, as familiar to Wynn as the weather. She was sharply reminded of the upcoming union talks. Not that she had anything against Local -117. Heaven forbid. On the contrary, before the unions came, her grandfather and her father before him had suffered great privations. Buffalo Bill drove until he was almost asleep at the wheel and was a mass of aching tension, agonizing low-back pain, even damaged kidneys from the constant jolting. Now Wynn Carson was in charge. And overwhelmed. She recalled with amusement some of Big Mike's notes, hastily scribbled at the hospital: "Take care of our men," he'd written. "Trim at the top, maybe." He'd always said you didn't skim cream from the bottom; Wynn was going to reexamine their executive team. "Watch Court," Big Mike had warned.

Enough. She'd have to phone another garage. The Fiat had to be fixed. Wynn's watch said six-forty-five. Goodbye, Councilman, she said to herself with a silent chuckle.

Howard would be fit to be tied. But it was too late to call him; he'd have left at least fifteen minutes earlier. She could set Greenwich Mean Time by Howard Bartley.

Wynn felt strangely relieved to be missing the date. Howard was really the dullest man she'd ever known in her life, and she wondered why she'd ever bothered. Immediately she wondered about the very strength of her relief—he hadn't seemed so bad before. Before what? she questioned. This black-haired giant at the counter? But that was too absurd. Nevertheless, Wynn headed toward the phone again, feeling as if she'd been let out of school for an unexpected holiday.

She stiffened her backbone and dialed another garage. Busy. So was the next. She hung up, indecisive, wondering if the Fiat could wait till morning.

"Miss." She wheeled around. It was the dark-eyed Galahad again. "Look," he said soberly, "I'm sorry if I offended you. Why don't you let me have a look at your car?"

He seemed so earnest, so sincere that she relented. "All right." That sounded rude, grudging. She amended, "I mean, thank you." She grinned and his eyes lit with a black fire at the grin, his mobile, sensuous mouth breaking into a smile that revealed straight, snowy teeth, startling against the tan of his face. "Thank you very much," she repeated.

"Shall we go?" he asked softly.

Wynn put some coins on the counter, and he followed her out of the diner. As they left, she thought she heard a suggestive murmur from some of the men. Wynn had a strong suspicion that Duke wanted to look at more than the car, but concluded, What the devil; I've handled these things before.

"It's the wire cap on the spark plug head, that's all it is," she said hastily, chagrined. "So simple. The problem is, I just can't reach it."

"Is that all? It won't take me two minutes." He opened the hood and reached with unerring swiftness under the engine, his long fingers disappearing. In what seemed a split second, he'd evidently screwed the cap down tight, because he said, "There she is. Should be fine now. You want to try her, just to be sure?"

Wynn nodded, her head a jumble of conflicting thoughts—how did he know so much about sports cars? She would have assumed that trucks were his forte. What was worse, she was also thinking how exciting it had been when they were leaning close together over the hood. She was sharply aware of his clean, male-musk scent, the play of tendons along his tanned, hard-muscled arm with its springing black hairs. Another strange, swift weakness overtook her arms and legs, gathering into a hot flow in the center of her astonished being. She got into the driver's seat, her fingers shaking a little as she turned on the ignition. She tested the engine. It purred in perfect, delicate rhythm. "Great," she called out to him. "Just right." Her voice sounded high and nervous to her own ears.

She got out and reached into her cream-colored shoulder bag. He was rubbing his strong, broad hands with a handkerchief. Replacing the handkerchief in his jeans pocket, he held up his hand in a deterring gesture. "Whoa!" he ordered, laughing. "You've got to be kidding."

"But, really . . ." She noticed that his companions were leaving the diner. One gave him a neat wave good-bye.

She realized then that he'd purposely delayed her, but somehow she couldn't be offended. On the contrary, she was faintly thrilled; she could feel her heartbeat accelerate and the disturbing weakness had returned to her knees. Something about him made her feel warm and good, the way she had with her father and brother. But something else was there, too, a feeling that was anything but familial.

"No, ma'am." He looked at her, and once again she was deeply affected by those penetrating eyes, sharp and soft at once, black as the wings of a crow, deeper than midnight, with all the night's bright mysteries. He drawled, "I wouldn't know how to figure the rate for thirty seconds. Too much math for me."

She doubted that—he looked sharp as a new razor blade. Intelligence fairly shone from those deep black eyes. How did such a man get to be just a trucker? Immediately she ridiculed herself. Big Mike had been "just" a trucker once. And look what Carson Trucking was today.

Now, for some reason she couldn't—or didn't—want to name, she wanted to delay this man a little. "I guess," she said companionably, "the Fiat looks like a kiddie car next to your rig. Where is it—over there?" She indicated a group of trucks across the street.

He looked nonplussed for an instant, which puzzled her. Then he answered quickly, "No. As a matter of fact, I don't have my . . . rig with me." She wondered at the hesitation. Surely *rig* was a common enough term to a trucker. He really was most unusual.

"And your friends have gone," she said with sudden realization. "I've done you out of a ride. Do you have far to go?" He shrugged, smiling. "I do feel bad," she added. "Can I drop you somewhere?"

Wynn surprised herself. Never in her life had she taken up like this with a perfect stranger, then offered him a ride. But there was something about the man that made her trust him, something that made her feel he was family. Maybe because he was a trucker. But that was silly. There were thousands of truckers in the world, and she'd never reacted to one like this. This was the most exciting man she'd ever run into; that was the answer. Duke was the best-looking man she'd ever seen. It was as simple as that, and the conclusion made her suddenly shy, hesitant.

He must have sensed it, because he asked softly, "Are you sure?" Those disturbing, level eyes, shiny as hard coals, bored into hers.

"Yes, of course. Quite sure." She didn't look away. She had an odd, chilly feeling that the words referred to more than just a ride.

She got into the driver's seat and shut the door as he folded his long length beside her. "A little snug for you," she remarked with a nervous giggle, wishing to heaven she could simmer down. It was worse than ever, having him so close, with his hard thigh brushing hers, a casual movement of his bare arm letting her feel the surprisingly soft black hairs on his forearm. His size, his massive strength, seemed to dwarf the small car almost as much as her. She thought, If my hands weren't on the wheel, they'd positively flutter. She had never been the fluttering type.

"Where should I drop you?" she asked, her voice still sounding high and thin, although she forced a casual tone. She idled the motor, glancing at the warehouses across Washington Street, the yards of empty trucks, glancing everywhere, anywhere but at him.

"To dinner with you, if you really want to know." Her heart thudded. Things were going too fast for her. She felt a little afraid, yet exhilarated, just the way she did in the car when she "high-balled" it, the trucker term for putting on speed.

"How about it? Have dinner with me . . . please."

Wynn hesitated. All of a sudden she knew it would be almost painful to see him go away. How she could know that so surely, so fast, she couldn't imagine, could hardly believe. But she did. The idea was so overwhelming that she got a funny, empty feeling in the pit of her stomach. She took a deep breath and said, "I'd like that. Where should we go?"

He grinned, and again that white grin in the tanned face did something to her pulse, tugged at every motion. "It should be someplace . . . loose, the way I'm dressed. Maybe I should go back to my place and change."

"Oh, don't do that," she protested. He looked pleased at her reply. She hoped he hadn't heard its hidden meaning—she hated the thought of even a brief separation at this moment. And that idea frightened her. She had not been dependent on any man since Don, and she didn't want to be. Get hold of yourself, Wynn Carson, she commanded, and managed to say casually, "I know just the place. The street's so narrow you can't park a bicycle, and you can't get there from here, but we'll manage." She laughed, feeling a bit more at ease when he laughed, too, at her reference to the twisting and turning Village streets.

"I don't really know the Village that well yet," she remarked. "I've only been living here a few months."

"Oh? I was born here. On Bleecker Street. I know it like the back of my hand; I can get us there. Where is the place?"

She blushed. "I can't even tell you. I just know how to get there. It's on West Fourth Street."

Wynn felt his glance as she maneuvered east. I was right to compare him to Marty and Big Mike, she thought. Bleecker and Thompson streets have a lot in common. She had a feeling that Duke was Italian, judging by the nightlike blackness of his eyes and hair, his gallant attitude and the Roman cast to his features, the almost operatic handsomeness.

She found a parking place on Perry Street and pulled in. "It's just about a block from here," she explained.

Duke was quiet all of a sudden. She wondered if he could be uneasy about her choice of a restaurant, if what she considered casual would seem so to him.

They got out and walked down West Fourth Street. She decided to chance speaking her mind. "Don't look so nervous," she teased him. "We're not going to an uptight place. Below this blazer beats the heart of a plain-living dame."

He beamed down at her, almost colliding with a roller-skater in jogging shorts, then with a lithe young man carrying a huge striped laundry bag.

"Oh. Sorry," Duke apologized to both, stepping down off the curb to let the second man pass. When he stepped onto the sidewalk again, the narrowness of the way made it necessary for them to walk close together. Wynn's heart pounded when Duke's hard thigh brushed hers.

"A 'dame' doesn't cut it. You strike me as a lady who's also a woman," he remarked in a soft tone.

She felt such a glow that she fairly floated the rest of the way. As a matter of fact, after they waited for a cab to pass and Duke put his strong hand under her elbow to cross the street, he practically lifted her onto the curb by the Spanish restaurant on the corner.

He laughed. "Hey, I'm sorry. You're just so light you bounced up like a balloon." He made her lightness sound so endearing and attractive that she

was actually glad to be small, the first time that had
ever happened to her. There had been nothing
condescending in his remark. On the contrary, he'd
made her feel feminine, pretty, protected and secure. And the comment made him, in turn, seem big
as a building, massive as a tractor trailer that could
pull twenty tons of freight. The contrast between
them was even more marked. It titillated her enor-
mously, and she had a sudden, wild desire to know
what his arms would feel like around her.

Wynn flushed. When she paused at the russet sign
a few doors down the street, over an easy-to-miss
doorway, he exclaimed, "Fedora's! Well, I'll be
damned." Wynn stared at him.

It couldn't mean he didn't like the place, because
his grin was wide, his eyes gleamed. "So you like
Fedora's," he said with great softness.

"Oh, yes. I've only been here twice," she said,
"but I love it. The food's wonderful."

"You're telling me! I've been eating here all my
life. Fedora's has been here since the Fifties. Well,
this is really something. Madame?"

Carefully she went down the steps to the below
ground-level restaurant, blinking a little as she entered the dim-lit, long, pleasant room with its lanterns, cream-colored walls and homey, relaxed air.

Wynn had liked it from the first—the neighborhood people lining the small bar at the left as you
entered, the comfortably spaced tables and hand-
lettered wine list on cardboard tacked to the big air
conditioner. To the right were portholed doors la-
beled "Fedora's Kitchen." People dressed any way
they wanted, from jeans to business clothes, and the
food and wine were superb and very moderately
priced.

As she smiled at a waiter she knew, Wynn heard

Duke call out, *"Enrico! Come va, paisan?"* and turning, saw the genial, gray-haired man behind the bar light up like a hundred-watt bulb, holding out his arms and answering, *"Donato . . . figlio! Bene, bene.* And you, how's it going?"

*"Molto bene,"* Duke emphasized, cocking his head at Wynn. Her face colored, whether from embarrassment or delight, she wasn't sure. Maybe both. She listened to Duke saying something about *"cavallos,"* and knew enough Italian to guess that Enrico played the ponies.

"Who is this gorgeous creature?" Enrico demanded. "I believe I've seen this lady here before. She's somebody you don't forget."

Wynn realized, dismayed, that Duke didn't even know her name. Quickly she held out her hand and murmured, smiling, "I'm Wynn Carson."

Out of the corner of her eye she saw Duke give her a look, partly grateful, she supposed, for her quickness, but compounded of something else, too. Something she couldn't quite read. Whatever it was, he recovered from it in record time, agreeing fervently with Enrico. "You've got *that* right." Then he glanced at the big clock over the kitchen, adding, "It's too early for Fedora, I see."

"Oh, sure, you know. About eight, eight-thirty." Wynn recalled that on her previous visits, between eight-thirty and nine at night, a petite gray blond woman, stunningly dressed in either gray or off-white, had made her appearance in the restaurant. It had been a charming, almost theatrical entrance; Fedora circulated swiftly from table to table, speaking to customers she knew, leaning to kiss someone's cheek, exuding warmth, vitality and graciousness.

Wynn had been amazed when one of the waiters told her Fedora had celebrated her sixtieth birthday.

The woman looked no more than forty at the most, reed-slim and incredibly chic, with short gilt hair, thin, fine-featured face, twinkling brown eyes and unlined skin. Her granddaughter's drawings adorned one part of the wall, and there were some very jazzy photos and cartoons of Fedora herself at intervals.

"Take that table, Duke," Enrico invited, nodding toward an isolated table in an alcove near the door.

"All right?" Duke asked Wynn.

She nodded. "Fine." They exchanged a quick look. All in an instant her appetite completely drained away.

When a handsome waiter who looked like a dancer "at rest" had taken their drink order, Duke remarked, "I'm sorry you won't meet Fedora. I call her my aunt, because she and my mother are like sisters. Enrico's her husband."

It seemed a strange and wonderful coincidence to Wynn. "Oh, I have met her. She . . . kissed me one night, when I was eating here alone and feeling a bit blue. It was the nicest thing. Maybe it was because we're both small and she empathized with me." Wynn laughed.

Duke looked serious. "Don't you believe it. She never does that unless she likes somebody. She's no phony, that lady." He was staring at Wynn in a new way—still with admiration, still warmly, but with that something else she couldn't figure out.

Their talk languished, as if both of them were finding it harder and harder to find something casual to say. As if, Wynn decided with rising excitement, there were things they were too new with each other to say yet.

When the waiter brought their drinks, Duke lifted his glass to her; they touched glasses. "To a very special night," he murmured, looking into her eyes.

She repeated the toast but had to look down. She was reluctant to let him see what might be in her eyes—an alien discovery, an almost unwilling openness. A sense of vulnerability that in all her twenty-nine years had never possessed her this way before.

He seemed to intuit her hesitation, her slight withdrawal. She was impressed by his apparent sensitivity when he abruptly changed the subject. "I love this place," he remarked in an easy tone. "Everybody here, including the waiters and kitchen help, is special." Seeing Wynn relax, he went on, "There's Joe the salad man. He and the 'pearl diver'—the dishwasher—Al, have a heavy punching bag in the back yard. Al set it up. We've all worked out on it from time to time. That Al is something else," Duke added, grinning. "I've talked to him a lot when I've come in here early. He's been everywhere, done everything, from shrimping to carpentry to selling mutual funds. He's brilliant, and a painter, too. I saw some of his stuff. Right now he's recovering from the sauce—the booze—and this is kind of a temporary job for him."

"I think I know the one you mean," Wynn said. "A good-looking man, very muscular, with an intense face. I like him."

"Hey, just a minute," Duke protested with a smile. "You're making me jealous." She looked straight into his eyes, absurdly thrilled by the light comment. Now she knew he could read her face and hastened to sidetrack him.

"Oh no," she said quickly. "He reminds me of one of my uncles. The reason I like him is the way he is with his wife, or girl friend. He never seems to look at women much, but once when I was here his friend came in and he lit up and kissed her in front of everybody. It was interesting, because she looked so chic . . . and she brought him some books. I like it when a man is a one-woman type . . . like my father, I guess." She blushed, feeling she might have said too much.

"I like it, too." Duke suddenly looked very open, serious. "That was Vivian. She's a writer, had four or five books published. I think they're going to get married pretty soon."

"Oh, that's nice." It was nice, she thought. They seemed to go together. But then it occurred to Wynn that this was a pretty heavy subject to discuss with a man she'd just met. She hurried on. "You've probably heard of my father. Big Mike Carson."

He didn't seem as surprised as she'd thought he would be. But his comment was sincere. "Sure. Who hasn't? He was quite a guy. I guess it must have . . . broken you up pretty bad when he died."

"Yes. Oh yes." She heard her voice shake. But she managed a trembly smile and remarked, "In his own words, 'Life is a celebration, not a wake.' And I don't want to make a wake out of this."

"This?" Duke picked up her hand and kissed the palm, much to the interest of Enrico and the waiters. "Nothing could do that, Wynn Carson." He took her other hand and turned it over in his, the smallness of her fingers dwarfed in his huge palm, and kissed it, too. A hot, throbbing tingle began in her hand, spreading up her arm to her breast, then swooping to the very center of her body. She'd never felt such an instant thing with a man before, not that her experience had been that vast. There had only been that one disastrous affair with Don, but even that had not been like this—this lightning, this glory.

She felt as if she were totally losing control. All of a sudden she wondered what she looked like; she hadn't looked in a mirror for hours.

It was wonderfully reassuring to hear Duke say, "You are so beautiful, the most beautiful woman I've ever seen in my life."

Her wineglass was arrested halfway to her lips; her fingers shook. Carefully she set the glass back down, incredibly touched by what he'd said, even if she'd heard it many times before.

Duke's words broke into her silent reverie. "Oh, thanks, Gene." The handsome waiter was setting their dinner before them. Duke had ordered Fedora's famous meat loaf for both of them. "This is the only place you can trust meat loaf, right, Gene?"

"Right on, Duke. You know what's in it here. Some places you have to wonder *who's* in it." The waiter chuckled and completed his service, then went lithely away.

"That gag was a little raw," Duke apologized.

"I loved it." Wynn laughed and met his eyes again. "It's the kind of thing my dad would have said." There was an earthiness in Duke that appealed strongly to Wynn. Her relatives would have described him as "all right," high praise from a male Carson. She almost said so, but was afraid she might have given away too much of herself already. Instead she said lightly, "Now, fair's fair. I've told you my name. What's yours? Duke or Donato? Were you christened Duke?"

"Mostly by the . . . truckers. Enrico said my 'church name,' Donato. Latin for 'gift of God,' my mother's idea. A sweet lady. But some potatoes for a mug like me, huh?" He looked sheepish.

She thought, The way you make me feel, it's a perfect name. Trying not to let him see that, she prodded, "And the last name?"

His smile froze on his face. His black glance dropped to the straw-jacketed wine bottle on the table. "Bardolino, like the wine. Would you believe it? I'm a good label."

For a second she didn't believe it; she thought he was kidding her. Maybe he was married. Maybe that was why he was giving her the wrong name. But would he have come to this place, where they knew his own mother, if he were married? Wynn didn't know. She was confused, apprehensive.

"I'll try," she answered. Some of the warmth and easiness had left her voice. He picked up on it right away. He set down his fork and reached for her hand.

"Believe me," he said in a pleading tone, "I'm not on the lam. Or a junkie. Or a runaround or a married man. I don't go that route, never have."

"Please. You don't have to . . . explain anything to me," she said coolly. The food, appetizing as it looked, was suddenly repugnant. Her whole body was in turmoil; she cared too much for this man much too soon, and she just didn't know how to handle it.

"Oh yes, I do," he said firmly. "I have to . . . it happens to matter to me what you think. A lot. I mean, what you think of me." He studied her closely. "Something's wrong, Wynn. I've done something, said something. Damn. Things were going along so nice with us."

"They still are." She lightened her tone and smiled.

"But you're not eating," he protested, looking at her plate. "But I'm not either," he admitted, laughing at himself. "All of a sudden I'm not hungry at all."

Oh, Donato, she said silently, I'm not either. The plain fact was, she wanted him too much. She had a feeling he felt the same way.

He looked around. "There are a lot of things I'd like to . . . say to you," he began. His voice sounded strained, excited, almost choked. "Somewhere quiet."

"I know." For the first time, Wynn didn't have that here-we-go-again sensation, that sinking feeling when the expected suggestion came. This was utterly, totally different. The whole world felt new and different, even herself—most of all herself. She didn't even know the woman she had become.

"I'd just like to get out of here," he said. "Take a walk . . . a drive. I could talk to you forever."

"I feel the same way," she confided, her voice so low he had to lean forward to hear her.

"But, *mamma mia*, Enrico's gonna have a stroke," he declared, starting to grin. "No one ever walks out on a Fedora specialty."

Wynn could feel the laughter bubbling up inside herself in response to his. It was very infectious, his hearty, almost gasping laugh, as vital as everything else about him was. "But what can we do?" she protested. "We can't just throw it under the table." She giggled.

The juvenile humor set him off, and they both burst into helpless laughter. Her eyes watered; she gasped for mercy, her stomach muscles hurting. Then, as suddenly as it had come, their laughter died and they looked at each other solemnly, almost grimly. A feeling this strong can almost make you grim, she thought, and felt that he was getting her vibrations just the way he had several times before. There was a true rapport between them.

"Look," he started, drawing a shaky breath, "let's pick at this and get out fast. Otherwise there'll be a *trambusto*, a hassle. Enrico will send the food back to the kitchen and yell at the cook; then Fedora will

come downstairs and yell at Enrico for yelling."
Duke grinned.

"We'll do the best we can," Wynn assented. They
fiddled with their meat loaf, poked at the salad and
took bites of their bread.

"I can't do any better," she said at last.

"I can't either," he confessed. "You'd never think
it to look at me, would you?"

"No." She stared at his hefty torso and muscled
arms. "You don't look like a picky eater."

"A vulture, usually." His black eyes gleamed.
"Shall we?" He signaled for the check. The waiter
brought it quickly and Duke threw some bills on the
table, hardly glancing at them. She couldn't help
being a little surprised at this rather cavalier attitude. Truckers were well paid, but all the same . . .
Still, she knew that he wasn't trying to impress her.
A juvenile trick like that seemed beneath him. He'd
been too up front about himself, his origins. This
was another small puzzle.

But she forgot it when Enrico predictably called
out, "Everything all right? Something wrong with
your dinner, Duke? If you don't like it, we can get
you something else, you know. Don't go running
out."

Wynn repressed a giggle. Duke reassured him,
"Everything's just great, Enrico. We didn't realize
how late it was, that's all. Have to get to one of those
seven-thirty curtains. Take care."

In a flurry of loud comments and farewells, they
stopped an instant by the bar where Enrico presided.
Wynn caught a glimpse of herself in the mirror. She
looked like a stranger to herself, another woman,
wide-eyed, glowing. They soon managed to escape
up the stairs to West Fourth Street.

It was nearly dark, that beautiful blue semidarkness that made spring nights so lovely in New York. Wynn took a deep breath. The exit should have made them laugh again, but suddenly neither of them seemed to feel much like laughing. It was odd that he had mentioned the theater, she thought. Some kind of curtain *was* going up for them.

Someone was playing a clarinet in an apartment on Perry Street. The horn was a plaintive, haunting sound in the failing blue light, piercing Wynn like the stare of Duke's black, glittering eyes. A cold thrill shot along her nerves when he looked at her again; she felt a winglike flutter inside her body. It was like the premonition of an unknown glory, the coming of a cataclysmic change.

# Chapter 2

"'SEVEN-THIRTY CURTAIN,'" DUKE REPEATED MOCK-ingly as they walked toward Perry Street. "It was nearly seven when we got there." He chuckled. "I should be able to think on my feet better than that."

That last expression puzzled Wynn. People who "thought on their feet" were generally public speakers, people in command of something or other. Why would a trucker have to do that?

But the small, teasing mystery was blotted out of her mind when they crossed the street between the Spanish and Japanese corner restaurants and Duke touched her elbow. Even the slight touch through the fabric of her silk blazer set her skin on fire. Wynn's knees felt so weak that she was afraid they were going to buckle. If his grazing fingers could do that, she thought in wonder, what would his kiss be like? She'd never felt like that before about any man, and it set her totally off balance. It was so thrilling that it transformed everything: The narrow Village street suddenly looked like a street in Paris; the small, plain brick houses containing walk-up apartments might have been artists' garrets right out of *La Boheme*. Even the scrubby, cockeyed trees that impeded their progress took on a new beauty and charm.

She was too breathless to reply to his comment. And all of a sudden he was very silent, too. A rising tension seemed to have taken hold of him, as it had of her. She glanced at his profile, so like that on an old Roman coin, so far above her. He looked solemn, almost sad, and she wondered if the depth of his feelings matched her own. The light graze of his fingers on the small of her back as they crossed the sparsely trafficked street with slow steps ignited another quick fire in her.

The hidden clarinetist reverted to scales. Nervously, feeling that she should say something, Wynn blurted, "My goodness, he sounds as dedicated as Greg."

"Greg?" She glanced up at Duke again and saw a peculiar glint in his deep, black eyes, a stiff expression around his mouth.

Feeling foolish, she explained, "My brother." Of course Duke couldn't have known who she was talking about. She was touched, absurdly elated, to see his lips relax, the hard sharpness leave his eyes.

"Oh," he said, smiling. His relief was plain. "I thought that might be your boyfriend."

"I don't really have one," she said with rash quickness. As Duke bent to open the car door for her, his tanned face lit up. It matters, she thought with delight. I think it really matters. She got into the driver's seat, and he shut her door.

When he got in the passenger seat, he asked, "Your brother plays the clarinet?"

Fighting the distraction of his nearness, the sensation of his massive body so close to hers in the little car, Wynn managed to answer with a measure of calm, "The flute. Can you imagine? Big Mike's son?"

Duke laughed. "It's hard," he admitted. "How did that come about?"

Wynn rushed into speech, telling Duke that Greg had been the "runt of the litter," only five feet ten in comparison to Big Mike's and Marty's six feet two and four, and not as strong as the others. "He's more like my mother . . . and me," Wynn added. She realized why she was talking so much—she was postponing the moment of deciding on their destination. She felt a strong temptation to invite Duke back to her apartment, something she rarely did with a man. She was not only fastidious, but a very up-front woman. She had told her more sophisticated and uncomprehending women friends that she never started anything she didn't intend to finish, that if there wasn't going to be any hanky-panky—and there never was—she just didn't invite a man to her place.

The others either said it was "all part of the game" to keep a man guessing, or they were more "liberated" in their attitudes toward sex. Not Wynn Carson. She had hardly ever asked even Howard to come in after a date. And now she was contemplating extending an invitation to this perfect stranger.

"Where would you like to go?" Duke asked her softly. His change of subject was not rude, but somehow eager and beseeching. Something cool melted inside Wynn. She said simply, "Home."

Their eyes met. He didn't say a single word, but

the light in his eyes spoke poems and sang ballads to her; a slow, incredulous smile broke out on his hard, tanned face, and he nodded. When at last he spoke, his voice shook a little. "That sounds just wonderful."

She felt a little apprehensive then and added quickly, "The least I can do is return your hospitality with a drink, since you've been so nice."

He didn't reply to that, and she realized how false it had sounded. She probably wasn't fooling him any more than she was fooling herself. Maybe he'd take it at face value, a friendly gesture without overtones of seduction. She just didn't know. His face gave nothing away, but as she glanced at his big hands on his knees, she thought they looked tense and expectant. She couldn't deny that she wanted him to kiss her, to hold her; she wanted to feel the hardness of his arms, his big, lean body.

The thought was so disturbing that she started the car a little awkwardly, for all her usual expertise. She'd been driving since she was sixteen, but suddenly she felt as if she were just learning. Everything felt new and different beside the man called Duke. They drove east. The Village streets and scenes looked different, too, more interesting and colorful, just as the houses and trees had looked on West Fourth Street.

"Here we go again," she remarked, laughing a little as they drove down Perry Street toward Seventh Avenue South. "We can't get there from here either. At least, not easily." She felt she had to keep chattering to cover her tension, but this was just making it worse. Her turn onto Seventh Avenue was incredibly amateurish for a seasoned driver.

"Where is your place?" he asked gently.

She told him, and he said, "Oh, that's easy

enough. I'll give you the best route." Wynn felt his probing glance on her.

"I walked from Fedora's last time," she explained, driving perilously close to a southbound taxi. "Duke . . . do you think you'd mind taking over? I'm really not driving well tonight. And since you know the best way . . ."

"Sure," he said easily. "Pull over right here." She found a convenient spot, and they exchanged places. Seeing him at the wheel, she felt utterly relaxed, impressed with his ease in a sports car. She supposed, though, that a trucker could drive anything.

He handled the car with a casual competence that she greatly admired, guiding it through the twisting and turning streets toward the east. "You said you had another brother," he remarked companionably.

"Marty." Her voice trembled. "He was killed in Vietnam."

"That's right, he got it in 'Nam," Duke answered in a gentle, regretful tone. "I'm sorry, Wynn. I should have remembered that."

Should have remembered, she repeated silently. Why? She wanted to ask, but somehow couldn't. Instead she said, "You were there, too, then. Everyone who was calls it 'Nam."

"Oh yes," he said soberly. Negotiating a knot of tangled traffic on Sixth Avenue, he kept his eyes carefully ahead, but she felt that he was checking her out on the rim of his vision, leaning toward her a little as if in empathy. "You've had it pretty rough, lady, losing your brother and your father. Good thing there's somebody left."

"Greg is a dear," she agreed. "I'm grateful for him . . . and Dolores, his wife. They've made me an aunt, too. The children are darling."

"You like kids," he stated. It wasn't a question.

"I love them," she said simply.

"So do I." This time he glanced aside at her, and his face was warm and open.

Oh dear, she reflected. Every time I talk about anything it seems to be a little indiscreet. I've only known the man a few hours, and already I'm talking about children. She blushed. He must have caught it, because he grinned and said, "That's not a mortal sin, you know."

She didn't answer, thinking how little she knew about Duke Bardolino—if that really was his name. That matter still bothered her a bit, but she resolved not to think about it. Now, this moment, was all that mattered. She was too happy, too warm and elated sitting close to him, to let anything spoil it for her. No, she decided, the words singing silently to her, this magic must not be shadowed or marred. Such loveliness had never come to her before, and she wanted to keep it, to treasure it, as long as she could.

"Here we are." He braked before the grilled gate to the mews.

"It's locked," she explained. "I'll get it." She got out and unlocked the gate with a key from her key case of lilac leather. Then she got in again, directing him to the garage under her place.

When they came out of the garage, he looked around the sequestered, tree-shaded group of trim, beautifully preserved carriage houses. "It must be hard to get a place here," he commented. "It's beautiful."

"Almost impossible," she said wryly. "A city commissioner just happened to move out to Westchester when her term ended." Wynn suddenly realized that this might sound snobbish and elitist and regretted the explanation, but Duke didn't seem at all overwhelmed, and she decided, I mustn't be silly. He can't think a pauper could afford this place, anyway.

When she unlocked the door to her apartment, she realized what a landmark occasion it was.

"This is a gorgeous place," Duke commented in a quiet voice. "Like you."

She was more gratified by that than anything else she could remember at that moment.

"Some smart decorator," Duke added.

"Thanks. The decorator was me." Wynn was prouder than ever now that she had dismissed a decorator in utter frustration and found her own perfect style.

"Twice as smart," he commented, grinning. His black eyes gleamed with admiration. "Some people pay a decorator a fortune and still don't get what they want."

"Please," she said. "Sit down. What would you like to drink?" She took off her blazer and draped it over a chair in the foyer, tossing her cream-colored bag onto a side table.

"Pardon?" He had been so intent on his examination of the apartment that he started. "Sorry. Anything. Scotch and water, if you have it." He smiled at her and her heart turned over. Not only was he as beautiful as a Roman warrior, she thought, he had intelligence and taste.

"Mind if I look around?" he asked, still on his feet.

"Of course not. Be my guest, which is what you are." Her laugh came out high and nervous again, and it was almost a relief to walk away from him to busy herself at the little bar, pouring out a scotch and water for him in a massive Swedish tumbler, sherry for herself in a minute etched goblet. Even the glasses, she reflected, as she prepared the drinks with trembling hands, reminded her of how deliciously opposite they were. He was so big, so heavy and strong. He made her feel like a leaf in a windstorm.

He sat on the long gray blue couch. When she handed him his scotch, their fingers brushed, igniting once again the blaze that was so confounding and so new.

"Thanks." Duke saluted her with the massive tumbler, then barely sipped from it, setting it down on the oblong milk-glass coffee table in its swirling driftwood frame. Almost gingerly she sat down on the other end of the couch. Not touching her sherry at all, she put the goblet down on the table a little distance from his tumbler.

"This place . . ." he began. "It's so much like you, Wynn Carson. I don't know much about these things, but it seems to me I see the color of your eyes all around me."

"My sister-in-law talked me into that." Wynn smiled. "She has a thing about blue eyes; Greg's eyes are blue. Dolores is dark." Wynn's glance took in Duke's own vivid darkness: the night-blackness of his hair, so black it almost had a sheen of blue; his onyx brows; those deep, mysterious eyes. Then she, too, looked swiftly around, happy to be offering him the serene beauty of this place. The furniture was a mixture of the treasured old, from the family house in Rye, which she had reluctantly put up for sale—it would have been absurd, as well as sad, to live there by herself—and the startling, attractive new.

Three of the living room walls were ivory, one hyacinth blue; the carpet was the same pale blue gray as the couch, giving one the casual feeling of almost sitting on the floor. Here and there, in accessories—pillows and small pieces of furniture—

were touches of clear, bright yellow, subdued magenta and golden green. The colors always reminded her of a terrace garden by the water, filled with daffodils and roses.

Duke got a cigarette, offering her his pack. His hands were unsteady. She shook her head, smiling. He replaced the cigarette in the pack and slowly put the packet on the table next to his drink. The silence between them was almost palpable, vibrating with unspoken words, crackling with the tension she had felt in them both ever since she had first looked at him in the Ceebee.

"Would you like some music?" she asked, to break the tense, ringing silence. His face drooped a little, but he said politely, "That would be nice."

She got up and switched on the tape deck. The trill of a flute concerto filled the dim room, lit by only one rosy lamp. Wynn recalled that she had last been listening to a recording of her brother's; it occurred to her that this music might be a bit rarefied for Duke Bardolino.

"I hope this is all right," she said almost apologetically as she returned to the couch, to sit where she had perched before.

"All right?" Duke grinned his slow, enchanting grin. "Mozart seems just right for this place . . . for you. I've always thought that flutes sounded like little birds."

She was astounded by his instant recognition of the piece, overwhelmed that this virile, tough man could even think something like that, much less say it. That's the sign of a real man, she thought, thrilled and titillated. He wasn't afraid to be thought effeminate or odd. He was secure in his unmistakable masculinity. It occurred to her that if Howard had said the same thing, he would have sounded effete.

"I've always envied birds," Duke said dreamily. "Flying so high and so free. I always wanted to be a pilot," he said, chuckling. "And where did I end up? In a tank. More like me, huh?"

She smiled at his joke but didn't know quite how to answer him. All she could look at was his mouth, and she was avid now to know what it would feel like, taste like. To divert herself—and him—she started to chatter. "That's Greg on the flute. Isn't he good? I was amazed when he told me Mozart didn't even like the flute. Imagine composing something like that when you felt that way . . ." Her voice died away.

Duke was staring at her with a half-smile on his sensuous lips, as if he weren't listening to her words anymore, only the sound of her voice. His breathing quickened. Almost unconsciously she moved closer to him on the couch.

"Wynn. Lovely Wynn." She could stand it no longer. She moved toward him, and he grabbed her by the shoulders with his steely fingers, as if he never wanted to let her go. He pulled her toward him, and now his tanned face was so close to hers that his eyes' black fire filled all her vision. She could see nothing but his eyes. She felt his hot, excited breath on her mouth and the wild, barbaric fever possessed her more strongly than before, that aching desire to know the taste of his lips.

Lightly she touched her mouth to his; then, suddenly, the touch was no longer light and tentative. His mouth had taken all of hers, caressing, tasting, wandering to learn the shape of her lips as if by Braille, until she and Duke were locked to each other's bodies, moaning. His thrilling hands stroked her trembling, vibrant sides; her small hands stole about his muscular neck to draw his head down to hers. The endless kiss was a shattering, titanic thing, and she felt as if the whole universe was centering on their melded mouths, whirling, whirling telescopically outward from that small, fevered, savage core that was their overpowering caress.

There was no time or space or meaning for her beyond the stunning pressure of his mouth, outside the tight, bruising circle of his massive arms. Under her closed, fluttering lids she saw repeated light explosions of little gold white stars and jagged redness. She realized that she was stroking his hard face, making faint, pleading sounds deep in her throat. Something in her was crying out, Forever and ever; this must be forever. I can't let go of him anymore.

At some point in their frenzy they were gasping, gasping for breath. He moved his mouth a millimeter away, speaking against her lips' softness. "Wynn, Wynn, my God, I've ached for this from the minute I first saw you. I still can't believe this; I can't believe it," he whispered, shaken.

"Neither can I," she murmured, her mouth still against his, tickling his lips with her speech. Groaning, he took her lips back again, and once more the world stopped turning.

At last, with an almost aching reluctance, their mouths let go, but he gave her nibbling kisses on her upper lip, her cheeks, her nose, until she felt as if her whole body was streaming fire. She was a hot, rushing fountain of flame, a storm of wild and obsessive need. His full, firm mouth gently touched her closed eyelids, first one, then the other, as he thrust his fingers into her tumbled hair, stroking and kneading her small neat head between his huge hands until he made her plead in a small, weak voice

she hardly recognized, "Oh, Duke, Duke, please
. . . please."

Astounded, she knew she was asking him to make
love to her. He stared down an instant into her eyes,
his own black gaze impenetrable, and then he shook
his head and dropped his lips to hers again, his hands
wild and uncontrolled, caressing her hard-nippled
breasts through the thin silk of her shirt, stroking her
stomach and her hips, tracing the slender, trembling
shapes of her upper legs, her knees.

Crying out, she reached up in a timid and unprac-
ticed way, fumbling with the buttons of his shirt,
unbuttoning it, reaching under it to rub his wide,
hairy chest with wondering hands. His outcry answered hers and he thrust his hand inside the
half-unbuttoned front of her soft shirt, fondling her
breasts until she almost wept with need and longing.
He whispered her name again and again in a tight,
hoarse whisper, as his exploring fingers caressed her
soft flesh, wandering from her breasts to the satiny
skin above her waist, skin that vibrated to his
masterful touch. She was dimly aware that her wild
desire had carried her hopelessly beyond the limits
of reason. There was no stopping now.

Still astounded, Wynn felt his hands unbutton the
waistband of her skirt, his shaking fingers move
down over the sheer surface of her pantyhose. He
was groaning, shaking all over, and she commanded
him in a low, choked tone, "Touch me, Duke. Touch
me; love me." Reaching out, she placed her small
hand tenderly on him, aware of the drumming
fullness of his own need.

"Oh, my God," she heard him saying. "Wynn,
oh, Wynn." Then he wrenched away from her timid
fingers, sliding his hand upward with great gentle-

ness from under the band of her skirt. He leaned back for an instant against the couch, breathing hoarsely, eyes closed, sweat breaking out on his face. When he could speak, he opened his eyes and looked at her with such tortured indecision, yet with so much tenderness, that even in the midst of her stunned surprise, she was unbearably affected by the caring she saw in his look. He leaned toward her again, taking her hands in his, bending to kiss each one, back and palm. His breath still came in short, quick gasps, and the tightness of his jaw attested to the iron control that he was exercising.

Wynn was still so excited that her arms shook with weakness, as if she had a chill.

"Stop, stop, Wynn," he whispered, stroking her arms in a soothing motion to warm her, then gathering her to him and kissing the top of her head. "Stop," he ordered.

"What?" Her voice was a squeak to her ears. "What did you say?" she faltered, dumbfounded.

"Wynn," he said more clearly, his warm breath tickling her hair, "you're too . . . you're so wonderful that . . . I can't . . . do this."

She was so confused that she could find no answer, no words to express her total bewilderment. He had wanted her, too; she knew that. It was so plain. And now he was telling her she was "too wonderful" to make love to. It made no sense at all. She was almost sick with confusion.

Still holding her head to his chest, Duke leaned forward. She saw his unsteady hand retrieving the pack of cigarettes from the table, shaking one loose. Looking up, she saw him put the white cylinder in his mouth and light it one-handed with a bent match in a paper packet. He turned his head aside, so he wouldn't get the smoke in her eyes, and exhaled with a sobbing whisper. Even the sight of his huge, competent thumb on the bent match, she thought, made her insides scrape with fresh desire. I can't bear it, she reflected. I can't bear it. Wanting a man so much is horrible.

Willing herself to attain a measure of calm, she moved away from his embrace and looked up at him. He turned his head and stared down at her; the peculiar gleam of dark pain was still there in the midnight eyes, and still she couldn't understand. In a trembling voice, she said so.

Duke murmured, "Of course you can't understand, not right now. But I can't . . . do this to you. Not now, not as things stand."

"What do you mean?" she demanded. A cold suspicion assailed her. She felt as if she had something big and hard in her throat that wouldn't allow her to swallow. "You're involved with someone else. You're married. That's it, isn't it?"

"I told you I wasn't married," he said miserably. After putting the cigarette into an ashtray, he rubbed his face with both hands. "I'm involved though. Yes, I'm involved, all right. But not with a woman, Wynn. I'm not married. There's no one else."

"Then what is it?" she asked in a soft voice. "Tell me, Duke. Please." She put her hand on his arm.

He took the hand and kissed it. "I can't do that, not right this minute. I should never have let this go so far. If I'd known . . ." He shook his head, then smiled at her. "I can tell from the way you touched me, you don't . . . do this often."

"I don't do this at all!" she cried. "Nothing like this has ever happened to me."

"I believe you, honey. I know it. I can tell." He bent and kissed her gently on her puzzled mouth.

"Believe me, leaving here is the hardest thing I've ever had to do in my life." He stood up, looking down at her with tender sadness. "You'll understand all this tomorrow, Wynn Carson," he said, smiling crookedly. It was the most sorrowful smile she'd ever seen; it almost made her feel like crying. "Maybe by then you won't feel like this anymore. Not about me." He started toward the door.

She jumped up. "You've got to tell me what you mean. It isn't fair." She was throbbing with aggrieved frustration.

He shook his head; his black eyes flattened with some emotion that might be a blend of hurt and shame. "You'll know tomorrow," he said in a horribly neutral tone. "And I pray to God it won't ruin everything." It seemed hard for him to go. He stood there staring at her hungrily, his whole body expressing his desire to return to her. Then he squared his shoulders and suddenly went out. The door shut with quiet firmness behind him.

Wynn sank down on the couch, staring at the ivory blankness of the closed front door. She was nonplussed, hardly knowing whether to be angry or to cry. But she knew that something had been torn from her very heart with his going. Nothing, nothing had ever been like this, or would be again. She had sublimated all her natural feelings for so long, kept herself remote, working like a madwoman to still her needs. The emotions he'd aroused had resurrected her, made her feel reborn. And then, just like that, in the wink of an eye, he'd rejected her. Gone. He'd said there was no other woman. What could it be? There was no lack in him, she was sure, no inability to love. His kisses, his hands, his body had been evidence of that. Finally she decided to give up the puzzle for the moment. It made her head ache, made her almost ill.

She got up and went to the door with heavy steps. She double-locked it and decided she'd get ready for bed. It was early still; the gilded French clock on the mantel indicated that it was only a bit after nine. But Wynn was drained.

The apartment was utterly quiet, except for the light ticking of the little French clock. Greg's exquisite Mozart concerto had long ago fallen silent; the tape had shut itself off. As she went about turning on more lamps to cheer the gloom, Wynn heard the traffic sounds from Fifth Avenue drift in through the open windows, interspersed with the cheerful noises of the evening crowd in Washington Square: transistors; guitars; an occasional bark from a happy, unleashed dog racing in the park; whistles; voices; laughter. Suddenly she felt alone in the universe, there in her beautiful, sequestered apartment.

But she wasn't the kind to wallow in self-pity—that was fruitless. She forced herself into brisk, normal activity. Retrieving her blazer and purse from the foyer, she took them into the bedroom, hanging the blazer neatly in her capacious closet, changing her purse to one that would match her outfit for the next day.

That was going to be very important indeed. She would have to be attractive yet very businesslike. The union reps were coming at eleven for their preliminary get-acquainted talk. In her superefficient way, she'd already called the weather service and knew that the day was going to be cooler. That would require somewhat darker, more dignified clothes than she had put on for her date with Howard. Howard. Despite her dejection, Wynn had

to laugh aloud. She'd totally forgotten Howard
Bartley, hadn't even checked to see if he'd left a note
or wondered why he hadn't called.

Shoeless, she padded back to the foyer. There on
the rug was a small, neat white note written on one
of Howard's rather pompous office memoranda
sheets. "From the Desk of Councilman Howard E.
G. Bartley" was printed at the top in bold script. She
glanced at his scribbled note. "Sorry I missed you,
beautiful. Guess you got held up. Will give you a
ting-a-ling tomorrow. Howard." *Ting-a-ling,* she repeated silently in disgust. A man like Duke would
never use a silly word like that. The remembrance of
him brought another wave of pain. Damn Duke
Bardolino, if that was his name. Damn Howard . . .
and all men, for that matter. She wondered all of a
sudden how Howard had gotten through the gate
and the downstairs door. A neighbor, no doubt,
impressed with his expensive clothes and kingly air,
had let him in. Well, she'd have a word with whoever
it was. What were her neighbors trying to do? Get
her mugged by any city councilman who happened
to wander in?

The thought was so absurd that Wynn had to
laugh at herself. Feeling really exhausted, she crum-
pled up the note and tossed it in a wastebasket. Then
she turned off the lamps, except the one she generally kept on for company, switched off the stereo and
returned to her bedroom.

It was a serene yellow and aqua bower that
ordinarily soothed and heartened her with its beauty, simple and uncluttered with that Japanese quality
of *shibui*—selective, minimal loveliness—she most
admired. With ivory and aqua walls, the room was
sparsely furnished with a platform bed having two
built-on side tables and an immensely long row of

chests. Built-in bookcases lined the windowed walls, and another wall held a solid, immense closet with sliding doors. The window curtains were a clear, exquisite yellow; between the two windows hung a Japanese painting, and to its right was a one-of-a-kind Rookwood vase with an arrangement of yellow flowers.

On the wall over the chests was one painting, a panoramic view of New York Harbor on a rainy afternoon. A TV set and radio were hidden behind one of the doors of the cabinet. The only other piece of furniture, if it could be called that, was a harmonizing "valet" in an unobtrusive corner behind the closet. It was on the valet that the methodical Wynn laid out the next day's clothes each night.

For some reason—she scoffed at herself; Duke was the reason—the whole place suddenly looked pathetic and cold and bare, like an old maid's prissy cell. Wynn determinedly shook off the unwelcome notion. She quickly undressed and padded barefoot through a little hall lined with more bookcases and mementos of Marty and Big Mike into her luxurious bath, which she'd had completely redone when she took the apartment.

She examined her naked body in the full-length mirror set into the back of the bathroom door. Nothing wrong with you, Wynn Carson, she consoled herself silently. From her wealth of shining blond hair to her full breasts and narrow waist, from her shapely hips to her slender legs and manicured, trim feet, there wasn't a blasted thing that didn't look good. If this wasn't good enough for Duke, then . . .

"Stop it." Wynn spoke aloud, sternly. He'd never said there was anything wrong with *her;* there was something wrong about *them,* together. But what on earth could it be? What in the name of heaven? Wynn's head began to pound with renewed frustration. She took some aspirin and showered, washing her hair, determined not to think of it again.

And yet, as she blew her hair dry and completed her preparation for the morning, the question kept nagging at her. She tried watching some TV to distract herself, then turned to music and a book. Nothing helped. She had to face the fact that she wanted that man as she had never wanted any other—for that matter, as she had never dreamed she could. After a time Wynn's headache was a little better, but her eyes were gritty from TV, reading and general exhaustion. She turned out the lights and settled down to try to sleep. But the image of a tall, dark giant kept haunting her. Heavens, she thought, I'll never get any rest, and I've got to be on my toes in the morning.

Irritated beyond measure, she turned on the light again and looked for another book. By some unlucky chance she picked up one with an inscription on the inner cover; it had been a gift from Don.

Oh wonderful, she reflected with sarcasm. That's all I need. If it's not Duke haunting me, it's the memory of that worthless—

Wynn tossed the book all the way across the room, painful and unpleasant memories of Don McKendrick flooding over her.

Big Mike had never trusted him, she recalled. A "lightweight," had been her father's judgment. But Wynn herself had been so besotted by his Irish charm, the reckless twinkle in his bright blue eyes, his carefree manner, that she wouldn't listen.

They had met at a New Year's Eve party three years earlier. The dateless Wynn had let herself be persuaded to attend the party with a woman friend. It had been enjoyable enough, but hardly exciting, until Wynn had noticed a red-haired man in a gray suit sitting by himself in a corner. He had been far and away the handsomest man at the party. When he caught Wynn's eye, he got up at once and came over to her.

"This can't be New Year's Eve," he said, grinning. When he grinned his blue eyes sparkled, and a deep cleft appeared in his chin.

"Why do you say that?" Wynn queried, returning his smile.

"Because you make it seem like morning. You look like sunlight, with that glorious hair and your eyes like the summer heavens." She couldn't help being excited by that lyrical outburst.

"Don't tell me," she retorted. "You're a poet."

"No such thing. I'm a lowly, banal financial writer." He named his newspaper. "Which is not to say," he rushed on, "that I don't have a poet's soul. You look like the women in Yeats' poems to me."

Wynn doubted that and said so, but she was very fond of the poems of W. B. Yeats. Before she knew it, they were deep in conversation on the subject. Wynn, of course, was enchanted, as she was meant to be. When they saw each other at his insistence two days later, she was dismayed to learn that he was married, with a child, but in the throes of an imminent divorce. He was living in an apartment with another man, he said, on East Thirty-second Street, and his estranged wife and child lived in Rye.

At that time Wynn was still living in the big Rye house with her father, Greg and Dolores. It seemed a rather spooky coincidence, but Wynn tried to ignore it. On their second date she had fallen hopelessly in love with Don McKendrick. But she kept running into his wife in Rye, and that made her feel uncomfortable.

The next year had been part ecstasy, part nightmare. During the first few months, of course, it had been mostly ecstasy: the courtship; the flowers; the gifts; riding the Staten Island ferry; the hansom cabs in Central Park; theaters and restaurants; a whirl of city gaiety, romantic and lighthearted.

Then had come their move together to an apartment on Manhattan's Upper West Side and her lies to Big Mike about sharing an apartment with a woman. Finally there had been the awful night when Don was working late and Big Mike Carson visited. He'd opened the closet door, mistaking it for the front door on the way out, and saw the men's clothes there. Her father's shock and pain and Wynn's solemn assurances that they were going to get married had followed quickly.

But somehow the divorce proceedings never quite proceeded. And then there'd been the painful, awkward times when Don had tried to encourage a friendship between Wynn and his small daughter, who, insecure and confused by her parents' separation, resented Wynn completely despite every effort on Wynn's part to arouse her affection.

Worse than all, far worse, had been Don's increasing restlessness, his pursuit of other women. Wynn would find strange lipsticks, scarves and other items in Don's jackets when she emptied the pockets to take them to the cleaner's. "I can't help it," he'd say, giving her an ingratiating look from his Irish blue eyes. "Just can't help myself, darling. It's you I love, you know." Feeling like a martyr and a fool, Wynn went along, telling herself she wouldn't put up with it much longer. And yet she did, for months.

Besides the women, there was the drinking. At

first his rollicking, laughing, occasional drunkenness amused Wynn; she accepted it as part of the romantic newspaperman image. But all too soon Wynn realized she was being treated like a wronged wife, without any of a wife's advantages. She got so desperately lonely she even called his favorite hangout a couple of times to see if Don was there, getting the expected "No" from the trained bartenders, who never gave any information to a female caller.

When one night Don stayed out drinking and gambling all night, then returned to the apartment bruised from being hit by a taxicab and threw bills of large denomination all over the bedroom, the brokenhearted Wynn realized she'd had enough. She packed her things as soon as daylight came and left the sleeping Don without even a note. After checking her suitcases in lockers at the train station, she went on to the office, where she was then working as an executive assistant to one of her father's men, and told Big Mike it was over. That night Big Mike helped her move back to Rye.

In the weeks that followed, she lost weight, looking hollow-eyed and puny. Big Mike had insisted that she take an extended vacation. Proudly she refused, but when her vacation time came, she did use her two weeks for a very restoring cruise.

After that she coped better, even when Don continued to pursue her. For months Wynn hung up on him, returned his gifts and tore up his letters. At last he ceased to pursue her.

Rest in peace, old affair, she thought now on this wakeful night, returning the book to the shelves. Maybe there was a reason why she had remembered Don, Wynn decided; maybe this was a warning to her not to get too deeply involved again.

It was a cold thought, but somehow reassuring.

When she still couldn't sleep, she sought out another book and found an old novel that had been her mother's, an agreeable, old-fashioned tale of true love and fidelity. It was sheer escape, and Wynn read it avidly. One particular passage stuck with her, a line about blue eyes hungering for brown, dark yearning for fair.

Don McKendrick had had eyes almost the color of Wynn's own, a related fairness. Duke was dark as night, all of him, from his inky hair and brows to his mysterious onyx eyes and his deeply tanned skin. She and Duke—the dark and fair. Like day and night, one naturally following the other. The idea haunted her. They were like the lovers in the story, magnetic opposites fated for each other.

In one romantic instant all her logic failed her. She could see nothing but images of him: Duke in the Ceebee, rising to tower over her; his practiced fingers adjusting the Fiat. Most of all, the feel of him beside her as they drove; the gleam in his eyes across the dinner table; the taste of his magical mouth; the hot touch of his calloused hands on the singing flesh of her willing body only hours earlier.

Wynn put the half-finished novel on her bedside table and drew a jagged breath. It was starting again, and she had to stop it. She had to get hold of herself. If she was exhausted in the morning, she'd lose the fight before it even began.

Determinedly she got up and went into her small, neat kitchen to heat a pan of milk. She drank it down, rinsed the pan and cup, then put them in the sink to drain. Feeling more relaxed, she turned out the lights and went back to bed. Some of her sanity had returned. She stretched out her legs luxuriously, sensing knots of tension loosening. Sleep finally seemed possible.

As Big Mike had said in his realistic way, "Things will look different in the morning, darlin'. Not better necessarily, but different. New problems are a kind of rest from the old ones." Well, she'd have tougher problems tomorrow than Duke; that was for sure.

Wynn was able to smile at herself, if a bit grimly, as sleep began to steal across her with its healing shadow.

## Chapter 3

WHEN SHE AWOKE AT EIGHT O'CLOCK THE NEXT MORN-
ing, Wynn's first thought was of how right her father
had always seemed to be. Things looked very different by daylight. The spring sun streamed through the
thin yellow curtains, giving them the look of daffodils' corollas. It was going to be a fine spring day. For
just a moment she believed that last evening had
been no more than a pleasant dream. She had to face
reality again.

A little tired from her restless sleep, but much
more energetic than she'd expected to be, Wynn got
up and hurried into the kitchen to make coffee.
While it was heating, she took a lightning-fast shower and made the bed. When she returned to the
kitchen, the coffee was just right. She sat down in
her loose terry cloth robe to enjoy her first cup in the
small green-white-and-yellow room. Like the big
living-dining area, the kitchen was also reminiscent

of a garden—replete with hanging plants and bright copper utensils, its narrow windows curtained in a thin flower-printed material of yellow and green against a white background, the panes affording a view of new-leaved trees.

In winter Wynn warmed the house with touches of scarlet and orange instead of yellow. A few weeks ago she had made her changes for spring, and it all still looked very new and inviting. Her spirits began to rise. She was too full of the day ahead to be hungry, so she decided to have some breakfast sent in to the office before the union conference. After quickly drinking another cup of coffee, she rinsed out her dishes and put them in the drainer.

Then she hurried back to the bedroom to dress. She wanted to look poised, every inch the executive. The clothes she'd laid out would give just that look; the softly tailored gray suit, with its silk bow-blouse in watery pastels of rose and blue and lavender, was perfect. She would look attractive yet proper. It was easy for her to look too cute, with her big eyes and small stature, so at the office she avoided ruffly things or too-busy prints. She coiled her hair in a gleaming French roll at the back of her head and made up almost imperceptibly. She used a little more makeup than usual on her long-lashed blue eyes because she planned to wear her big blue-rimmed glasses to look older, serious.

She didn't even think of Duke until she got in the car and listened to the perfect rhythm of the engine. After all, he was the one who'd adjusted the wires. An unexpected stab of excitement pierced her whole body. The previous night hadn't been a dream; his arms and mouth had been all too real. Resolutely she paid full attention to her driving, weaving in and out of the heavy traffic. She felt that his ghost was

exorcised, at least for the moment, and her mind
leaped to the matter of contract negotiations.

She'd studied past contracts, read her father's
notes until her eyes were blurry. But this next
contract contained so much that was new—demands
for new safety devices and other benefits that might
be a real squeeze for Carson's over the next three
years. Wynn blessed Big Mike for his curt but
invaluable directions.

"Good morning. Ummm . . . that blouse looks
good enough to eat." Ruth Wiley, Wynn's secretary,
glanced up from the mail as she spoke. There was a
pleasant grin on her wise, middle-aged face; she was
a pleasant sight altogether, with her short, curly
salt-and-pepper hair, twinkling eyes of golden hazel
and attractive cream-and-russet dress.

"Don't tell me," Wynn quipped. "You're dieting
again, so you're ready to eat anything." She grinned
back at Ruth. "How are you this morning?"

"Fine . . . and I *am* dieting again." Ruth had
always been in a calorie battle, Wynn recalled. She'd
known the older woman for years, first as Big Mike's
secretary. Wynn was touched that Ruth didn't resent
working for the girl she used to mother; on the
contrary, Ruth seemed to love it. She sometimes
remarked that working for Wynn was almost like
having Big Mike back again—they were both bright
as buttons and stubborn as mules.

"Well, rotsa ruck." Wynn's smile widened.
"What's with the crises this morning?"

"Nothing much. The messages are on your desk—
the Honorable Howard B. phoned twice and wants
you to call him *tout de suite*. Dolores was more
patient, as usual. The construction boss at that
Broadway site is screaming for the trucks, but Wilson took care of that. I put the union file on your

desk, too. That's about it. I'll bring the mail in shortly."

"Don't lose too much weight," Wynn ordered, "'cause every ounce is gold, lady." Ruth flushed with pleasure as Wynn entered her own sanctum. She'd left Big Mike's office almost exactly as it had always been, adding only a few personal things of her own. She saluted the big oil portrait of him that hung between her wide walnut desk and the corner conference area, with its round table suggesting a wheel and its comfortable chairs of bright blue leather shaped somewhat like the plain, upright seats of a massive truck.

Tossing her patent leather bag in a desk drawer, Wynn got out her owlish glasses and looked at the messages. Howard's she tossed in the wastebasket, thinking, Let him call. Dolores's she put aside to deal with a little later. The others, she judged, could wait until that afternoon. However, she dialed Tommy Wilson's extension on the interoffice phone. Hearing his clipped voice answer, she said, "Top of the morning. How goes it with that jerk at the Bascom site?"

"He's managing fine," Tommy assured her. "The rigs rolled in while I was on the phone with him. You know the drill. He always wants everything before he orders it."

"Right on, Thomas. Thanks a lot. I always count on you."

Wilson's brassy laugh rattled the receiver. "Wynn, you're a sound for sore ears."

"Relax. Put away the butter. You don't need it; you know this place would collapse without you. Gotta go." She replaced the receiver.

Ruth came in with the morning mail. "Get some coffee and sit," Wynn invited, "after you get your pad. I want to get through this stuff so I can get on to union business."

"Right." The secretary was back in a moment with pad, pen and coffee.

Wynn leafed through the mail, putting most of it aside. When she glanced at the memos, she muttered, "Scrooge again." She and Ruth privately called the treasurer, Jonathan Court, Scrooge, both for his austere appearance and his crabby manner.

"Oh yeah." Ruth made a face. "He was here as soon as I was, asking for you. Wants to discuss the first bargaining session."

That would be fun, Wynn thought darkly. She had a feeling that Court and the others would expect her to go along with whatever they wanted, since she was so new at this. Well, they'd all have a big surprise coming, she decided. She would conduct the talks as Big Mike would have.

Wynn raced through the more important items. When the dictation was done, she asked Ruth to order her some breakfast.

Tsk-tsking, Ruth chided, "Again? You're going to waste away."

Wynn accepted the comment as she did all the other evidence of Ruth's mothering. She poured herself a cup of coffee from the coffeemaker in a small separate kitchen and brought it back to her desk. She'd have breakfast as she worked. Asking Ruth to hold her calls for a half hour, Wynn shut the door. She'd avoid Court; they'd talked enough already.

She took the massive union files from the drawer and once again went over her own notes, comparing them to Big Mike's. There were items, she'd discovered previously to her surprise, on which she agreed with the more conservative board members, in opposition to her own father. But generally she and Big Mike were of the same mind—a reasonably generous stance.

Wynn turned to Ruth's typed sketches of the union's negotiations, prepared so Wynn would have a personal slant on the men she hadn't met. Ruth had a delightful way of penciling in personal comments so they could be easily and discreetly erased. Grinning with anticipation, Wynn took a fresh pencil from the pewter mug on her desk. Knowing Ruth, some of the comments would be lulus, and she'd have plenty of erasing to do. They were. By the name of the president Ruth had lightly penciled, "A knockout. Ha ha."

Smiling, Wynn erased. She did a double take when she read the president's name again—Donato Bellini. A knockout named Donato. No, it couldn't be; it would be just too ridiculous. Duke so-called Bardolino was a trucker.

Or was he? She remembered his hesitation before the word *rig*, his familiarity with the entrails of sports cars, his reference to "thinking on his feet." Then there were his cavalier attitude toward money, more in keeping with sixty thousand a year than thirty-six or so, and his air of command.

Wynn glanced at the last signed contract. The bold, familiar scrawl made "Donato" look like "Ronald." But it wasn't an *R*, it was a *D*. The stabbing excitement that she had felt in the car that morning plagued her again. With an annoyed exclamation, she made herself read the other sketches. Aaron Weinfeld, vice-president, a "real legal eagle, complete with beak—Damascus steel"; Bernie Halloran, secretary-treasurer, "looks like Santa Claus but thinks like the original Scrooge." The recording secretary and trustees, on the other hand, were characterized as "pieces of cake." But that didn't console Wynn much. She didn't doubt that the three top men were the prime movers, just as Big Mike had always found. She glanced back at the thumbnail sketch of Donato Bellini, president of 117. "Tough, dedicated, but eminently reasonable."

The coincidence of the name bothered Wynn all morning, as she returned her sister-in-law's call, accepting an invitation to dinner that night and made some quick notes on less urgent correspondence. Before she knew it, it was eleven o'clock. The hands of her watch were just touching the hour when she heard Ruth buzz and her well-modulated voice over the intercom announce, "The delegation from 117 is here, Miss Carson."

"I'll be right out." Wynn's desk was clear, the union folder at the ready; blue cups and saucers, a pot of fresh coffee, a tray of pastry and gray paper napkins were conveniently arranged on the conference table. Wynn got up, straightened her shoulders and opened her door, smiling. She recognized most of the men at a glance, for Ruth's sketches had included, as she humorously put it, mug shots. Her mind registered them, but all she could see in that first instant was Donato Bellini. She realized how remarkably Ruth's description had coincided with the looks of Duke so-called Bardolino.

He looked taller than ever, impressive in a lightweight gray chalk-striped suit worn with a berry-red cravat that had little silver wheels printed on it. In the fluorescent light she noticed taut lines in his face that had not been revealed by the gentle twilight the evening before, nor by the soft lamps of her apartment and Fedora's. His expression was almost comical, as if he were waiting nervously for her reaction.

Wynn's heart was crowding her throat. She

thought for one horrified moment that she couldn't speak. But she took a deep breath and calmly said, "Good morning. Mr. Bellini . . ." She held out her hand to Duke, properly recognizing him first as the chief officer. He took her hand, giving it a gentle squeeze. The touch nearly undid her, but she turned to the others with equal poise. "Mr. Weinfeld," she said, smiling. "Mr. Halloran." Weinfeld was civil, but far from charmed; Halloran pretended to be, but Wynn wasn't fooled. But she was happy with her foreknowledge and poise; they seemed impressed in spite of themselves when she also succeeded in recognizing the attorney and the director of their pension fund.

She hadn't expected the latter two and was a bit annoyed that she hadn't been informed, but Ruth got them extra coffee cups and napkins with smiling grace.

Wynn carefully avoided looking into Duke Bellini's eyes as they settled themselves at the conference table, joined by Carson's dour treasurer, Court, and James Noble, one of the company's more forbidding attorneys. Noble's frankly antilabor stance had often annoyed Big Mike, and he was one of the executives Wynn wanted to keep an eye on.

Duke Bellini seemed impressed by Wynn's tough, self-assured manner as she opened the meeting. Things became less genial when the two sides got down to cases. The company also had demands. Court and Noble referred frequently to tight money and the economy.

Weinfeld snapped back with a reference to Wall Street's recent rally. Once, when Noble went too far, appearing to speak for the company, Wynn interjected quietly, "I'll go on record now. Only Wynn Carson speaks for Wynn Carson." She regretted having to say it, however; the union, sensing inner dissension, could use it as a club. But she saw a gleam of amused respect in Duke's dark eyes.

"Shades of Big Mike," Halloran commented, smiling. He looked up at the portrait on the wall. Duke commented, "The toughest, fairest adversary 117 ever had. My own dad said a man can't be too careful in his choice of enemies." Duke grinned. "Mike was a hell of a guy, and you're a spoke off the old wheel. I have a feeling it'll be a pleasure to do business with you, Miss Carson."

"Don't count your fringes before they're trimmed, Mr. Bellini," she punned. It was easy to joke at this stage, the sweetness-and-light phase. Later it would be eye to eye and far less sweet. Her heart thudded, though. It seemed to her that Duke Bellini was talking about more than negotiations. She was relieved when the conference ended. Her poise had been stretched to the limit.

When the group was leaving, Duke Bellini stayed a step behind, near Wynn. He asked in a low voice, "Are you free for lunch? There are a couple of things we didn't get to, and I'd like to talk them over, if we could."

You bet we didn't get to them, she thought. And we're not going to. "I'm afraid not, Mr. Bellini," she replied coolly. "See my secretary, Mrs. Wiley. She has my book. Maybe she can set up an appointment for you." Wynn was fully aware that her book was jammed.

He couldn't hide his disappointment, but he answered levelly, "Thanks. I'll do that."

"Thank you for coming, gentlemen." Wynn gave a general smile, a nod of farewell.

Duke Bellini looked up once more, a pleading

expression in his black, shiny eyes. Wynn ignored the look. Turning on her heel, she went back into her office and shut the door.

She stood with her back against it, listening to the murmur of his voice, interspersed with Ruth's soft replies. That phony, Wynn raged in silence. What kind of fool did he take her for? Bardolino, indeed. Had that been some kind of ploy, to get her in the palm of his hand so he could maneuver a good deal for his members?

Wynn walked to her desk and sat down, putting her head in her hands. But no, that didn't make sense. How could he have known he'd run into her at the Ceebee? And she remembered how taken aback he had looked when she'd introduced herself to Enrico as Wynn Carson. He hadn't known. And when he found out, she reasoned, he hadn't allowed himself to make love to her, much as he had wanted to, because the situation was too loaded. Natural competitors couldn't become lovers.

She dropped her hands and looked up, staring with unseeing eyes at the conference area. So *that* was it. Somehow that seemed to explain the whole thing. On the one hand it heartened her that their professional lives had been impeding him, not another woman or any lack of desire. But on the other, things looked grimmer than ever. How could she and Duke Bellini ever get together, when they were fated to oppose each other every step of the way?

It was a dilemma too knotty for her to handle. Not right then, at least. She could see no way out of it, no solution. Anyway, she might be reading more into things than existed, making it all up in her own mind and giving him credit for subtleties, for nobility he didn't possess.

There were no voices from the anteroom anymore. He must have left. Wynn wanted to ask Ruth if she had set up an appointment, but somehow she didn't dare. She knew she couldn't inquire with a straight face. She might give herself away, so she dismissed the idea and turned back to the papers on her desk. However, underlying her surface calm was a rolling confusion that persisted throughout her solitary lunch and the rest of the afternoon.

She planned to leave a few minutes early. Her dinner date with Greg and Dolores was at six-thirty, and she wanted to try to beat the thick after-work traffic. Generally, Wynn didn't leave the office much before six. Ruth, as usual, said goodnight at five. Wynn was preparing to go, a little after that, when a florist's employee came in with a huge parcel.

Puzzled, Wynn tipped the man and ripped away the wrapping. It was potted lilacs, lavender and white, in a beautiful gray glass urn. She found the card. In a bold, familiar hand was the message, "April is a cruel month, when your name is Duke Bellini."

Wynn was titillated. First Mozart, now a paraphrase of a line from T. S. Eliot's poetry. She had to admit that it was something of a paradox, an exciting one—a tough, down-to-earth unionist, born in a tenement, sending her lilacs that symbolized the sweet ache of spring.

She breathed in the scent of the fluffy blossoms and then sat down at her desk, staring at them. She couldn't remember the exact words of Eliot's poem, but there was something about lilacs and remembering . . . remembering and desire. And April rain waking the earth. It was like the afternoon and evening past. Something had bloomed out of her own remoteness; the late-night memories of Don and of her mother had mingled with her desire for Duke Bellini.

The only thing lacking was an April shower. If it started to rain that evening she'd feel haunted. Wynn was overwhelmed by it all. Then it occurred to her that this was just a little *too* wonderful, too smooth. Maybe Duke Bellini courted all the women bosses he knew with poetry and flowers.

The idea was depressing, and yet it was what she needed to get her going again. She was wasting time; traffic would be bumper-to-bumper, and she had to get uptown. Sighing, she got up and threw the florist's wrapping into the wastebasket, along with the card. Fortunately the florist's delivery man had had the sense to put the heavy urn on a side cabinet where it wouldn't interfere. She had to admit that it looked beautiful against the white wall, in keeping with the blue and gray of the office.

Something made her retrieve the card from the wastebasket and slip it in her purse before she turned out the lights and left.


"You look wonderful, Wynn," Dolores Carson said, studying her sister-in-law with big, soft eyes. Probably the marvelous dinner, Wynn thought, and the wine, plus the general lazy comfort that this place always inspired.

She glanced around the pleasant living room of the apartment that overlooked Lincoln Center Plaza. It was solid and inviting, with predominant greens and earth tones in the furnishings. Greg taught at Juilliard, a mere half block from the apartment, so it was a perfect location for them.

"You look . . . different, Wynn," Dolores added in her low, vibrant tone. She'd made similar remarks earlier, and Wynn wondered uneasily if the experiences of the past two days could possibly show. But that was a fanciful, silly notion, and she tried to dismiss it.

"Probably my hair," she said lightly. She'd taken it down after she'd arrived, and brushed it out for greater freedom and relaxation. "Nothing's new," she said mendaciously. "Just another day, another dollar at the office."

Her sister-in-law looked a little skeptical. Nevertheless she gave Wynn her sweet smile, a slow, confiding smile that lit her dark eyes with greater warmth and crinkled the smooth skin of her tanned face. At thirty-five Dolores Carson was a beautiful woman, with black, heavy hair which she habitually wore in a coronet around her graceful head, and an aquiline nose at odds with her full and very feminine mouth and voluptuous body. No one, Wynn reflected, could have been more different from Wynn's gaunt blond brother. Again the idea of "fatal opposites" flashed into her mind, as it had the night before.

To divert both Dolores and herself, she remarked, "I'm sorry to miss 'The Man,' but this is very nice, just the two of us."

"You are so right." Dolores grinned, revealing small, white, very even teeth. The Spanish half of her, inherited from her father, who had been a fine classical guitarist, was very evident. She was wearing an easy-fitting robe of dark red printed with gold and purple; the strains of a Segovia recording filled the peaceful room. "No matter how I love my men, it's very restful to have two of them asleep and one away."

Wynn smiled. The children had been put to bed, and Greg had accepted an evening "gig," recording a commercial at a studio on West Sixty-ninth Street.

He had told Dolores he might or might not make it back before Wynn left, depending on how things went. Such jobs, which he did on occasion, were a financial boon, and he didn't like to pass them up.

"Every time I see those kids, they seem to have grown a foot, even if it's only been a week," Wynn commented. She could feel Dolores studying her and turned to meet the dark, level gaze.

"You're evading, kiddo." Her sister-in-law made an inventory of Wynn's face. "I've been saying there's something different about you ever since you got here tonight. I said it with the first martini, and again with the paella, and then with the dishes. I admit," she chuckled, "I have a one-track mind. But every time I've said it . . . or a variation . . . you've talked about the great martini, the great paella and how much fun it is to help me with the dishes," she ended dryly.

When Wynn didn't answer, Dolores prodded, "What's up? You haven't looked like this since . . . well, since Don McKendrick. Wynn . . . you haven't met someone else like him?"

This frontal attack was so uncharacteristic of Dolores Carson that Wynn was surprised. Dolores never pried and she'd never made reference to the Don disaster since it ended, although she'd made no secret of her disapproval while it was going on.

"Oh no," Wynn assured her. "Not like *him*." She could have bitten off her tongue. She hadn't wanted to mention any of it to Dolores; the whole thing was too difficult, too bizarre. And the last thing she needed was to get her brother's and Dolores's hopes up when the whole incident would end in nothing. Now she'd given herself away for sure.

"Aha!" Dolores grinned, triumphant. "Then you *have* met someone. I knew you couldn't look this glowing about the Honorable Howard." It was an accepted fact between them that Dolores did not admire Howard Bartley any more than she had Don.

Wynn had to laugh at her tone. "You're a perfect bloodhound. I'm sorry to tell you, but I haven't really 'met' anybody."

"Haven't met him? What on earth does that mean? Either you did or you didn't." Dolores sounded exasperated.

I wish I hadn't spilled the beans, Wynn thought. To mask her nervousness, she looked away, leaning forward and pouring herself another half glass of port from the decanter on the table. "Well, I mean, I met someone, in a manner of speaking, but it'll never work."

"Now you're driving me mad. Why won't it work? Who is he? What's he like?" Dolores's eager questions tumbled out. She sounded like a teenager discussing football heroes with a classmate. "He's not married, is he?"

"No, no," Wynn said hastily. "It's just that he's somebody I could never . . . we couldn't . . ." She stopped, at a loss to explain. It was too embarrassing to describe how they'd met. It had been no more than a pickup, in simple terms. And Dolores would be disturbed to know that Wynn had invited him to her apartment on such short acquaintance. She was always saying how she worried about Wynn living alone.

"Well, I hope he's not a terrorist . . . or a convict," Dolores commented, her brows raised in mock concern. Wynn sensed that Dolores was embarrassed about intruding and was trying to cover it with a joke.

"Oh, neither, neither," Wynn retorted, keeping her tone light. "Actually, he's a sixteen-year-old rock star with hair to his waist. And I couldn't do that to you and Greg, or my lovable nephews." Embroidering the fantasy, she went on, "How would he look, after all, in church on Easter or by the Christmas tree? Besides, he tried to assassinate Jean-Pierre Rampal." At this reference to Greg's idol, Dolores let out a hearty laugh. Then she sobered.

"Look, Wynn, I'm sorry I poked at you." Dolores patted Wynn's face. "It's just that, you know, we're always hoping." She added, in her earthy way, "It's a long time between drinks."

Wynn flushed.

"Speaking of which," Dolores said hastily, as if fearing she'd said too much, "can I give you anything else?"

"No, please. I am wonderfully replete." Wynn leaned over to kiss Dolores on the cheek, then retrieved her shoes and slipped them on. "I'd better hit the road. You know I get up with the truckers."

She realized what an unfortunate remark that was and felt her cheeks grow pink again. Dolores gave her a keen glance. Oh dear. Now she'd think Wynn had been talking about a trucker, maybe think her all kinds of a snob for finding the mysterious suitor impossible on that account.

"Give Greg my love," Wynn said, putting on her jacket and slinging her purse over her shoulder. "And kiss the heirs."

"I will." Dolores hugged Wynn and gave her a wide, sweet smile. "Look here, I'm sorry if I was out of line."

"You weren't. Really," she answered, and meant it. "Honestly, there's nothing going on, Dolores. Just a rig that passed in the night."

But after she'd left, while she was driving down-

town again, Wynn wondered if it was going to be
that easy, dismissing Duke Bellini. A misting rain
began to fall.

It wasn't easy, she found the next morning when
she arrived at her office, hanging her damp rose-
colored raincoat in the closet and leaving her umbrella in the small kitchen to dry. Next to the potted
lilacs on the cabinet was a vase of American Beauty
roses. No card was in evidence, there or on her desk.

"Ducky weather," Ruth quipped, coming in to
bring the morning mail. "Those came when I did,"
she said, nodding at the roses. "No card." Her hazel
eyes twinkled with enjoyable curiosity. "Howard B.
getting anxious?"

Wynn shrugged, avoiding her eyes. "Could be."

"I take it lilac time began last night, after I was
sprung." Ruth was still grinning as she put the mail
on Wynn's desk.

"Uh-huh." Wynn was noncommittal, seemingly
fascinated with the messages and letters. "No card
either," she lied.

"Really? How exciting." Ruth stood there for a
moment longer, as if eager to talk about it. But
Wynn continued her perusal of the mail, and out of
the corner of her eye, she saw Ruth leave.

She thought, I'm doing it again—shutting out
another friend who's dear to me, someone I've
talked to as much as I have Dolores. But somehow
she couldn't bring herself to tell either woman about
Duke. Why get their hopes up when nothing was
going to come of this strange affair?

Wynn's face grew warm to the roots of her hair.
She wondered why she had referred to the incident
like that, even to herself.

It became increasingly difficult to concentrate as

the day wore on. Howard called twice. The first time she refused the call, telling Ruth she was busy. She took the second one, apologizing for the other night but declining his invitation to lunch.

She was inundated with work, but when lunchtime came, instead of ordering her lunch sent in, she went out and took a long walk in the drizzling rain, grabbing an unsatisfactory sandwich at a crowded coffee shop. She felt a little irritable all afternoon. Somehow she'd expected Duke Bellini to phone.

On succeeding mornings she found other floral tributes when she got to the office. They were the colors of her living room, she realized with a thrill—daffodils the third morning, white roses the fourth, and then, on the fifth, hyacinths.

On the morning of the hyacinths, her private phone rang. It was Duke Bellini. For a second she wondered how he'd gotten that number. Of course, she reflected, he would have had Big Mike's number for labor-management emergencies. "Miss Carson? Donato Bellini."

She was touched that he was so formal. Neutrally she answered, "Yes?"

"I just wanted to issue a personal invitation," he said in the same formal way, "to the truckers' art exhibit. It's opening this afternoon. Three to seven." He gave her an address on West Sixteenth Street. "I thought you might like to drop by. We have a couple of exhibits by Carson employees." He waited.

She took a quick breath. She'd been aware for some time of the union-sponsored art program and had visited their exhibit once before. But she hadn't met any officers there. Several of the trucker-artists had made humorous remarks about how hard it was to get the union "bigwigs" to come. And here was the president of 117, personally asking an employer to attend. Obviously it was just an excuse to get to see her. Wynn didn't know whether to be annoyed or delighted; she see-sawed between both.

"Miss Carson?" he repeated.

"Yes, Du—Mr. Bellini," she amended quickly, imagining she heard a quick intake of breath on his end of the line. "I'd be delighted." Suddenly she identified her emotion. Delight *was* what she was feeling. She wanted to see him again, very badly, and she might as well face it. It was very subtle of him, too, very sly, not to breathe a word about the flowers. "The lilacs were lovely," she said on an impulse.

"I'm glad you liked them," he replied gruffly. "What time will you be coming?"

"Oh, I think about four," she said in a casual tone.

"Four," he repeated. "Great. See you there."

She hung up with a sense of rising elation. It was clear to her now how much she had actually missed him. Missed him, and it had only been a few days since they'd last met.

She smiled, realizing that she hadn't thanked him for the other flowers. But she could hardly do that, could hardly assume they were from him, when they had arrived without cards. Could they have been from Howard? No. She laughed off that idea. Whenever Howard Bartley sent anything, he always asked her how she liked it. He had the subtlety of an eighteen-wheeler.

Wynn was disturbingly glad to see four o'clock approach, even gladder that she had happened to wear a very pretty dress that morning. The weather was almost as warm as May, unseasonable for a New York spring. And in tune with the day, she'd chosen a soft, bright yellow long-sleeved jersey, almost the color of the daffodils that she'd missed the last couple of days. More fragile than the other blossoms, they had withered the morning after they were delivered.

Giving herself a last-minute check in the ladies' room mirror, Wynn noticed that the yellow dress gave her blond hair and blue eyes an interesting new value, that her color was high and she looked her best. She was wearing her hair loose. It brushed her shoulders in shining near-waves.

She picked up her taupe yellow and aqua envelope bag, switched off the lights and said to Ruth, "I've got a dental appointment, so I won't be back."

"Ooh, I hope it's not too bad," Ruth Wiley sympathized.

Wynn shook her head, smiling. "Only a cleaning. See you Monday morning. Enjoy the weekend." She paused, then added, "Take off now if you like."

"Thanks, I will." Ruth sounded pleased. "That'll give me some shopping time before my big date." The big date was her regular Friday evening dinner out with her husband of many years.

"Enjoy." Wynn waved and went out, thinking, I've got a date for a change, too. But actually she was as nervous as if she really were going to the dentist.

She ridiculed herself for the notion. Maybe, now that he knew who she was, this was just a ploy, like the flowers. And yet that didn't quite compute. He'd known who she was when he kissed her and caressed her, when he revealed how much she excited him. Now she was beginning to feel the same wild, romantic feelings she'd had when they were driving crosstown to the mews.

She garaged the Fiat at her own place and took a cab to Sixteenth Street to save time, knowing that parking places were few and far between in that busy area. As she got out of the taxi, she almost wished she hadn't come. She was so excited that her breath was coming in short gasps, and she felt uncomfortably warm. Calm down, Wynn Carson, she ordered, hearing the quick patter of her heartbeat in her ears.

She took a deep breath and walked up the stairs to the little gallery, which she remembered as nothing more than a big, simple, sunny room, a converted store. She heard recorded music and the buzz of voices, punctuated with laughter.

The sun-flooded space was crowded with dressed-up truckers and their pleased families, and a couple of newspaper people with cameras; some TV equipment was being set up in a corner. There were long rows of paintings and drawings lining the walls and wooden display racks; the sculpture section was located by the big plate-glass window, near a bower of green plants. Wynn was thankful that the place was air-conditioned; she was feeling warmer than ever in her nervousness.

Then she caught sight of Duke Bellini. He was immaculate but casual in dark brown slacks and a camel-colored sports coat worn over a creamy shirt open at the neck. The dark pants seemed to whittle his narrow hips to panther leanness; the light shirt and jacket made his shoulders look as wide as the door. His jet-black hair gleamed in the sun, and he was smiling, his dazzling teeth snowy in that tough, tanned face.

He was holding one of the sculptures in his big hands, apparently admiring it, to the delight of the man standing next to him, who must have been the artist. The figure was that of a voluptuous female nude. Duke said something to the other man in a low voice, and they both laughed. Duke's caressing hands on the figure reminded Wynn of his touch on her own thrilled flesh, and her heartbeat accelerated. She felt a flush rise to her face and she stared at his exploring hands.

At that moment he caught sight of her, and his smile widened, his face changed. He no longer looked sophisticated and carefree. His eyes were as eager as a child's and his face expectant, his smile welcoming but shy and hesitant.

"Miss Carson," he called out to her from the other side of the room and strode toward her. She noticed that heads turned; people were staring. Wynn was well aware that superficial social contacts between employers and labor union heads were, at least on the surface, friendly. But to the more down-to-earth union members, bosses were bosses and unions were unions; the twain should never meet with too much cordiality, in the members' view. Duke's enthusiasm didn't look good.

All those things whirled in Wynn's brain, aggravating her already nervous condition. It was impossible, she found, to see Duke Bellini or to be near him and talk to him without getting flustered. Ridiculous for her to react like a smitten teenager around her first love, but there it was. She did, and she couldn't seem to help it.

Duke Bellini held out his hand, smiling down at her. Half willingly, she put her hand in his and, as she had expected, felt the same electric shock she'd experienced the first evening they met.

"It's so good to see you," he said earnestly in a low voice, his dark gaze holding hers.

She was saved from answering when an acquaintance of his came by, grabbed Duke by the arm and demanded in a gruff voice, "How's it going, boy? How was the conference? You have a drink for me at the Red Lion?" The man looked huge to Wynn, bluff, red-faced and hearty, with the veined nose of a heavy drinker.

"I couldn't have as many as you'd want, Charlie," Duke chaffed him. "The conference was the usual—" He caught himself, glancing aside at Wynn, and she imagined he was repressing a rather randy word, just as Big Mike used to do in her presence. She couldn't help grinning. ". . . the usual non-sense," Duke finished weakly. "I'm glad to get back."

So he'd been away, she thought. Maybe that was why he hadn't called. Things began to look different to her.

"Oh, I'm sorry." Duke introduced Wynn to the red-faced man. She recognized his name as that of a prominent official on the state's labor mediation board. When the man walked away, Duke comment-ed softly, "He looks like a clown, but he's the hardest-headed son-of-a—" Again he stopped and amended, ". . . gun in Albany."

Then, indifferent to the staring crowd around them, Duke added, "I've missed you, Wynn Car-son."

"But you did send flowers," she said in the same low tone, unable to control her trembling smile. "They were lovely. I noticed the colors, by the way."

"I knew you would." His nearness was so disturb-ing that she fervently wished they weren't in such a public place. Surely her excitement was plain to everyone who looked at her. The traitorous pound-ing of her heart was loud enough to echo in her ears, and she was convinced her cheeks were red as fire, they felt so hot.

It was an enormous relief to hear her name. "Miss Wynn."

She turned at once to see a smiling, heavy, gray-haired man standing at her elbow. "Sam!" she exclaimed with delight. "Sam Sposato." It was Carson's garage manager, a man who'd been with the company since its founding. "Don't tell me you've entered some artwork here. You're not union now."

"All right, I won't then," Sam Sposato retorted in his genial baritone, adding, "Hiya, Duke. Didn't think the big bugs'd be here today."

"You know how it is, Sam. All that p.r. stuff. Anyway, I wanted to see what you guys do with your spare time besides watch TV."

"Who's got time?" Sam demanded. "This lady keeps me busy, and with the family and my stuff over there, I don't have time to . . . breathe." Wynn was getting the familiar feeling that these men were really pulling in their horns wordwise, in deference to her. While she appreciated their respect, it made her feel like an intruder. But nevertheless, she had really begun to enjoy herself. Sam was like an uncle to her, and she was eager to see what kind of work he'd done.

"Well, at least you don't have to be a shop steward anymore." Duke gave a short laugh. "We lost a good man when Big Mike pulled that fast one on us."

"Fast one?" Wynn asked. Then she understood. "Oooh yes. _Now_ I remember." She chuckled. Her encyclopedic knowledge of personnel stood in her good stead at times like these; she clearly recalled the battle between Big Mike and 117 over Sam Sposato. The union hadn't supported Sam in his request for reconsideration of mandatory retirement —some balderdash about uniformity of treatment or something. To get around it, Big Mike had changed Sam's actual title from foreman to manager, making

him management and setting him out of the reach of
union jurisdiction.

"Big Mike was the grandest twister that ever
breathed," Sam declared, grinning. "He sure saved
my . . . er, neck, Miss Wynn." He paused, then
studied them both. "Now you're gonna have to deal
with this mug. How da ya like that? Big Mike's little
girl, eyeball-to-eyeball with Duke Bellini. Ain't that
a kick in the head?"

Duke and Wynn glanced at each other. Neither
spoke. She wondered what he was thinking. As far
as her own thinking went, she'd stopped short—
again—at the realization that she and Duke Bellini
were on opposite sides of the fence. That fact made
it harder than ever to face the truth. She was
inevitably drawn to him, all of him, his face and
body, his mouth and hands. Even the sound of his
voice made her feel that she was being undressed.

Wanting to fill the awkward silence, afraid that her
desire was written in her eyes and echoing from her
words, Wynn said quickly, "What are we standing
here for, Sam? I want to see those paintings."
Deliberately she added, "That's what I came here
for, after all." She didn't look directly at Duke, so
she had no idea whether the shot had gone home,
but she heard him say levelly, "So did I."

The three of them walked to the opposite end of
the room. Sam Sposato's paintings were tagged with
his name, "Carson" and "Local 117."

"Wait a minute," Wynn said, puzzled. "If you're
management, Sam, how come you're in this exhibit
at all, not to mention with Local 117?" She turned to
Duke, her brows raised questioningly.

Duke smiled a triumphant smile. "Big Mike's not
the only twister, Miss Carson. I heard from one of
the other guys that Sam's stuff is good, and we

needed all the good stuff we could get for the TV cameras today. Besides, I wanted to give Sam a break."

Now Wynn was really confused. Duke Bellini favoring Sam!

"It was the executive board, not me, who turned down Sam's request for continued employment," Duke went on. "If it had been up to me, well . . . But the board doesn't give a damn about art exhibits, frankly. And I said a word to our membership clerk . . ."

"You see, Miss Wynn? This is why I joined that union in the first place. This guy here." Sam punched Duke lightly on his arm. "Before that, I didn't see why we needed one, with a guy like Big Mike at the wheel. They had a tough time convincing me." Sam laughed at the memory.

"Be fair now, Sam," Wynn chided. "Where was Buffalo Bill Carson without a union?" She felt that was something that had to be said, in all justice.

Duke's face lit up. "Well, well. What is this?"

"It's the lamb saying hi to the lion," Sam said, laughing. "But listen, Duke, did you come here to talk or look?"

"*I* came here to look," Wynn asserted, and she did. Examining Sam's oil paintings, she was truly astounded at his skill. She found it amazing. This big, down-to-earth man could paint pictures like these? One was a still life of a rose, a simple red rose in a blue white vase. But it wasn't really simple when you studied it. It was an unearthly rose, like the bright ghost of an actual flower, and the watery shadows of the painting further enhanced the romantic air of the work.

"How much is this, Sam?" she asked him abruptly.

"For you . . ." he began.

"Uh-uh," she negated. "No 'for me' about it." She peered at the little tag on the frame, seeing that it listed the price. "I want it, I want it," she said as excitedly as a child. "Now." She reached into her bag and got out her pen and checkbook. "Do I make it out to you?" she asked him. He told her no, to the art center. She scribbled a check and handed it to Sam.

His broad face was shining with pleasure. "Gee, you really seem to like it," he said in wonder.

"Like it? I love it!" She really did, and couldn't wait to get it home and hang it. Or maybe she'd put it in the office. "Can I take it with me now?"

Duke laughed at her eager question. "What do you say, Rembrandt? Can she?"

"Sure," Sam assented. "They've already shot it for the TV. Let me get it." He unhooked the picture and handed it to Wynn. "Thanks, Miss Wynn."

"Thank *you*," she countered, studying the picture.

She was so intent on it that she hadn't noticed Aaron Weinfeld, 117 vice-president, and the secretary-treasurer, Bernie Halloran, hovering nearby. But she caught a soft male chuckle, heard a murmured, "Sure as hell looks like it," and her every sense became alert. She realized then that it was Weinfeld who'd spoken, and listened to Halloran saying, ". . . if it's a sweetheart deal on their side or ours." Then Weinfeld whispered, "Not so loud, damn it, Jim."

Wynn couldn't prevent herself from casting a lightning glance at Duke Bellini. The triumphant Sam has rushed off with the check, and she heard several people talking about the first sale. Duke's face was utterly impassive, so Wynn couldn't tell whether or not he'd heard the men's talk.

But the unpleasant hint of collusion between Wynn Carson and Duke Bellini couldn't be forgotten. Here it was again—the constant hint of more than met the eye. And now it was Wynn's turn to wonder. Did it mean that Duke Bellini was romancing Carson's and not her, instead of conspiring?

The idea was so off-putting that she felt herself withdraw into suspicion.

When Duke made the expected suggestion, "Can I help you take that home?" Wynn found herself going cold.

# Chapter 4

"No, thank you," she said stiffly. "It's very light. That's not necessary at all."

She had thrown him completely off base apparently, because he looked bewildered. "Is there something the matter?"

"Nothing at all," she said with cool formality. "I'd better be running along."

"But you haven't seen the other pictures . . . and the statues," he protested, attempting to take her arm.

Wynn moved out of his grasp smoothly. "I'm afraid I really don't have the time."

He was very persistent. "But there's a lot of other stuff here by Carson guys. I wish you'd take a look. Come on," he added coaxingly, trying to take the painting from her. "Let me put that in a safe place while you look around. Then at least let me put you in a taxi. Or did you bring your car?"

She realized that they were attracting attention. Blast him for putting her in this position. "Very well," she said resignedly, handing him the painting of the ghostly rose. Irritated, she watched him take it away and put it near the sculpture section, where someone stuck a red sticker on the frame proclaiming "Sold." Blast Duke-Donato Bellini absolutely to hell, she fumed.

But she was really mad at herself for letting him get away with it. To cover her angry confusion, she wandered among the exhibits, looking at them with unseeing eyes. Duke rejoined her. More than ever she was shaken by his towering presence, his upsetting nearness. She could catch the faint aroma of that clean male-musk scent, free of cologne, a blend of faint, healthy sweat, immaculate clothes and his own undeniably masculine smell that affected her so strongly.

As soon as she decently could, she said a little less coldly than before, "I'm sorry, I've really got to go now. I have a dinner date," she lied.

Duke's sensuous mouth tightened, but he answered calmly, "All right. Could I carry the painting for you, Wynn?"

"No, thank you. Really." She was firm.

"Okay." He shrugged. "I'll get it." He did so and returned, handing it to her. "Well, thank you for coming, Miss Carson," he said coolly, nodding. "See you in negotiations."

She was perversely chilled by his sudden compliance with her wishes, wanting him to demur, wanting to reverse the situation again somehow. But she'd cast the die, so all she could do was return his nod just as coolly, wave to Sam and walk out the door.

A few minutes later, while waiting on Seventh

Avenue for a taxi, she heard a shrill whistle right behind her. A cab was approaching. Determined not to let someone else pirate her taxi, Wynn moved out farther into the street.

The cab screeched to a halt. Before she could shift the painting comfortably to open the taxi door, a large male hand reached out from behind her and opened it. "This is *mine*," she said savagely, turning.

Duke Bellini was towering over her, grinning. "Ours, Wynn Carson."

"Hey, buddy," the cabbie snarled. Horns were honking behind him. "Ask her inside. Are you comin' or goin'? They're pilin' up t' Twenty-third."

"Goin'," Duke growled, fairly pushing Wynn into the taxi. He got in beside her, slammed the door and gave the driver Wynn's home address.

As the taxi shot forward, Wynn hissed at Duke Bellini, "I won't be bulldozed like this. You got in my cab without my permission."

"Why, Miss Carson!" he teased her. "You own a fleet of cabs now, besides all the trucks? I'd better get my guys on this tomorrow—are you trying to run a nonunion shop?" He shook his head in mock consternation.

"Damn it," she blurted, "you know what I mean." She never said things like that and was even more annoyed that her temper had made her swear.

"My goodness gracious," he said in a falsetto voice, "what language." He grabbed her hand. The cab had already reached the eastward turnoff at Greenwich Avenue and was taking the turn with squealing tires, just avoiding an irate pedestrian about to cross illegally.

The lurching taxi had paused for a red light at the corner of Sixth Avenue and Village Square before Wynn got her breath. She started to say something, but then thought, What's the use? I can't argue with him now. But just let him try to come in! Mere seconds, it seemed, elapsed as the taxi sped along Eighth Street, threatening a bicyclist, a wandering musician and two dogwalkers before stopping on Fifth across the avenue from the mews.

"This all right?" the driver growled.

"Yes," Duke and Wynn answered at once. He paid the driver and got out, taking the picture from Wynn to help her.

On the sidewalk Wynn said curtly, "Thanks." She held out her hand for the painting, her bag slipping from under her left arm.

"I'll take it," Duke insisted. "You're dropping your purse." Fuming, feeling helpless and frayed, she waited for the light at Fifth and Eighth to change. When the traffic stopped she darted across the street, so Duke had to use long strides to keep up. She unlocked the mews gate and snapped, "Thanks. I'll take it now."

"I'll carry it upstairs for you," he returned in a stubborn tone.

"No, *thank* you." A really good scream, Wynn thought, would help me immensely. It was unbearably irritating, even maddening to be so attracted to a man she couldn't trust as far as she could throw him. And yet, in spite of all that, she had to admit that he looked wonderful, immovable and strong.

"I told you," she repeated, feeling almost desperate, "I have a dinner date. I've got to get ready."

"Break it," he said calmly. "Please, Wynn."

"I can't do that. Or rather, I won't. Are we going to stand here all evening, or are you going to give me my painting?" she demanded.

"I'll carry it upstairs," he said flatly. "I want to talk to you, lady, and damn it, I'm going to. If you want it to be here, then that's fine with me." His jaw was thrust out pugnaciously, and her will felt battered. To make it worse, a neighbor of hers passed by with a pleasant good evening, giving Duke an interested glance.

He's blackmailing me, she raged inwardly. He probably knows I hate scenes and is taking full advantage.

"All right, then," she said savagely. "Carry the wretched thing upstairs, if that's the only way I can get rid of you." She flounced on into the mews, almost letting the front door slam in his face, going ahead of him up the carpeted stairs in angry silence. She unlocked her apartment door and stood aside with an unwelcoming face to let him enter.

"Can I have it *now?*" she asked him sarcastically.

He handed it to her with a chagrined expression, but continued to stand by the door.

"Good night," she said coldly. "Thanks for the haul and delivery."

"Uh-uh, boss-lady. Not yet. Not until I do this." He gently took the painting from her hands and put it down, leaning it against the wall. Then he grabbed her in his massive arms and, as her bag fell to the floor, forced her face up to his for a long and hungry kiss.

She closed her lips, struggling in his hold, but it did no good. He was too strong for her, his big hand holding her small face while he ravaged her mouth with his. Dismayed, Wynn felt her lips parting under his, her very will slipping away. His strong arms were tight around her body; pressed to the length of him, she was aware of every contour of his hard, commanding, steely frame, and her softening flesh caught fire. She was without volition, overwhelmed, her reason snatched from her and blown away like flower petals on the wind.

She had no measure of sense or time, no memory of anything between them but this instant. She only wanted this never to end; her small hands, balled into fists, relaxed, moving up his mighty arms, caressing, stroking, stealing about his sinewy neck as her trembling, eager mouth returned his endless kiss. She was shaking all over, tongued by the flames of a wild, barbaric need.

He made a primitive, groaning sound deep in his throat, and she felt his body quaking, too, as his mouth relearned the shape of hers, as his big hands kneaded her vibrant flesh and traced the form of her sides, descending to the curve of her slender hips to draw her closer, tighter, breathlessly tight until she could feel the desperation of his arousal.

Suddenly he raised his face from hers, gasping, whispering her name over and over, the heat of his breath igniting her mouth, her cheeks and hair. He held her in a bruising grasp, saying hoarsely, "Wynn, oh, Wynn, let me stay, let me stay. At least talk to me. Tell me what happened back there. I was so glad to see you, but all of a sudden you turned so cold."

Leaning back a little, she let her dazzled eyes span the distance from his creamy shirtfront upward to the strong, tanned neck revealed by the wings of its open collar, where a drumming pulsebeat hammered at the hollow of his throat. Her gaze caressed the features of his face, meeting at last his black, piercing eyes. His look was no longer hard and bright, but soft and pleading as he repeated, "Darling, talk to me, talk to me."

It was going too fast, too fast, her mind cried out.

It always went this way whenever Duke Bellini touched her, and now that she could think a little, a kind of sanity came back to her. Something deep in her protested. This was too grave a thing, it said, too gigantic a commitment to make in a fevered moment.

He must have sensed her withdrawal, because his eager expression died with the bright light in his coal-black eyes. Giving her a crooked smile, he said gently, "Sit down with me, Wynn. We've got to talk."

Reluctantly, still half under the spell of his kisses and his close embrace, she moved out of the loose circle of his arms and walked to the couch, sank down on it and leaned back on its comforting cushions. She was more confused, more vulnerable than before. Her treacherous body had betrayed her again, mocking her anger and suspicion.

Duke came slowly after. He stood for an instant looking down at her with a tender expression; then he sat down close beside her. She moved slightly away, not wanting her senses to be overwhelmed by him so soon again. She had to have a minute to gather her thoughts. If he touched her, she would hear only the sound of his voice, not what he had to say.

He didn't touch her. Reaching into his jacket pocket, he got out a pack of cigarettes. "Do you mind?" he asked softly.

"Of course not," she murmured, and he lit one and put lighter and pack on the milk glass table with a soundlessness an absent part of her mind admired. It was clear that he had extraordinary control, over his motions as well as his feelings; that he was far from calm was evidenced by his flared nostrils and still-shallow breath.

"What happened at the Center, Wynn?" he asked her quietly. "In just a minute you changed from . . . from sunshine to ice."

"It's not just what happened at the exhibit," she answered, her voice trembling a little. "It's . . . it's the way it's been from the very start."

"What do you mean?" He put his burning cigarette in an ashtray and reached for her hand. She moved her hand away, noticing the look of hurt around his mouth when she did.

Even this far away from her, she thought, he had the power to confuse and disturb her. Already she was finding it difficult to get her thoughts together. She took a deep breath all the way from her stomach, the way she did when she wanted to calm herself, and managed to reply, "That masquerade the first night we met."

Duke leaned forward and picked up the cigarette, taking a long pull from it. "I'm sorry about that. I really am. But you see, when I heard you introduce yourself at Fedora's, it knocked me off kilter. I realized the position we'd find ourselves in . . . and I still didn't have the guts to tell you who I really was. Not then. I had to put it off a little longer." He smiled at her, and the smile was so open and warm, so devilishly charming, that Wynn began to feel that fatal distraction, stroked by the deep tone of his voice. "I had to go on with the 'masquerade,' as you call it, because I couldn't stand to blow it—that great feeling, that thing we had going between us."

"I felt the same way," she admitted softly. "I couldn't let myself be suspicious of you. Suspicious that you were married . . . taking advantage . . . because . . ." Her words trailed off, and this time when he took her hand, she didn't pull away.

"Because what?" he demanded, his eyes bright and eager.

"Because it was so lovely."

"Wynn. Wynn Carson, you're so sweet, so beautiful." She knew that he was going to kiss her and submitted to his new caress, knowing things were getting out of control again but unable to do the slightest thing about it. All she could do was submit, savoring the taste of his mouth. When he let her lips go for an instant, his breath had quickened. "Wynn, this was meant to happen," he insisted, his strong hands kneading her shoulders. "When I saw you the next morning, at your office, I wanted to take you in my arms right then and there. But you were so cool, and then when you turned me down for lunch . . ." He shook his head. "And then, damn it, I had to go out of town. That's why I sent all the flowers. I was afraid to call you, plain afraid. But I hoped the flowers would . . . remind you of me, maybe."

"Oh, they did. They did, all right," she said a little dryly, moving away from him again.

"What happened today, honey? You've got to tell me," he demanded, caressing her arm through the thin yellow material of her dress, circling her fragile wrist with his fingers, looking at the wrist as if he were amazed at its smallness.

"I heard Weinfeld and Halloran talking," she answered curtly. Some of her earlier anger and suspicion were returning. "Discussing . . . us, obviously."

"What in hell did they say?" he asked her, a steely anger underlining the softness of the question.

"I couldn't hear it all—something about a 'sweetheart deal,'" she said shakily. "They couldn't tell who was conning who." Wynn leaned back against the couch, staring grimly ahead.

"Why, those stupid—" Duke bit off the word. "Wynn, there's no conning here, on your part or on mine. You know that—you *should* know that. The way I feel about you, it's a whole other thing from our positions."

"Is it?" she protested. She felt like crying. "What can there be between us, Duke, but problems?"

"There's this between us," he retorted, moving to her. He took her in his arms again, forcing her head back so that his ravenous mouth could taste hers, exploring, caressing, overpowering it with his own hard lips. She emerged from the kiss breathless and undone. "There's a fire between us," he said. "And it's raging out of all control. *That's* what there is, Wynn Carson, and it means more than anything else. You know it. You feel it. I can tell."

"No. No!" she cried out, wrenching herself out of his insidious hold, trying to avoid his commanding hands. "It won't work, Duke; it just won't work. Everybody will be saying we're . . . we're in cahoots with each other. Nobody will ever let us be together." He tried to touch her again, but she got up from the couch, shaking her head. "No. Please don't do that anymore. This is no good, Duke."

He looked up at her and said solemnly, "This is the only good thing that's ever happened to me." He got to his feet and towered over her, staring down into her eyes with his mesmerizing black stare. "And, lady, if you think I'm giving up on you, you'd better think again." He cupped her face in his hands and kissed her lightly on her nose. "Now, are you coming to dinner with me?"

That traitorous warmth stole over her again. "I told you," she whispered, repeating her earlier lie, "I have a dinner date." She almost wished she hadn't lied; she didn't really want to see him go. She couldn't stand to see him go, she admitted in silence.

"And you won't break it?"

She hesitated. Then she shook her head.

He let out an exasperated breath. "Okay. Okay, then. But tell him it's the last time." He kissed her again and walked out the door.

That does it, she thought. She was seething again with anger and frustration. Of all the arrogant, conceited . . . He actually assumed that she would tell her mythical date that it was the last time.

Some of the tenderness and magic aroused by his kisses evaporated. Now that he was gone, she was more in command of herself. That fact alone, she reflected, should tell her something. It told her that she mustn't let him get the upper hand again. Wynn kept telling herself that, even as her titillated senses kept protesting.

"What did you do, stay here all weekend?" Ruth Wiley quipped when she brought in the mail on Monday morning. "I guess not," she answered herself. "You changed. That's a gorgeous outfit, Wynn."

"Thanks." Wynn, wearing owllike glasses, looked up and smiled at Ruth. It was an overcast day, so she'd chosen a brighter and dressier ensemble than she usually wore to work. She'd needed something special after her really rotten weekend and to compensate for the need to come in early to make up for leaving early Friday.

"Oooh, what's this?" Ruth asked excitedly. The ghostly rose painted by Sam was leaning against the wall cabinet. Wynn had decided that it would brighten up the office and was planning to have it hung that day. "I love it!" Ruth enthused, staring at the picture.

"Do you? Well, take it. It would look great in your office." Ruth's sanctum was a rather austere ivory and gray, which she'd brightened with touches of red. "It might jazz up that blank wall over the files, where you were planning to hang something," Wynn added.

"Oh, I don't want to take it from you." Ruth's rather guilty tone couldn't hide her eagerness to have the painting.

"I insist," Wynn said. "You'll be doing me a favor; Tony'll be banging on your wall instead of mine." Now that she thought of it, she'd just as soon not have a constant reminder of Duke Bellini to stare at all day. If Sam came to the office, which he rarely did anyway, he'd be complimented to hear that her secretary liked the picture so much that she'd stolen it from Wynn.

"Oh yeah? It seems to me people are always doing you favors, taking things off your hands. You're a very generous person. Still, you've twisted my arm." Ruth laughed with pleasure. "I'll take it." Obviously delighted, she took the painting into the outer office.

Wynn started reading the mail, thankful that Ruth hadn't asked her about the artist. Sooner or later she'd notice the signature "Sposato" and inquire, but right then Wynn didn't feel like talking about Friday at all. She'd hardly slept Friday night, making up for it on Saturday by sleeping so late that she couldn't close her eyes until about three Sunday morning, repeating the pattern that night. So she was tired to begin with and feeling strangely vulnerable. Duke couldn't have called her over the weekend, she realized, because her home phone was unlisted. But she had the feeling he'd call today, and she both wanted that and dreaded it. That was the worst part of it, she raged inwardly, this stupid indecision. Wynn Carson was usually a very decisive woman, but when it came to Duke Bellini . . .

Wynn shook her head and forced herself to concentrate on the mail.

Her mood didn't improve greatly when, while she was in the midst of dictation, the company treasurer, Jonathan Court, stuck his austere head around the frame of the open door. "Have you got a minute, Wynn?" he asked her in his curt, unsmiling fashion, ignoring Ruth. Wynn noticed that he was holding a sheaf of stapled papers in his thin hand.

Good morning, Mr. Sunshine, Wynn said to herself dryly. Court never asked anyone how the weekend had been or anything else as human as that. "I'll be through here shortly," she answered in the same manner as his, nodding at Ruth. It forced him to mumble, "Ruth," and the secretary smiled at him, nodding back.

"Have a seat, Jon," Wynn said, calling him by the same shortened form of his first name that Big Mike had always used, although he unfailingly called himself Jonathan. If ever there was an appropriate Jonathan, Wynn judged with the day's first real amusement, it was Court. He was really more like Cotton Mather than Ebenezer Scrooge, with his tall, forbidding thinness, his aristocratic features and the drab colors he always affected. Ruth had commented once, to Wynn's delight, that Mr. Court was the color of the file cabinets in the typing pool, all tan and steel; his eyes and hair were steel colored, and he invariably wore a succession of sandy beige suits that varied only in the weight of the material, with ties the shades of invalids' complexions.

Wynn repressed a grin at the memory and dictated the last letter to Ruth while Jonathan Court paced pointedly over the carpet in the conference area, as if to reproach her for keeping him waiting. "Thanks, Ruth," Wynn said when they were through, and the secretary seemed thankful to go back to her own desk.

"Sorry, Jon," Wynn said in as friendly a voice as she could muster. "Please, sit down."

"No thanks," he said coldly. There had been trouble between them from the first. He had barely been able to hide his disapproval of Wynn's inheriting the wheel at Carson's, and she disliked having to deal with him. "These demands," he said brusquely, "are outrageous." He thrust the stapled sheets at her, and she could see underlinings and scribbles. He acted like it was his own money.

"We've discussed this before," she said a bit impatiently. "Is there anything new here?"

He stiffened with resentment. "I think you'll find that I've gone into the matter in greater detail," he countered in a huffy tone. "Unless there's a sharp downward revision, we're going to be running a charity here." *His own money.*

She ignored the last remark. "Give me a chance to study this, and I'll get back to you as soon as I can." Jonathan Court had a sublime disregard for increased living costs and all the human factors involved in contract negotiations, as Big Mike had told Wynn many times. He lived with figures. Certainly he looked like someone who had no interest in anything else. Wynn spared a compassionate thought to the sad-faced Mrs. Court, who looked as if she might drink a little too much—perhaps with reason. He was probably just as stingy at home.

"I'll look this over right away," she repeated.

"Please do," he said austerely. "We've got to present a united front in three days, you know. At this point, I'm not too sanguine about the talks."

*Sanguine.* Good heavens. He was always using expressions like that, right out of a bleak, old-time novel.

"Because I'm president?" she asked belligerently. If there was anything that got to him, it was plain speaking from a woman, in particular the young shrimp who had the temerity to be his employer.

"That's a rather rash way to put it," he said stuffily. "I was referring to your somewhat permissive attitude at the preliminary meeting."

"Well, what would you prefer?" Wynn inquired coldly, as her temper slipped its moorings. "To have me grump us right into a strike?"

"There's no need to use such extravagant language," Court objected, and Wynn was annoyed at herself for losing her cool. "But I think that, in your inexperience, you are showing a too generous attitude, which is not practical. Your views are much more liberal than your father's. I can only hope," he continued with a frosty smile, "that some of Mike Carson's toughness rubbed off on you. We're going to need that."

"You can bet it did, Jon." Wynn looked up, meeting his metallic eyes with a confident stare. "Now, if you'll forgive me, I've got a meeting with the lawyers in a little while. I'll look over your comments as soon as I can."

"Of course," he replied stiffly. Without another word he stalked out of the office.

"Heavens," she exclaimed. He was the living end; she imagined that, if he had his way, she'd be shut up in a drawing room with an embroidery hoop until the proper fellow came along to make an honest and domesticated woman of her.

Her buzzer sounded, and Ruth's voice came through. "No rest for the weary. The Honorable Howard B. on two."

That's all I need, Wynn decided. "I'll take it," she said, resigned.

Howard's tone irritated her at once. "Wynn, my darling girl." He'd missed his calling. He should have been an actor, with that brassy, resonant speech that hardly needed a phone. She wondered why he didn't just lean out of a City Hall window and call out over Broadway. "You've been avoiding me, beautiful."

"Have I?" she parried. "I've been awfully busy, Howard."

"Saturdays and Sundays and nights, too?" he inquired in a skeptical way. "You're not locked up with the dese and dose guys yet. That's not till Friday."

Her anger caught fire, both at his snobbish reference to the union men and at the fact that he knew so much about Carson's business. "Well, aren't you the private-sector expert?" she demanded with acid sweetness. "What has Carson's got to do with City Hall?"

"Not nearly enough, as far as I'm concerned," he said smoothly. "If I had my way—and you know it very well—the president of Carson's would be a political wife."

"Howard," she said hastily, "I've got a meeting in about five minutes. I've got to go."

"Not yet, cruel lady, *ma belle dame sans merci!*" His pompous, perfect French belled out, hurting her ear, and it occurred to her again how different it had been when Duke Bellini had shown an interest in Mozart and T. S. Eliot. Every time Howard made a reference like that, it came off as affected, elitist. "Not yet," he pleaded in mock horror. "Have lunch with me, darling. You've probably been living on pizza, considering—" He stopped abruptly, and she wondered what that meant.

But she passed over it, saying, "I don't think so."

"Look, please." He sounded less phony now and she thought, Why not? He'd keep bugging her until she consented.

"All right," she accepted without grace.

"Wonderful!" he boomed. "You name the place. I'll make the reservations."

Suddenly feeling spoiled and contrary, perversely glad to be running things again instead of being led, Wynn named a newly redecorated Italian restaurant not far from the office.

"Gaudy, gaudy," Howard scoffed. "But you're the boss-lady," he acknowledged. "What time?"

"I'll meet you there at one-thirty." After enduring his effusive good-byes, she hung up.

The meeting with the lawyers went well, and the afternoon seemed to be on an upswing when Wynn walked out of the light drizzle into the restaurant. Howard got up from the bar, and his face lit up when he saw her. She had to admit he was a very good-looking man, but when he spoke . . . A memory of that first night, with Duke, assailed her. Howard was blond, just like her. He was not the "fatal opposite" of her mother's romantic old story.

It occurred to her, for the first time, that she had purposely chosen an Italian restaurant. Some devil, she thought, had made her choose it, a mean and childish trick, because Howard wasn't fond of

Italian food. But it was more than that, she knew. Somehow this place brought back Fedora's.

She was unsettled, disturbed, when she walked toward Howard Bartley, submitting to his peck on her cheek.

"You look glorious," he said, his blue gaze taking in her vivid, graceful ensemble. "A sight for sad eyes on this dreary day."

She managed a smile as they were shown to their table, glad for the light warmth of the jacket that matched her dress, because the place was air-conditioned to accommodate weather like the previous day's and hadn't yet caught up with the cool rawness of today. And yet she wondered if the temperature was what was making her feel cold. She had a suspicion that it was Howard's company, and also the fact that the very Italian atmosphere reminded her so sharply of Duke. The room seemed full of big, dark, macho men, not the Ceebee kind, but attorneys, politicians and businessmen. Still, they weren't far removed, she mused, from the simpler days. She recognized an official who'd started out as a construction laborer but was now a bigwig at City Hall; he had owned half of a huge construction company as well.

She gave Howard her cocktail order, while from a speaker Caruso cried out *"Vesti la giubba,"* from *Pagliacci,* with heart-rending lyricism—"On with the Play."

"Enrico always puts so much pasta in it," Howard remarked with contempt. His brassy voice jarred Wynn, whose heart always melted at the aria, reacting to the almost impossible sweetness in Caruso's tone.

But it was the sound of the first name that made

her repeat, significantly, "Enrico?" It was the first name of Duke's "adopted uncle."

"Enrico Caruso, lovely one. An odd question from an opera buff like you." Howard rapped his fist lightly on the table, asking humorously, "Wynn . . . Wynn . . . are you there?"

She pulled herself together. "I'm here." But she was still flowing with the plaintive aria, still reacting to the stirring music. "On with the play," she reflected. I've got to go on with it, too, no matter how awful I feel. She recalled the engraved plaque of Big Mike's that was still on her desk. "Keep 'em rolling," it said in copper letters on a walnut ground. She, Wynn Carson, would have to keep 'em rolling in Big Mike's place.

"What's that dreamy expression for?" Howard demanded, putting down his glass and leaning toward her. "Somebody else taking my place?" he asked, trying to keep a light tone. But his eyes were earnest.

Poor Howard. He didn't have a place to be taken. Wynn answered with a tight smile, "Sorry. I guess it's the negotiations."

"Tough for you, the first time around," he said sympathetically. "But their demands, in essence, aren't too different from the last time, only the usual. Keep up with inflation and all that." Suddenly he seemed to bite off the words, as if realizing that he'd given something away.

"How did you know that?" she demanded. This knowledge and his earlier remark about pizza—did he have some inside track at Carson's, some knowledge of her association with Duke? The idea made her very uneasy. "How did you know?" she repeated.

"Jonathan Court." Howard looked chagrined, annoyed at himself for his indiscretion. "He disagrees with me, naturally."

"What does he have to do with it?" Wynn asked coldly.

"Didn't you know? Jonathan's my mother's cousin. We were having dinner at his house the other night. Naturally the subject came up." Howard looked down into his drink.

"No, I didn't know. That's very interesting." Wynn couldn't keep the acid from her voice. "So you have a little spy right in my office, it seems."

Howard didn't answer, merely looked rather sullen.

"And what was that remark about pizza?" she prodded. "What was *that* supposed to mean?"

Howard smiled at her, but it wasn't a pleasant smile. "I saw you that night, taking that . . . taking Bellini home with you. And he stayed a good long time, which is more than *I've* ever been allowed. Naturally I assumed that by now you'd be haunting pizza parlors, so I wanted you to get a decent meal for a change. Unfortunately, you chose this place."

He had raised his voice, and the men at the next table must have heard. Glancing over, Wynn caught sight of the expression on the face of her acquaintance, Mario Raguso, whose sons ran the construction business. Mario had resigned when he was elected to city office, so there wouldn't be any conflict of interest, but there was no way he wouldn't tell this tidbit to his sons, Eddie and Sal, whom Wynn knew and liked. Carson's trucks delivered material to all Raguso construction sites. Now she caught an irritated gleam in Mario's dark eyes. He had obviously overheard Howard's denigration of Duke Bellini and the restaurant.

She took a spiteful pleasure in the occurrence. Mario Raguso had the power to help defeat any of the bills introduced by Howard Bartley, and Howard certainly wasn't covering himself with glory now. Wynn saw Howard become belatedly aware of the neighboring table's occupants; his smooth face reddened with vexation.

He was even more dismayed when Wynn said abruptly, "You'll have to forgive me, Howard. This is absolutely awful of me, but I have an appointment that slipped my mind. I simply must go. I'm sorry." He had hardly scrambled to his feet when she was at the door. She rushed out to the street a moment later.

Relieved, she inhaled the moist air on West Broadway and walked quickly uptown toward the office.

Ruth could hardly hide her surprise when Wynn passed her, saying over her shoulder, "Order me a sandwich, would you? Anything."

A little later, when Ruth brought the order in, Wynn asked calmly, "How much?"

Ruth told her and she reimbursed the older woman. "Gee, Howard B. must be some big spender," Ruth commented. "Where did he take you, to a hot dog wagon?"

Wynn just laughed, not answering. After she had wolfed down her lunch, she went back to work with renewed zest. Good-bye, Councilman, she decided. First Howard Bartley spied on her personal activities, then he used his direct line to the Carson treasury. Wonderful, just wonderful, was her silent, sarcastic judgment.

It was four o'clock before she knew it. She felt unduly tired, but then, it had been quite a day. To ease her tense neck muscles, she got up and wandered to the broad corner window, resting her weary eyes, too, by staring at the trees in City Hall park. They were damp and green, the grass bright emerald, a refreshing sight. Starlings, pigeons and sparrows vied for the gloomy, gunmetal gray air. There was something wistful and haunting about the hues at that time of day. A sharp sensation of loneliness and loss pierced her.

When the private line rang, she hurried to answer. It was Duke Bellini. His rough yet gentle voice was all she needed to send a shiver along her every nerve.

"It was a long haul this weekend, Wynn." His words were quiet and solemn. "How are you? Are you all right? Can you forgive me for coming on so strong . . . again?" The questions tumbled out.

She was almost too overwhelmed to answer. As always, his voice affected her like hands on her naked body. But at last she managed to reply, with a hint of humor, "One thing at a time, Mr. Bellini. It wasn't such a great weekend at that. I'm partially all right."

"What does that mean?" he asked with quick anxiety. "You're not sick, are you?"

"A little sick of being chairman of the board," she answered with an honesty that surprised her.

She could hear his relief when he said, "I couldn't get your home number from the operator. I tried to convince her it was life or death, but even that didn't work. It *was* life or death to me, though, Wynn. I nearly came over, but I was afraid that would just . . . get you mad." His voice was so serious, so eager, that she felt herself melting again, warming to him more and more.

Oh, Duke, Duke, her mind cried out in silence.

"Are you still there?" he asked.

"Yes, yes. I'm here," she said softly.

"Then I tried to get you all day today—rather, I tried a couple of times this morning. You were in a meeting; then you were out of the office. This afternoon you were out to lunch." Wynn recalled that Ruth mentioned going to the private phone twice to answer, but that the caller had hung up. "And then," Duke rushed on, exasperated, "I had to go out in the field, and I ran into three ripped-off phones and one in a bar that was out of order. I thought about calling from a job site, but there were things I wanted to say privately, and the damned phone was on the foreman's desk."

An even greater warmth flooded Wynn. "There are days like that, aren't there?" she murmured.

"Look, lady," he interjected, "you've got to let me take you to dinner. Please." He paused. "Please." When she didn't reply, he went on, "The toughest bosses at least consent to listen to a guy." She could almost see his dawning smile, the dazzling whiteness against his tan face. The image of that sensuous mouth sent a hot thrill to her very core.

"All right," she said, her voice a little shaky with emotion. "I'll listen."

"Can we negotiate dinner, then?" he asked, his tone jubilant.

"I don't see why not," she replied with deceptive casualness. She was dying to see him, had been for the last three nights and three days. He named a restaurant on Desbrosses Street. "Where's Desbrosses Street?" she demanded. "I've never heard of it."

His vital laugh echoed along the line. "You're a phony trucker if you don't know Desbrosses Street. It's almost nothing but rigs and warehouses, and right in the middle of it is this great, great restaurant. Can you make it right after work? I know I'm not giving you much notice," he apologized.

Especially glad that she was wearing a lovely dress, she answered quickly, "I don't need that much notice today. After work would be just fine."

She heard his raggedly exhaled breath. "You don't know what good news that is. I guess it would be better if I didn't pick you up there," he said awkwardly.

"I'll get a cab."

"No way. That district's not safe enough, even if you're in a cab." She couldn't help being gratified by his protective insistence; it made her feel extremely feminine and romantic. "I'll pick you up next door to your office at, say, five-thirty? Okay? I'll be in a red Porsche."

"Fine," she agreed. A Porsche. So that's why the Fiat had been duck soup for him. "See you then," she said.

*"Arrividerla,"* he said softly and hung up.

Wynn was glad when Ruth left and she had the office to herself. She worked late so often that her secretary took it for granted. But as soon as Ruth was gone, Wynn got an extra makeup kit out of her desk and hurried to the ladies' room. She decided to do a complete overhaul. She wanted to look very special for this dinner date.

As she began making up anew, Wynn stared at her excited reflection in the glass. They were carrying dangerous cargo, she and Duke Bellini, considering all they both had at stake. But surely this couldn't hurt, she tried to convince herself, seeing him again just for dinner.

## Chapter 5

WYNN WALKED OUT OF THE LOBBY RIGHT ON TIME. As soon as she saw the dark red Porsche draw up, indifferent to honking horns and police whistles, she had a feeling that it was going to be more than just a dinner.

Duke was about to get out in the midst of it all, but she waved and hurried to the low-slung car to prevent that. He opened the passenger door for her, and she quickly got in. Traffic was at a standstill, so he was able to sit and stare at her for a long moment. His dark gaze slowly wandered over her, taking in her casually waving golden hair, curlier with the day's moisture. Her blue stare locked with his. The bright black look seemed to caress her every feature; she saw it linger on her mouth, descend to the vivid ruffled collar of her soft dress, all the way down to her small, narrow slingbacks of taupe suede.

"You're so beautiful," he said with wonder. Suddenly it seemed to her that they were utterly alone in the raucous sea of traffic clotting Broadway on this ordinary Monday evening that wasn't ordinary anymore. It might have been the first light of creation, the first awareness between a man and woman, alone and bemused in a world that housed no other people, no one but them. She was dazzled and transformed, knowing that she had never felt such a titanic, mysterious thing before. She could find nothing to say at all.

He reached out one strong hand to touch her hair and stroke her cheek. "So beautiful," he repeated, the words fading in the traffic noise that drifted through the window open to the mild twilight air. It was no longer drizzling, but the faint wind was still heavy with the smell of rain, and he was so near that her nostrils quivered at his inimitable scent. With enchantment and delight, she breathed his smells of crisp, immaculate fabric and tobacco, the clean and leathery male musk of his vibrant skin.

The strange and wonderful sense of altered time persisted when he urged the Porsche into motion. She watched his big hands take control of the car as they drove slowly away, not noticing at all what streets they passed, what turns he made with absent skill, because her body was so near his, her hip beside his hard thigh. Even though he kept his dark eyes trained ahead in the blue light of evening, she could tell that another part of his attention never left her for a moment.

The Porsche entered an area of solid factories and warehouses, massive and plain in the gathering dark, surrounded by fields of gigantic trucks that were like huge, benign animals crouched in the thickened dusk. Astounded, she heard faint music and caught sight, to the right of them as he turned, of a brightly lit building that should never have been there at all. Her sense of magic deepened. This was like some urban fairy tale. There in the midst of that deserted, workaday place was a fabulous restaurant right off the Riviera. The building was white, with a brilliant entrance of shining glass, a plaza with a fountain and tall, potted palm trees.

Duke eased up the drive and slowed. He glanced aside at Wynn, smiling at her expression. *"Ecco,"* he proclaimed. "Here it is—Bravura's."

"I feel as if a wizard had waved his wand," she said softly, smiling into his dark, shining eyes. She could tell from his expression that her reaction filled him with delight. He raised one of her hands to his lips and kissed it; a tingling warmth began from the point of his touch, wild flames licking her excited nerves.

The fairy-tale sense grew stronger and stronger as a genial man with a ruddy face, dressed in a dark red uniform with gold buttons and gilded braid, opened the passenger door and handed Wynn out as if she were a breakable treasure that required the most delicate care. Then Duke was at her side, the Porsche was being driven away by an unseen attendant and they were entering the tall glass doors in the golden light.

A pale, tuxedoed captain with dark, brilliant eyes and features like a Roman prince bowed to them, saying *"Buona sera, signorina; Signor Bellini."* He gave Duke a faint, discreet smile of congratulation, so faint that it was almost imperceptible. The whole thing carried with it a splendor that Wynn had never quite experienced before, in spite of her acquaintance with the elegant places of New York. She felt as if they were, at that moment, no longer merely a woman and a man, but a princess with her prince.

Nothing that followed detracted from that buoyant impression. A headwaiter almost as stately as the captain at the door led them through a blur of widely spaced tables glittering with crystal and silver and china, past walls draped in purple red velvet to a flight of carpeted stairs. The music that Wynn had heard faintly from afar surrounded her now— honeyed violins sobbing "Mattinata." A tenor joined the sound of mellow strings as they came nearer to the top of the stairs, and his poignant voice caressing the Italian words aroused a new and melting warmth in her whole thrilled body.

Upstairs they were given into the smiling charge of still another waiter, this one very young, and he seemed to bless the two of them with his wistful smile. Wynn fairly floated over the thick wine-colored carpet to the table designated for them. The waiter held out her velvet-covered chair and she sat down. Duke stood until she was seated, and for the first time her dazzled eyes took in the full view of him, towering above her in the golden light. He was dressed in a flawlessly tailored suit of some dark, soft-looking fabric, his shirt a pristine ivory, his tie a melange of rich, swirling burgundy and gray and jade. She had never seen him look quite so magnificent; he had never had quite that kind of majesty before. In the instant before he took his chair, staring at her as if enchanted, she imagined still another wondrous thing: Donato Bellini, once in exile, had come back to the palace he had once owned. He was in his rightful place at last.

The strolling violinists, followed by the tenor in

his dark red clothes and still rendering "Mattinata,"
wandered to their table. Duke reached across its
small white-covered circle, over a low bowl of blood
red roses, to take her hand, and a flood of almost
unbearable longing swept over Wynn in a mighty
wave. A molten thread of fire was drawn along her
every vein. She could tell that he sensed it, was
drowning in it, too, because his dark eyes burned
and widened as they stared into hers; his sensuous
mouth relaxed and trembled. He held her small hand
in a bruising grasp, his breath quickened, growing
shallow.

When the young waiter handed him the list of
wines, Duke looked at it almost without recognition,
like a man rudely aroused from sleep. He put it
down, giving her a bemused and sheepish smile.
Then the man ceremoniously awarded them the
bronze booklets of menus. Wynn opened hers with
trembling hands; the Italian names of dishes, in
flowing script, swam before her sight.

"I'll leave it to you," she said to Duke, staring
helplessly into his night-black, steady eyes. She was
only dimly conscious of his directions to the waiter,
only half aware that the violins and tenor had
wandered away again, that cocktails were being set
before them. She took a sip of hers from a fragile
stemmed glass.

She glanced around. This room was far quieter
than the room downstairs and sparsely populated at
this early hour. Again she had the sense that she and
Duke Bellini were separate from the world.

When her look returned to him, she saw that he
was taking a quick, substantial drink from his massive highball glass. He set it down and said in a low,
serious voice, "Oh, Wynn, there's so much I
planned to say. Now, looking at you like this, I can

hardly remember. I never thought I'd meet someone who . . . belonged here, who belonged with me."

She was so overwhelmed that she couldn't answer. He put his hand over hers again and continued in a slow, hesitant fashion. "I never thought that Duke Bellini could talk like this"—he smiled a little—"but you're like . . . like a jewel in a ring tonight. The lady of the *belle maniere,*" he added, giving her a sudden, brilliant smile.

*"Belle maniere,"* she repeated after him. The words sounded like music, like the trill of a bird. "How beautiful that is," she said. "What does it mean?"

"The beautiful manner," he translated, his look pausing on her mouth. "Or, as the fancy people used to say, 'good breeding.' I got that from my mother. She's Florentine and very proud. My father," he said, chuckling, "was a Siciliano, very rough and very plain."

"Like my mother and my father," she answered with delight. So that explained the puzzle that was Duke Bellini—the almost royal pride from his mother, the strength and earthiness of Sicily from his father. But nothing, she reflected, could ever explain this particular magic, this enchantment between them that transformed the ordinary world into a place that she had only dreamed of before.

She hardly noticed what the waiter set before them, nor, apparently, did Duke, because he ignored it totally. When the waiter had gone away, he rushed into speech again.

"When I first saw you, I reacted the way any man would have—I wanted you, pure and simple. Wanted you from the top of your little golden head down to your feet. I couldn't believe how small you were"—he smiled—"how dainty. Your shoes looked like a doll's, they were so small." As on that first evening, she felt no resentment at all at his reference to her size. He always made it sound endearing, lovely. His big hand slipped up her arm and practically burned her skin beneath the soft print fabric of her long, belled sleeve.

"And then," he continued, "when we were in Fedora's and you gave your name, I suddenly realized who you were. I'd seen your picture, I guess, in a paper somewhere. I was afraid my real name would turn you off. So I played a foolish game, to be with you a little longer, as long as I possibly could. But after, when we were at your place and I knew how . . . sweet you were, how much it meant . . . to both of us, the whole game changed. I couldn't take advantage. Do you see? Do you at least begin to see?"

"Yes." She nodded slowly. "Yes, I do." She was feeling even more vulnerable with him than she had before.

"We're dangerous cargo for each other," he said in a sober tone. "But there's no way I can stay away from you, no way at all. And I have a feeling it's the same for you. Tell me it is, Wynn. Please tell me."

"It is the same." Her words were so soft that he had to lean forward to hear them. "The very same with me."

Looking up at him shyly, she saw his face light up with complete and sudden and overwhelming happiness; his dark eyes were smiling, glittering brighter than the candles. "Let's get out of here," he urged her, a hint of laughter bubbling in his voice. "I won't be rushing off tonight. I give you my guarantee."

The very core of her ignited at the implication of his words.

She nodded, giving him a shaky smile. "This will be the second dinner we haven't had together."

He shrugged, grinned and signaled the attentive waiter for the bill. Trying to hide his shocked surprise, the young waiter withdrew, returning in seconds with the check for Duke Bellini.

And then everything was moving again with dizzying speed; almost before she knew it, they were downstairs, bowed out by smiling, puzzled attendants whose hands neatly received Duke's folded bills. Sooner than she had expected, they moved down the golden-shadowed drive again to the dark, abandoned street. The Porsche shot along a dimly lit block and abruptly halted. "Wynn." Duke braked and, turning to her, grabbed her by the shoulders, pulling her to him so their hungry mouths could meet.

"I couldn't stand it another minute," he whispered hoarsely when he finally let go of her. With a new boldness she hardly recognized as hers, Wynn took his hard, smooth-shaven face between her own small hands and coaxed his lips downward to cover her eager mouth again. This time she sensed even more surely the desperation of his need, the flaming height of his desire, fanned by her caress. Yet all the while she knew, with an amazed, sudden conviction, that his wanting was no greater than hers. She was all flame and longing, lapped and rocked and battered by rhythmic, increasing waves of desire. His hands found her just-awakened breasts, traced their sweet shape below her jacket until she began to quake with the wild, barbaric yearning to feel his fingers on her naked skin.

She felt her nipples bloom in excitement, moaned softly as his hands kneaded and stroked a downward

path from her throbbing breasts along her stomach
and her thighs to grasp her shaking legs. Then his
dark head was in her lap, and she quivered to the
hot, quick breath of his mouth caressing her through
the fabric of her dress. A car passed them with
stunning quickness, its garish headlights rousing
them.

Duke straightened, breathing hard, and declared
hoarsely, "This isn't the time, the place. I'll take us
home."

Still trembling, she lay back against the leather
cushions of the car, unbearably touched by his
saying "take us home," as if from then on their home
would be together.

He started the car again. "Come here," he ordered with tender roughness, and obediently she
moved close to him so he could cradle her in his arm
as he drove.

After the darkness, the lights of the busier streets
were an unreal blur of blinding, phosphorescent
stars. He slowed a little and gently withdrew his arm
so he could put both hands on the wheel. She leaned
against him, placing a timid hand on his hard knee.
She felt his leg tremble, and the Porsche swerved
slightly; she took her hand away.

Regaining control, he took his right hand from the
steering wheel and guided her hand back to his knee.
They were already at the foot of Sixth Avenue. He
was obliged to slow down, threading the way between the thickening traffic. When they stopped for
a red light, he glanced at her and grinned.

"I've almost forgotten how to get there. You'll
never know what you do to me, Wynn Carson."

Heedless of the people crossing the avenue, she
leaned toward him and buried her face against his

shoulder. His whole body was shaking slightly; she returned her hand to his knee. When he accelerated again, she thrilled to the play of hard muscles in his long, lean leg and closed her eyes to the carnival of Eighth Street as he turned, not wanting to meet the staring eyes of crossing strangers, not wanting to look into any eyes but his. Not this hour, not tonight, she thought, and the thought sang in her. Oh, don't let there be anyone in the mews when we get there, she prayed in silence. Just this once, she needed the continued sense of their utter apartness from the rest of the world. She had no idea of the time, but was unwilling to open her eyes to look at the gold watch on her wrist. The actual hour seemed a paltry thing in the face of this enchantment.

She kept her eyes closed until she swayed with the turning Porsche and knew they were on Fifth Avenue, heard nothing pass them as the car turned again and drew up in the mews. "We're here," he said softly in her ear, and she opened her eyes, alert to the need to get out and unlock the gate. She opened the car door eagerly, seeing him get out, too. He stood with his arm around her as she fumbled in her bag for the key. Then he took the key from her hand and put it in the lock and turned it.

He gave her back the key, smiling down at her tremulously, keeping his hard hand on her waist while they moved slowly, close together, toward her door, their thighs brushing like bemused performers in an exhibition dance.

Somehow, she was hardly aware how, she had given him the door key and he had admitted them, and they were going swiftly up the one flight of carpeted stairs; he was letting them in her apartment. She felt too hypnotized to handle even the simplest mechanical thing. He must have known that, because he'd taken over calmly, and she was grateful for it.

Gently he placed her keys on the table in the foyer and closed the door. Letting her bag fall to the rug, she went into his arms. He held her loosely, taking off her jacket as if he were undressing a child, placing it carefully on the foyer chair.

"Come, darling," he said with extreme softness and led her by the hand to the long couch, urging her to sit down. Her knees were trembling. Gratefully she sank down onto the familiar, welcoming cushions, looking up at him while he took off his suit jacket and tossed it carelessly onto an easy chair. She was certain the worship in her eyes was clear to him. The big, dimly lit room, where she had left a lamp burning, as usual, was a quiet haven. Faint city sounds drifted in through the open windows.

"Would you like some music?" she asked in a small, shaky voice.

He shook his head. "We don't need music, Wynn." He knelt down on the rug in front of her and lowered his head to her knee, stroking her thighs rhythmically as he spoke against her legs. "This is music enough," she heard him say softly against her, the loving declaration muffled by the material of her skirt, his heated breath seeming to penetrate the fabric and the straining nylon of her pantyhose. "Don't move," he ordered gently. "Lie back. Be easy. Let me love you."

Melting, submissive, she obeyed, letting her whole body go slack and soft as she leaned back again on the well-known sofa. She closed her eyes. He took off her shoes, sliding them off her feet, and his touch was so excruciatingly sweet that she gave a low cry.

She felt his hands ascending her ankles and her slender calves, stroking her thighs once more until she trembled and moaned. Her cry was wordless, pleading, but she heard him murmur, "Easy, baby, easy and slow," his words drawn out cajolingly.

She said in faint protest, feeling a dreadful shyness, "The lamp . . . the lamp." He must have understood at once, because he let go of her, and she saw him stride to the lamp and turn it off. The room was almost dark. Only the golden lanterns of the opposite mews dispelled the shadows, and Wynn felt free and daring once more. In an instant he was back, kneeling down again to take up his soft caresses.

A flame leaped up her body, gathering into a ball of heat in the very center of her. She arched backward with the dreadful power of her need; it was like a bolt of lightning in her. She heard a sound like sobbing emerge from her own throat; then his quickening hands were rising commandingly up her calves, over her thighs, easing back the pleated skirt of her dress, moving toward the throbbing, aching center of her desire, which thrust upward, waiting for the ultimate caress.

He peeled away the snug, constricting panty hose, and in the dark she heard him hoarsely cry out her name. He had moved closer to her, kneading her naked hips, lifting her upward so that his mouth could taste her bare skin.

With teasing, excruciating leisure, that unseen mouth moved open-lipped and moist over her vibrant flesh, licking her knees and her upper legs, traveling upward in an arrowing path, nuzzling the golden luxuriance of her secret body for so long that she thought a scream would be torn from her lips.

Then his questing tongue found at last the key to all her frenzy. At the first electric contact, her whole self leaped and shuddered; thrashing in his hold and moaning, she was lost to everything. There was nothing, nothing in the wide world left but that one flaming point of desire, that magic frenzy, and she quivered, arching as his rhythmic tongue continued and continued and continued, waves of pleasure lapping at her, washing her like sea waves in a fiery dream.

The waves began to narrow, drawing to a high, thin peak; she balanced on its perilous summit. Then it broke. A shrill, faint, almost mourning cry was pulled from her, a cry so deep that it seemed to come not from her throat, but from her throbbing core. She shook her head, turning her face from side to side in a crazy gesture of protest that was the ultimate assent.

She felt the hard hands on her upper legs again, stroking, then his mouth caressed her thighs as he grasped her ankles in a steely grip. She reached out to find him and discovered the desperation of his own desire. Sensing his withdrawal, she waited, listening to the sounds of his undressing. Then his hands were on her hands, drawing her upright; his naked hardness was pressed against her, seeking her through her clothes. She reached up to the back of her neck and undid the fastening of her dress; he realized what she was doing and moved back. She undid the zipper of the suddenly intrusive garment, then raised the dress over her head with his eager help. He unhooked and snatched away her thin brassiere.

Then he took her in his arms again, and they moved into each other. She felt his imperious maleness ask for her secret body. With a low exclamation he lifted her, scooping her naked body into his arms, striding toward the one dim light that streamed outward from the bedroom.

He laid her on the wide bed and stood looking down at her. Now she could see him, and she feasted in the sight of his bare and powerful body, drinking it in, from his tousled hair to his black eyes, blazing in his tanned face, almost mad with wanting. His chest was darkened with black, soft-looking curls that grew in a triangle to his narrow waist, and her emboldened look followed it lower.

He lowered himself to her, and from beneath half-closed lids she saw his eager mouth approaching hers. His midnight eyes blotted out the room as they at last came together, his thrusting, quaking body bringing both of them to a swift and shuddering release. The world rocked for her, exploded. For one breathless instant he winced with a joy that seemed almost agonizing. A sobbing cry, inchoate words, escaped his quivering mouth, and then he lowered himself to lie at her side, drawing her at once into his hard embrace.

She lay weakly against him, her parted lips tasting the salty tendrils on his chest, moistened with his clean, sea-smelling sweat. She kissed him with the same small, nibbling kisses he had given her in that dark, mad interval in the living room. His arm was like a vise around her back, pulling her closer and closer. She nuzzled into him, burrowing until her head was hiding in the hollow of his shoulder.

He chuckled softly. "Where have you gone? I can't find you. You've disappeared, and I want to kiss you . . . *cara mia, fata bellezza.*" She melted with an almost painful tenderness at the beauty of the words and came out of her hiding place. He kissed the top of her head, then stroked her tumbled hair, her shoulder and her slender, satiny arm.

"No, no," he instructed gently, "not *that* far away." He half-lifted her whole body with one strong arm until she was lying closer against him, their legs entwined.

She leaned her head back and looked up at him; in the dim light his black eyes gleamed like coals, devouring her.

"What did you call me?" she asked him with a smile.

"My darling," he translated. "Beautiful fairy." His voice was husky with emotion, his huge hand still stroking her side.

"Oh, Duke." She detached herself gently, drawing her body upward until she was lying on him, their bodies pressed together. She took his cheeks in her hands and kissed his face again and again, at last meeting his delighted mouth with hers. "It's so wonderful, so strange that you should call me that. Because I had the oddest feeling tonight that we weren't even in New York, that we were in a kind of fairyland. Oh, I have so much to tell you, about what it was like for me."

He squeezed her closer to him. "Well, you'd better not do it this way," he retorted with tender humor.

"Why not?"

"*That's* why not," he said breathlessly as, amazed, she felt the springing renewal of his desire.

"How can that be?" she teased him.

He could hardly speak; his words were choked and strained as he answered. "You get me crazy. I can't get over this; I can't get over you. Oh, Wynn, you're so . . ."

And then there were no more words. Wildly, she was kissing him and he was holding her closer, ever closer, until she was boldly making love to him, her softness surrounding him. She moved with frenzied and unaccustomed motions for his delight, heard him groan and cry out, brought him joy in ways she didn't know she knew. Wilder and faster, totally abandoned, she moved until she felt still another sharp, painfully pleasurable stab of thin, high ecstasy, and her innermost and secret body knew his answering fulfillment.

He gave a loud, astonished cry, holding their bodies bruisingly together. She fell upon him with her face resting against the throbbing pulse of his sinewy neck, conscious of the heavy drumming of his heart against her breasts. Very gently, after a long moment, he relaxed, circling her body with his arms and sighing.

She started to move from him, down to the bed, thinking she might be heavy on him. "Where are you going?" he demanded softly, tightening his hold.

"I must be heavy," she murmured.

"Heavy!" She could feel him shaking with quiet laughter. "You're about as heavy as a powder puff." He squeezed her closer. "Wynn, oh, Wynn, I can't believe this is true; I don't believe this is happening."

His strong, calloused hands caressed her back, tracing the roundness of her. "So soft," he whispered. "Like silk, like satin."

She trembled at the words, at the touch of his powerful hands, and kissed his neck and the hollow of his throat.

"Tired?" he whispered.

"Yes," she admitted. "So tired." She heard her thickening reply; her tongue felt heavy. She realized the extent of her exhaustion. She was drained from sheer emotion, lulled by her unexpected happiness.

"Sleep a little," he murmured, lifting her from him, easing her down on the pillows.

She tried to keep her eyes open, but failed. She lay on her side and his arms went around her, gently caressing, stroking. She plummeted into sleep.

Wynn didn't know how long she'd slept. When she opened her eyes, it was still dark and Duke was staring at her with an indulgent smile on his sensuous mouth. The smoke of a smoldering cigarette rose in delicate gray wisps from an ashtray on the other table.

"You look like a Roman prince," she murmured sleepily.

He gave a quiet laugh of sheer delight. Leaning forward, he kissed her nose and smoothed her hair away from her face. "Did you have a nice sleep?"

"Wonderful." She smiled at him, touching his chin. He responded to her touch like a great, contented cat, rubbing the hard chin against her fingers, making a purring sound deep in his throat.

She laughed, feeling inexpressibly happy. Then she said, "Good heavens."

"What?" he inquired lazily, kissing her fingers.

"You must be starving." She had just realized that they'd had no dinner.

"I could eat something," he admitted.

"A bear, no doubt. I'll make us something." She started to get up, then felt suddenly shy in her nakedness. "I'm . . ." she looked down at herself.

"Gorgeous," he finished, grinning. "Do you want something to put on?"

"Yes, thank you." She looked at him gratefully, throwing the sheet over herself.

He went to the big closet. "Where?"

"A robe. At that end." She gestured. He fumbled among the clothes, saying, "Pretty." Then he made a triumphant sound. *"Ecco."* He came back with a jade satin robe and handed it to her, after rubbing it against his face, remarking, "This is so soft and smooth, it's too pretty for me to handle." He chuckled. "These paws could rough it up." He looked at her. "I hope they didn't rough *you* up."

She stood up and got into the robe, belting it around her. "They did—it was wonderful!" She recalled with pleasure the feel of his calloused hands on her skin. "Wonderful," she repeated.

He grabbed her to him, saying, "You feel so good through that." He looked down at her. "And you'd better not look at me like that if we're going to get any food, lady."

"I'll make you some, as soon as I've had a shower."

"Have your shower. I had mine while you were asleep. I'll be the cook," he offered. "I have two specialties—hamburger and eggs and bacon. Which have you got?"

"Eggs and bacon. It sounds wonderful. There's already coffee." She moved close to him and kissed his bare chest.

"Not any more," he told her, grinning widely. "I've had it all. It's real truckers' coffee. I'll make another pot."

"You are a very useful man," she said, "in more ways than one."

He patted her in an intimate place and ordered, "Take your shower before I change my mind."

When she came out of the bathroom, padding barefoot to the kitchen, she smelled the appetizing aroma of bacon and freshly made, strong coffee.

Duke was pouring it out when she entered the bright yellow and green room. He was wearing his dark trousers and his ivory shirt open at the collar.

"This is wonderful," she said, sitting down opposite him at the small table, tenderly amused that he had managed to use all unmatching dishes and silver. "But I wish I had a robe for you to wear," she remarked.

"You don't know how glad I am that you don't," he retorted with significance. She blushed but was suddenly glad, too.

As they ate he said, "This is so pretty—this room . . . your place. I've never known a place that looked so much like the person who lived in it." He cocked a dark, ironic brow at her. "Not that I'm an expert on women's apartments." He described his own place to her, saying that it looked like a monastery compared to her apartment. "Pretty bare . . . a bed, books, TV, a place to hang my hat."

He lived in a rather ugly modern apartment building at Sixteenth Street and Sixth Avenue, a place she'd often passed going uptown to shop. It was right around the corner, however, from the union. And as he talked about *that,* Wynn gathered that the union was pretty much his life. She knew something about unions from Marty and Big Mike— the long hours, the pressure, the backbreaking, exhausting strikes. Duke said that he'd often slept on a couch in his office during strikes, when he slept at all, going home only to shower and change clothes.

Pausing, he studied her with dark, serious eyes. "I guess that's a hell of a thing to bring up now," he commented. "Maybe it reminds you of . . . problems."

She reached across the table and touched his hand. "Not tonight. It doesn't matter tonight, Duke . . . not at all."

He looked only slightly reassured. To lighten his mood she began to talk about the restaurant and its magic spell. She could see him brightening, easing. As she told him what the evening had meant to her, that wondrous sense of altered time returned, the feeling that they were utterly alone in an older time of brave, adventurous men and women who gave their hearts with total fire.

"It's great," he said softly, looking at her with gratitude and tenderness. "You make *me* feel like that . . . like we're living in another world together."

She was overwhelmed with happiness that she had made it so. Then their mood lightened, and they laughed, carefree together. He helped her wash dishes and clean up the kitchen.

They lounged together on the couch, listening to music, talking very little, enjoying each other's nearness until she happened to look at the small French clock.

She said with surprise, "It's one o'clock . . . it can't be." She discovered that he usually got up at seven in the morning. "But I won't make it tomorrow," he told her, smiling. They agreed to get up at eight, her usual time for rising.

Falling asleep in his tight embrace, Wynn knew that she had never felt such gladness or such peace.

Even in the light of morning, the spell he cast persisted. Neither of them was a heavy breakfaster, so after they were dressed they had coffee together. Before they went out, he took her in his arms again and kissed her deeply. Then he stepped back and inventoried her. "You're beautiful," he said. "More beautiful than before, if that's possible."

"I'm different from before," she told him solemnly. It was a bright, sunny morning, with almost cloudless skies, hinting at the warmth of May. She was wearing a shirtwaist dress the color of new cream, printed with flowers of soft gold and hyacinth blue, with pale accessories.

"You look like spring," he murmured, touching her hair.

She had never felt so treasured or so beautiful.

Although she'd suggested taking a cab downtown, he insisted on driving her, then going back to his place to change before he went to the union. "I'm not going to let you get away now," he declared. "You think I'm going to waste that hour in downtown traffic with you?"

She giggled at his reference to Manhattan's daily clog of trucks and buses, cabs and cars, settling contentedly into the Porsche.

"Closer," he directed, and she obeyed, sitting very near him as he drove. "The highways are faster," he observed, "but who's in a hurry?"

"I'm not." Already she had a peculiar dread of going to the office, something she couldn't remember ever having felt before. Usually she looked forward to it. "Oh, I wish . . ."

"So do I, baby. I'd rather face a firing squad than go in today." She had a strong and certain feeling that this was very unusual for him, too. "I'd like to take off for about a year. In fact, I'd like to be alone with you until the six guys come in to carry me out."

His black humor couldn't conceal his deep seriousness. She was thrilled and touched. She put her hand on his knee.

"Dinner tonight?" he asked. They were approaching the downtown tangle of truck traffic, and he was forced to slacken their speed. He was looking at her eagerly.

"Yes."

"And every night, if it's okay with you." She met his black and pleading stare.

She nodded slowly. "That's very okay with me."

"Wynn, oh, Wynn." They were stuck in traffic. He took his hand from the wheel and pulled her to him, kissing her unashamedly in the bright, public sun. A truckdriver whose rig was stuck next to the Porsche leaned out of his cab, yelling, *"Bravo, bravissimo!"*

Wynn blushed, but Duke laughed, giving a thumbs-up signal to the trucker and calling out, *"Grazie!"*

She felt as giddy and warm as a honeymooner. A honeymooner. The word echoed in her mind. She thought, How wonderful he is. None of this neurotic nonsense her friends had confided to her about their lovers—their need for "space," their "having a thing" about staying overnight, the silly limitations of most so-called modern affairs. Duke Bellini was a man, all right, a man who knew what he wanted. She looked up at his strong profile; he was staring straight ahead again, intent on the traffic, which had resumed its slow forward pace.

He probably knew what he wanted in every area, certainly in the area of bargaining. He would be a tough opponent across the bargaining table Friday. And this magical thing between them would make no difference at all, wouldn't keep him from fighting her every step of the way.

Duke glanced at her. "Why are you sitting all the way over there?" he asked her, grinning as he maneuvered the Porsche between a truck and taxi. She moved close again, thinking, I love him. I love him already.

"Penny for them," he said.

"I was thinking about how decisive you are," she said with ambiguous truth. She couldn't say she was worrying about Friday, when both of them would become, for all practical purposes, two other people. He had his interests to protect, his people; well, she had a double responsibility—to her employees and also to the tradition that was Carson's . . . to Big Mike, to keep what he had so painfully built. And yet she didn't want to spoil this golden, enchanted morning with thoughts like that.

When they stopped for a red light, Wynn idly observed the crossing pedestrians. One of them was a lean blond man in a crisp tan suit; he turned and looked into the car, directly into Wynn's eyes. Howard Bartley.

She repressed an angry, anxious exclamation. Howard was proceeding across the street, but he turned and looked back, a sarcastic smile on his handsome mouth.

Oh, Lord, Wynn thought. That's all we need—the office spy's own cousin, seeing me with Duke Bellini in *his* car at this hour of the morning. Howard was bound to put two and two together and come up with twenty-two.

Wynn glanced at Duke; apparently he hadn't noticed the incident. He had a happy, contented smile on his lips.

He slowed the Porsche in front of Carson's. Looking at Wynn, he said, "Damn it, honey, I hate to see you go."

"I hate to go," she assured him, already hearing the angry honking of a horn behind them. She put her fingers on the handle of the door. "But I'd better."

"When do you go to lunch?" he asked quickly.

"About one."

"I'll call you. Maybe we can get together before tonight." He gave her a hasty kiss and she got out.

She stood a moment to watch him drive away uptown. And then the world closed in around her.

## Chapter 6

WYNN KNEW RUTH WILEY WOULD SENSE THAT SOME-
thing was up when she hurried by the secretary's
desk with a quick, rather self-conscious "Good
morning." Wynn didn't stop, as she frequently did,
to pass the time of day.

She sat down at her desk and looked around.
Everything looked different to her this morning,
even the office where she'd spent so many busy,
devoted hours. The portrait of her father seemed to
smile at her; she wished he could be there to give her
his blessing. She had a feeling he would. He'd often
spoken of Duke with respect, but had almost always
referred to him as "that boy." How odd it seemed to
think that Duke and her own father had spent so
much time together, while she, Wynn Carson, had
never happened to meet the union leader. He had
never fully registered with her. Well, he had now,
she reflected, leaning back in her chair. More than

registered. She felt as if she still carried his mark on her.

Ruth, looking springy and chipper in yellow, pranced in with the morning mail, messages neatly on top. She stood waiting the customary few minutes for Wynn to glance through the pile and give her directions.

Wynn saw a message from Howard Bartley, and an unpleasant coolness skittered along her nerves. Already? There was also a message from Jonathan Court. "Scrooge, at this hour?" Wynn demanded humorously.

"He's in a tizzy," Ruth commented in her dry way. "Negotiations come up Friday, sez he, and you still haven't met with him and the board."

"Oh dear." Wynn shuffled the mail with vast disinterest, noticing nothing that seemed urgent. "Not much here," she muttered. "Maybe you'd better get me Scrooge on the office horn."

"Right."

Wynn looked up, a little puzzled. Usually her alert secretary suited the action to the word, but this time she was still there. "Right away, Ms. Carson," she said, grinning. "But first I've got to know what's happened to you."

"What does that mean?" Wynn felt a slight impatience; sometimes, she thought, this office is too small.

"You look like you went on an overnight cruise to the Caribbean. You're absolutely glowing."

"Must be the dress," Wynn said with forced casualness. "And my new vitamin regimen. I figured I'd be needing them for Scrooge and the board . . . not to speak of negotiations. Now, will you get out of here and get me Scrooge?"

"*Tout de suite.*" Ruth was gone.

Waiting for her buzzer, Wynn thought, The negotiations are starting in three more days. And then we'll be lovers at the breakfast table, antagonists at the bargaining table. It was an unsettling idea.

When the buzzer sounded, she picked up the phone. Jonathan Court said curtly, "We've got to get that meeting set up, Wynn." No "good morning," she reflected with her usual resentment.

Answering him with like brusqueness, she snapped, "Four this afternoon all right with you?"

"That late?" he grumbled. That late was exactly the time she wanted. Everyone would want to get away at five, just as she was so eager to do, so the late start would discourage people from rambling on and on. She hoped she hadn't outsmarted herself, though. There were some who would be undisturbed by the lateness of the afternoon and could talk till doomsday.

"Best I can do," she retorted mendaciously.

"All right. Four in your conference area. I'll notify the others." He sounded grouchier than ever.

"Thanks," she said briefly and hung up.

She called out to Ruth, "Snow White and the Seven Dwarfs, four o'clock, conference area."

"Oh dear. Okay. I'll have it ready."

Wynn went back to her perusal of the mail. Thank heavens there was nothing complicated in it—her concentration was shot. She was dictating memoranda and replies to Ruth when her private phone rang. In a way, she hoped it wasn't Duke. She knew that her expression, the tone of her voice, would give the whole game away. And though Ruth was nearer to the phone than she, Wynn reached over hastily, saying, "I'll get it." Ruth studied her with surprise.

It was Howard. "Good morning, duchess. Hope I

didn't catch you at a bad time." He clipped off his words and his ironic tone belied the polite disclaimer.

"Not really," she said coolly, not bothering to hide her impatience. "I'm dictating."

"Why, you little dictator," he quipped. She made a restless movement. "I won't keep you. Can you make it for lunch?"

"Sorry. I'm all tied up." She listened to his resentful silence. He was still smarting, no doubt, from her desertion of the day before, not to speak of the scene he'd witnessed that morning.

"More union business?" he asked dryly. "I notice you're starting negotiations earlier and earlier in the morning."

Damn him, she thought savagely. She wondered if he'd already been tattling to Court. "Sorry, Howard. I've got to go. I'm right in the middle of dictation, as I mentioned."

"Well, excuse me for living," he snapped back, and she heard the line go dead. Hanging up, she went back to her dictation without another word to or from Ruth. That was unusual, too, she realized. The irrepressible Ruth nearly always made some remark about "poor old Howard B."

They finished in record time. As good luck would have it, Duke phoned on the private line when Ruth was in the ladies' room. "Hello, baby." Her heart jumped into her throat when she heard his rough, deep, caressing voice.

"Well, hello," she answered, her voice shaking a little. "This is the nicest call I've had today."

"It's the nicest one I've made. I miss you already. Isn't that crazy?"

"No. It's not crazy at all. The feeling's very

mutual." She pictured his sensuous mouth close to the receiver and a small quiver ran over her body.

"Honey, I feel like an A-Number-One jerk. You know, when I left you this morning, I was so nuts I didn't even remember tonight. We've got a membership meeting scheduled to finalize the demands before negotiations. It might be a very late night; those guys go on and on."

"Tell me about it." She chuckled. "They sound like my board."

"Damn it, honey, I don't like to ask you to see me so late, but . . . but I want to see you. I've got to see you, in the worst way."

"Sounds like the best way to me," she returned in a soft, caressing tone. "Come on over to my house . . . whenever."

"You mean it? Oh, Wynn, that's wonderful. You'd do that for me?" He sounded so impressed, so overwhelmed by the simple gesture, that her heart ran over with tenderness.

She found it difficult to control her voice when she answered. "I'd do more than that."

"You're the best thing that ever happened to me, Wynn Carson." There was a pause, and then he went on, "After that, I'm ashamed to tell you I can't make it for lunch either. I've tried to wangle the time, but I'm up to my ears. The guys are waiting for me now, to take me out on the sites. We're covering terminals all day."

"It's all right, it really is," she told him sincerely.

"When they made you, lady, they broke the mold and threw it away. All right, all right, hold your horses!" She heard him yelling through the covered receiver. His voice came on more clearly again, low and caressing. "All right, beautiful. I'll see you tonight. It may be ten-thirty, eleven, something like that."

"Whenever. I'll be waiting." Hearing his soft good-bye, she hung up the phone. The glow lit by his call lasted throughout the afternoon, through the uneasy meeting with Court and the members of the board. From Court's manner, she thought she could read evidence of a call from Howard Bartley. He made several suggestive remarks about her "soft stand" on the demands. She held onto her temper, however, proud that she'd made points with the other board members about the reasonableness of 117's hourly-raise demands. As before, she admitted that the retroactivity clauses might be revised in Carson's favor, that certain fringe benefits might be curtailed. But she couldn't help reminding them that Big Mike Carson had started out as a trucker and had always tried to give the union a fair shake.

Court asked contemptuously, "Are you going to give them built-in bars and wall-to-wall carpet, like limousines?"

"I think you've forgotten our no-drinking rule," she snapped. Court reddened, chagrined, and Wynn regretted the remark. She and Court had trouble enough already. There was no point in starting an internal battle before they went to war. In one thing he'd been right: They had to show a united front.

The martial simile haunted her after the board had left—to her relief, at ten till five—and she was freshening her makeup. She hoped she and Duke wouldn't have to go as far as war. Not now, she pleaded with fate. Not so soon after their magical coming together.

She knew she should stay and go over Court's notes again, make her final decisions. But she had a strong desire to go shopping uptown. Housewares and nightgowns, she thought dreamily. She didn't have anything that was really glamorous. She hadn't needed things like that till now. After an indecisive moment she gave in to the itch to do some shopping. She'd leave the car in the Carson garage just one more night.

Later, too jubilant to mind the crowds rushing along Thirty-fourth Street, Wynn walked swiftly east. A frivolous pair of gray satin bedroom slippers with high heels and marabou on the instep caught her eye in a window. She went in and bought them. Swinging the little drawstring bag on her wrist, she hurried to a department store and bought some new sheets and pillowcases. Instead of her usual flowered patterns, she chose bolder prints on backgrounds of aqua and bright yellow. They'd make Duke feel more at home, less like a visitor to a feminine bower. She took one set with her, asking to have the others delivered.

Laden with the sheets and pillowcases, she went on to look at lingerie, splurging on a filmy blue green chiffon nightgown with simple, Grecian lines, and another, a heavenly shade of gold satin. Unable to resist, she added a ruffled and pleated yellow nylon gown and several teddies and chemises. All of the gowns, she thought, would look wonderful with a full, mandarin-collared ivory robe she had at home. Nevertheless, she still yearned for something to match the gray slippers, so, feeling quite mad, she also bought a gray satin robe with pink appliqués like wings on its front. "Angelic." The saleswoman grinned. "It's perfect for you."

Now the dilemma was, how was she going to get it all home? She finally decided to take some of the chemises and the blue green Grecian gown. The rest she would have delivered to the office. She put the purchases on one of her credit cards and left the store, feeling buoyant.

At last she found a cab on Fifth Avenue that delivered her to the mews. Struggling with her packages, she let herself into the apartment. It was already nearly eight, and she was very tired. But she went out again to a delicatessen on Eighth Street and bought some cold cuts and beer. In another shop she picked up some yellow candles, and finally, at a florist's, an enormous bunch of fresh daffodils.

Home again, she distributed the daffodils among the bedroom, living room and kitchen and put yellow candles in the silver candlesticks in living and bedrooms.

After grabbing a hasty sandwich, she undressed and took a leisurely scented bath, perfuming herself and fluffing out her hair. It was already nine-thirty, and she still had a lot to do.

She slipped on the aqua gown and buttoned the ivory robe over it. She proceeded to put the new sheets on the bed and turned out all the lights except for a few dim ones here and there. She left her study light on in the living room. It was after ten by the time she got to the papers in her briefcase, a guilty reminder as to how she should be spending her time.

But it was hard to concentrate. She'd been working so long, enjoying herself so little. For a few hours she'd felt like other women, happily engaged in women's pursuits. She put the papers in the briefcase and stashed it in the hall. At a quarter to eleven the doorbell rang. She rushed to push the buzzer and light the candles.

She opened the door. Before she could speak,

Duke grabbed her in his arms, kissing her as if he couldn't bear to let her go, as if they'd been away from each other for weeks. Breathless and quivering, she leaned against him. He said, "I'd better come in, hadn't I?"

She gave him a trembly smile and, when he'd stepped over the threshold, softly closed the door. "Let me look at you." He took her hands and stretched out her arms, watching the full sleeves of ivory silk bell outward with the motion.

"I must be dreaming. I've got to be." He studied her minutely, from her soft, sun-colored hair to the small manicured toes peeping out of her ivory slippers. Then he released her hands and held her close to his hard body. She put her arms around his waist, pressing herself against him, hearing him say, "You smell like all the gardens in the world. Oh, honey, I never knew one day could be so long. It's crazy as hell, but I feel like I haven't seen you for a week." His big hands kneaded her back.

She shook inside at the touch. "I felt the same way, all day long," she admitted. She heard the steady, vital pounding of his heart. His fresh, open-collared shirt was damp.

"You must have hurried," she murmured.

"I practically ran. So I'm all sweaty again, and I just got out of a shower ten minutes ago," he confessed.

"Ten minutes ago!" She moved back to look up at him and smiled. "You didn't run, you flew." He looked weary but jubilant.

"The guys are probably wondering what's gotten into me. I bulldozed them through that meeting like a high-balling hot dog, and then I sprinted to my place to get cleaned up." He chuckled, still holding her lightly by the arms, looking at her with raw hunger. "I feel about sixteen years old," he said with amazement. "Duke Bellini just doesn't work that way . . . or never did before."

"Come on," she urged him, "sit down and relax. I'll get you a drink."

He shook his head. "I'm drunk enough now, Wynn Carson. No man could be *that* tired." He grabbed her close again and with sweet astonishment she recognized the swift returning of their wild, inevitable desire. His hands were on her everywhere, as he lowered his head to hers so their eager mouths could meet, savoring the taste and shape and hunger of each other's parting lips until he made a sound of primitive longing, deep in his throat, and picked her up in his massive arms.

He strode with her to the sequestered bedroom, pale gold with candlelight. Setting her carefully on her feet, he began to fumble with the fastenings of her concealing robe. She swayed with a hot and melting weakness as his fingers opened the voluminous garment, parting it, letting it fall to the carpet in a whispering aureole around her ankles. She stepped out of its center, watching his eyes light up when he saw the clinging, transparent gown the color of tropical water that barely veiled her white, curving body. He kneaded her breasts through the diaphanous fabric; she could feel her nipples bud and tingle. Then slowly, with great gentleness, he lifted the gown over her head, making sounds of wonder as her flesh was gradually revealed.

The fabric was so thin that she could see his features through its curtain while it was being lifted over her head. Then she was free of it and it was drifting to join the fallen ivory of the robe. He gazed in bemusement at the pale, liberated globes of her breasts; her whole self drummed and pounded with abandoned and awakened need.

He stooped to kiss each breast, his wild tongue darting out to encircle one rosy tip, then the other, drawing at the rigid nipples until the very depths of her cried out in singing silence for completion. Marveling, she saw him kneel before her in the candlefire, grasping her soft hips, holding her with a grasp of steel as his trembling mouth sought out her throbbing innerness, her most secret longings.

His steady tongue probed like a narrow and relentless tongue of flame, caressing with an unvarying and skillful rhythm. She was trembling so much that she felt she could scarcely stand, shaking her head from side to side with that peculiar gesture of protest that seemed to indicate utter disbelief in the magnitude of her ecstasy but was really the ultimate pleading for it never, never to cease. Her head fell helplessly back, and she sensed the light, whispering descent of her own fine, belling hair on the skin of her shuddering back.

Somewhere in that timeless frenzy, the sensation that was almost agony began to climb to that perilous peak where she balanced, swaying, before pleasure so titanic it threatened to stop her heart. The focused sensation broke, began to eddy and widen. She gave a high, wailing moan, collapsing against Duke.

Still lapped in the widening pleasure waves, she was dimly conscious that he was supporting her with one steely hand as he removed his own clothes with the other. She heard his hoarse gasping, felt him lifting her to him, and instinctively her shaky legs encircled his hard and narrow waist. They moved together, deep in the final closeness, his loud, gasping breath in her ear like a stormy wind, and her breasts flattened to the dampness of his chest, his great hands gripping her, guiding her as they met in a mad and all-forgetful dance. He filled all that had ever been empty in her, bringing her, astounded, to another pleasure peak far greater and more shattering than the one before.

When the giant flood of his release rocked him, her final bliss was claimed. Her every nerve vibrated to his outcry, echoing through her breasts. His frame trembled convulsively so that her own body shook with his. And yet the big hands never slackened their relentless hold on her. His strong, quivering arms held her securely against him until he lowered her safely to the wide softness of the bed.

He lay down beside her, drawing her into the comforting circle of his embrace. When he could speak again, he murmured against her hair, "Nothing in my life has ever been like this for me. You know that, don't you?"

"Yes, oh yes." She burrowed into him. "Or for me." She took a shaky breath and added, "Do you know, last night, when we fell asleep together, I hadn't felt so good, so happy since I was a little girl? I haven't slept like that since then. So deep, so peacefully."

He stroked her. "I know. Oh, darling, as great as it was to . . . love you . . ." He sounded hesitant, uncertain. She sensed that it was hard for him to speak of these things, so his attempt to do so touched her with an almost unbearable tenderness. "As great as it was," he went on more surely, "the thing I thought of most today . . . as crazy as it sounds . . . was just this. Holding you. Falling asleep with you in my arms. It's like one night of you, one night, Wynn, and I want to fall asleep like this with you for the rest of my life."

She was so overwhelmed that she couldn't answer. All she could do was kiss his lazy flesh repeatedly and listen to his contented, lazy murmur. She noticed that his hold gradually loosened, and she knew the depth of his exhaustion. His eyes were closing, his breath becoming regular and deep.

With cautious tenderness she slid out of his slackening embrace and left the bed. She took a silk comforter from a cabinet and covered him with it. Then she padded soundlessly into the living room, locked up and blew out the candles. Touched, she noticed that he had brought a small canvas bag that she had been too excited even to see before. She unpacked it, handling his things with new affection. She put his shaving things in the bathroom cabinet, then went to the bedroom with the other things, laying out the robe on the chest at the foot of the bed, placing the slippers on the floor by his side. Then she stashed the small bag away and, retrieving her nightgown, took it with her to the bath.

She made her quick preparations for bed, perfumed herself and slipped on the gown again. In the bedroom she glanced around once more, lingering on the sight of his big, tanned body sprawled in sleep. The power of him was undiminished by that vulnerable position. He looked like a drowsing warrior, with his massive limbs and proud, fine features. But a very different side of him seemed evident to her. The open, relaxed hands seemed to be asking for something and at the same time giving it. She was overcome with an absurdly protective feeling.

Suddenly melting, eager to be close to him, she

took one more swift look around the room, blew out the candles and lay down beside him. "Here you are," he mumbled, only half awake. "So nice, this is so nice." Reaching out, he encircled her. She brushed her mouth against his; then she lay down near him on her side and he enfolded her tightly, kissing her neck, her shoulder.

Drifting to sleep, she thought her last drowsy, fading thought—it was only in the old love stories that something like this happened, this instant magnetism, such rightness so soon. And yet it was happening to them.

They woke up early, less solemn, and made love again with a slow, rich familiarity that was new between them. She lay dreamily in shafts of bright sunshine, listening to him singing in the shower. He had a surprisingly melodic baritone.

She got up with a delicious sensation of well-being, smoothed the bed, rescued the dropped ivory robe and hung it in the closet. She stripped off her nightgown, put it in the hidden hamper and buttoned herself into a ruffled robe printed with bright green and yellow daisies.

"That bathroom is something else," he said admiringly. "And so are you." He kissed her, complimenting her robe, and began to gather up his fallen clothes.

"Be with you in a moment," she said, going in to shower. She lathered herself with a bar of jasmine-scented soap and showered fast. When she was dry and lightly made up, her rich hair combed in loose, shiny waves, she heard the sound of music from the living room. He was sitting on the couch, smoking a cigarette; his eyes shone when she came in.

"Come here," he directed. She went to him and he pulled her onto his lap, hugging and kissing her as if she were a small, petted child. "Now," he said briskly, setting her upright, "get yourself dressed and let's go out to breakfast. I'm starving."

She patted his face, got off his lap and went to the bedroom, where she expeditiously got into her clothes for the day, a lavender scoop-necked blouse and soft companion skirt. After putting small amethyst buttons in her pierced ears, she checked herself out quickly in the hall mirror and rejoined him. "How's that for speed?" she demanded with a grin.

"Incredible. Impossible," he amended. "Nobody looks that good that fast." He was on his feet, holding out his arms. She went into them for a breathless moment, and then they hurried out together to the bright new day.

Both would be heading west, so Wynn suggested a place she liked on Eighth Street, pleasant and sparsely peopled at this early hour in a neighborhood where most places didn't open before eleven. When Duke saw the ice cream parlor sign, he teased, "I'll do anything for you, honey. But ice cream for breakfast?"

"Read the rest, wise guy," she retorted, indicating the breakfast sign. "If your eyes are that bad on Friday, Carson's will have it made." She wished she hadn't said that. He laughed, but there was a slight constraint between them as they breakfasted in the dim restaurant, with its postered walls and casual service.

Yet when they were outside again, heading for Sixth Avenue, he took her hand tightly in his and the bad moment passed.

They paused at the corner of Sixth Avenue and

Eighth Street, smiling at each other, looking up at the glorious clear spring sky. "What a day," he said.

"It's heavenly. Don't you love that building? It always reminds me of a castle in a fairy tale, especially when there's snow on it in the winter." She indicated the Gothic Jefferson Library building, with its gables and turrets, banded brick and stonework, carvings, belfries and balconies. A passing flight of pigeons, their breasts gleaming in the sun like abalone, fanned out above the towers and a faint wind caressed the green gold trees on the avenue.

Duke gazed up, shading his black eyes from the glare. "You know, it does at that." He looked back at her again. "You always make me see things differently. I've lived here all my life, but when I'm with you I really see New York. It's so good with you, Wynn."

Unashamedly he bent his head and kissed her. She bloomed with a wild exhilaration. Public displays of affection had never been her style, but somehow this was different. Suddenly it didn't matter a bit. "Walk with me a little way," he coaxed her. "All right?"

"Very all right." He took her hand again, and they headed uptown. He slowed his long, loose stride to match her shorter steps. He squeezed her hand, remarking, "The world looks good today, Wynn Carson."

She returned the pressure of his hand, but didn't answer. Hearing her last name had reminded her that the day after next they'd be meeting across the bargaining table. Suddenly she remembered that Howard Bartley lived on Twelfth Street—she didn't know exactly where, because there'd never been any need to—and she wondered uneasily if they'd run into him. So at Eleventh, when she realized that several empty cabs had already passed her by, she said, "I guess I'd better flag down a taxi, darling."

"I know. I hate like hell to see you go, but I understand." He raised his hand to stop an approaching taxi. "We'll drive in together tomorrow, okay?"

"I'd like that."

Duke opened the taxi door for her and handed her inside. She had the same buoyant, weightless feeling she'd had that night on West Fourth Street when they were walking to Fedora's. Leaning in, he kissed her soundly, saying, "I'll call you this afternoon." She nodded.

When the cab was pulling away, she watched him as long as she could. He looked back and waved, then strode quickly up the avenue as her taxi hurtled westward, blotting him from sight.

All morning Wynn went through the motions of work as if she were moving in a dream. He called before afternoon, in time to lunch with her. He suggested the same Italian place she'd gone to with Howard, which would be convenient for her and offered prompt service. She hesitated; they would both run into a lot of people they knew.

"What's the matter? Don't you like it?" he asked her.

"I love it," she said sincerely. They made an appointment to meet. As she had suspected, they did run into a good many people they both knew. That circumstance put a damper on everything for her, and Duke was quick to notice her rather stiff manner.

"You don't like it here," he said dolefully. She leaned toward him and took his hand despite the interested glances from neighboring tables.

"I do," she protested. "I love it. I've never been so happy here before." His face lit up. "It's just that it's about as private as Grand Central Station," she went on in a rueful tone. "Acquaintances, you know."

"Yeah." His face fell as he looked around. "We're some lion-lamb team, aren't we, lady?" He smiled uncertainly.

"Just not very discreet."

"Damn discretion," he said boldly. "Let 'em talk."

But she had a feeling that he wasn't as sure as he sounded. He gave an almost imperceptible nod toward the table of the Raguso brothers, who had been covertly staring at them. "Maybe you're right, baby. We could play it a little cooler."

She gave him as reassuring a smile as she could muster, feeling saddened, hunted and somewhat resentful. After all, they weren't doing anything criminal. Yet their position as opponents made her feel like a fugitive. It wasn't fair. To atone for the pall she'd cast over their lunch, Wynn began to chatter about other things. Soon she noticed with satisfaction that Duke's expression had lightened, and they were enjoying themselves again. And it was heavenly, she thought, to feel so good when only the other day she'd hated the place because she was there with Howard. Now the romantic atmosphere and the recorded voice of a soulful tenor seemed to have been created just for her and Duke Bellini.

Her good mood lasted through their hasty goodbye and the rest of the afternoon. The store delivered her packages, and Duke called again at four.

"Dinner out tonight?"

She shouldn't . . . but she would. She said joyfully, "You've got a date. But let me meet you. I have a package I have to drop at the house, and I'd like to change." She gave up the idea of restudying the demands.

"I'll pick you up. I can't have you carrying things. How big's the freight? Big as you are?" he asked with caressing humor.

"Just about," she admitted.

"That settles it. Five-thirty . . . outside your office?"

She assented, thinking, We're getting more and more indiscreet. And the Fiat would spend still another night in the garage. What the men would think she couldn't even imagine. But then, they weren't paid to think about her private business, she told herself.

When Duke saw her with the immense bundle, he shook his head, grinned and got out to relieve her of it, putting it in the trunk of the Porsche. They caused quite a traffic snarl, but got a laugh out of it. It was so good to be together that nothing else seemed to matter much. Wynn was happier and more secure than she had ever been in her whole life, even in her childhood days with Greg and Marty and Big Mike. She'd thought she was totally independent before she met Duke Bellini. But now, just the fact that he was able to do simple, physical things for her—the simple hoisting of a package that was heavy for her and a feather for Duke—made her realize how wonderful it was to feel taken care of.

She told him that as they drove uptown, and he was so touched by it that he drew her close against him, hugging her, kissing her hair. "I always want to take care of you," he murmured. She wondered just how much that implied. A silence fell over them both, but she didn't want to ask what he was thinking.

In the apartment, he asked, "Where does this go, honey?"

"The bedroom would be fine."

"The bedroom's always fine," he retorted over his shoulder as he took the package in and put it on the chest at the foot of the bed. She followed.

"Speaking of which . . ." Her heart thudded. "How hungry are you?" he inquired.

"Not very." She grinned up at him. "Is this another dinner we're not having together?"

"It's another one I'd like to postpone," he countered, drawing her into his arms.

"Can you control yourself until I take a shower?" She rubbed her head against his chest.

"Not if you keep doing that." She looked up at him and saw that he was teasing. Then he sobered and added, "Honey, I've waited for you for more than thirty years, ever since I was born. A few more minutes won't make that much difference."

She hugged him and directed, "Put on some music and make yourself a drink. I won't be long at all." She hurried into the bedroom and undid the package, put the things away except for the lovely gray satin robe with its winglike shell-pink appliqués. She undressed and took the robe and matching slippers with her to the bath.

She found him in the living room when she emerged perfumed and relaxed and eager. He got up from the couch and strode toward her, saying, "Why do I get the feeling that I'm dreaming when I look at you? It never fails."

He led her into the bedroom, shadowy in the

twilight and silvered with the flames of the fresh blue green candles she'd put in the candlesticks that morning and lit a moment before. He undressed her slowly, with a worshipful face, and their coming together was even more fulfilling than the last time.

Later, when Duke remarked how beautiful the house was, saying it was a shame to go out, they decided to have Chinese food delivered and ate it companionably together in the pretty dining area.

Over coffee he made a sudden gesture of exasperation.

"What is it?"

Not answering, he got up, strode to his discarded jacket and took a satin box out of one of the pockets. He returned to her, grinning sheepishly. "I was feeling bad about not sending you flowers," he said softly. "Things have been so hectic. So I figured I'd get you some that would last a few days." He handed her the satin box. "I completely forgot," he confessed. "When I see you, I forget just about everything, Wynn."

She snapped open the lid and inhaled a quick, gasping breath. "Ooooh . . ." was all she could manage.

"I don't know much about these things . . ." he said awkwardly.

"I do," she said with truth. She knew a good bit about antique jewelry, and this piece was exquisite, a delicate brooch in the shape of a spray of turquoise forget-me-nots, with leaves of gold. "Oh, Duke. It's magnificent . . . wonderful." She jumped up, feeling as eager as a child, and hurried to a mirror.

"Where are you going?" he demanded, laughing.

"To put it on." She had changed into a soft ivory pajama suit, and she pinned the brooch on its plain neckline. The turquoise flowers fired her eyes to a deeper blue, the gold leaves echoed her hair. She turned for his inspection.

"I'm better than I thought," he boasted. "I knew it looked like you. And a forget-me-not's the best flower to give a lady like you. Maybe you'll think of me once in a while."

She came to him and took his head between her hands, lifting his mouth to hers for a loving kiss. "Once in a while," she mocked him. "Oh, thank you, thank you. I love it!"

"I'm glad. But it's not much when I think what you give me." He looked up at her with his heart in his eyes, then drew her down to his lap to cradle her in his arms. The glow from the few simple words warmed her for the rest of the happy evening and through the long, close night.

On Thursday morning she chose a turquoise blouse to wear with her lightweight pearl gray suit, because it went so perfectly with the flower spray. The weather was cooler but still bright. Her happiness persisted throughout the morning, but late that afternoon she realized that trouble would start the very next morning; the bubble would burst.

Nevertheless she greeted his phone call with joy. That evening, he insisted, they would not miss dinner. He'd pick her up at the apartment at seven. She decided to drive the Fiat home. She had a feeling they might not be driving in together the next morning. That wouldn't be appropriate at all. As she drove, the idea cast a shadow over her to match the graying skies of evening. Clouds were forming. It was humid and warmer, with the unsettled feeling of an approaching storm. That was appropriate enough, she reflected somberly, garaging the Fiat and rushing upstairs to bathe and change.

They dined at a wonderful restaurant just a few

blocks up Fifth Avenue, full of golden light and furnished with the accessories of a 1930s dining saloon on a luxury ocean liner. Duke's eyes gleamed when he studied her, noticing that she was wearing the pin again.

When they emerged it was misting; they got to the apartment just before the downpour. It was a calm and pleasant evening, yet both of them seemed to be avoiding any mention of the following morning. By tacit agreement they decided to have an early night. They watched some television in the bedroom for a while, but their sweet caresses soon caught fire. Duke snapped off the set, and they came hungrily into each other's arms.

When they awoke in the morning, it was still pouring. As Wynn had guessed, he opted to leave early; there wouldn't be time for breakfast. In a cheerful apricot hostess gown to brighten the morning, Wynn gave him coffee and offered him a big black umbrella, the only masculine-looking one she had.

"Never touch them," he joked. "But thank you, darling. Thank you for everything." He kissed her. "Today's the day, Wynn. We'll be all right, baby. I love you."

The three brief words, words that he had never said before, sang in her heart as he went away.

She showered and put on a bright pink dress the color of cyclamen to keep her courage up. The spray pin was vivid against its soft cowl neckline. She made up with extreme care to hide the evidence of her restless sleep; her blue eyes were shadowed with fatigue. She coiled her hair into a smooth French roll that made her feel poised and in command and got into her raincoat of taupe cire.

This was it—today was the day. And even though

Duke had told her he loved her, it couldn't bring her the security and joy it would have if she were another woman. It couldn't change the day to come, when they would not be lovers, but antagonists.

Wynn took a deep breath and plunged into the morning.

## Chapter 7

BY THREE-THIRTY THAT AFTERNOON WYNN FELT LIKE A
wet rag. Her head ached and she was so gloomy and
irritable that she couldn't face the thought of talking
to anyone. Ruth apparently understood, because she
hadn't asked any questions, hadn't come near ever
since Wynn had stormed by fifteen minutes earlier
and shut her office door.

Wynn sighed and took a pack of cigarettes from
her desk drawer to have one of her rare smokes. She
inhaled deeply, leaning back in her padded leather
chair. She watched the wispy haze curl up from the
white cylinder, reviewing the past few hours, blessing the fact that it was Friday, that she would not
have to meet with the Carson team again until
Monday morning prior to afternoon talks with the
union. What a mess the whole thing was, she reflected. She was on trial not only with 117, but with her

own people, and she hadn't measured up with either side.

And Duke . . . That was the thorniest problem of all. When the union delegation had arrived at eleven and gone into the big board room to start the talks, he'd looked more overwhelming, more attractive, than she had ever seen him. He had been wearing a faultlessly tailored suit of cocoa brown with a pale beige shirt and a tie striped in bright gold, russet and brown, so handsome he took her breath away. And he had, she thought dismally, leaving her unable to cope.

His manner had been as assured as ever, but perfectly formal; only she had seen that one quick glance, suspiciously like a wink, that he had given her. But now she thought resentfully that it had been as if he'd thought she was no competition, that there was really no contest, that Duke Bellini would be the winner, come what might.

Wynn had found it difficult to meet Weinfeld's and Halloran's eyes, had had to exercise the utmost force of will to keep her poise and calm, remembering what she had overheard them saying. What was worse, she had felt that Jonathan Court and Noble were monitoring her—her words, her manner, even her expressions. It had been the toughest four hours she'd ever endured in her whole life. The talks had begun promptly at eleven, continuing almost without a break, except for a hasty, ordered-in lunch, until three. Court and Noble had taken issue with her several times.

At lunch, of course, through a process of natural selection, the two sides split up. Duke, surrounded by his stalwart supporters, seemed as cool as a cucumber. Wynn, on the other hand, uneasy with

Court and the sticky new situation, felt that she was utterly alone, with no allies at all.

And the upshot of it was that Monday promised to be a hundred times more difficult. After the superficially amiable beginning, both sides were toughening up. When the session ended, Duke Bellini's face had been hard and impassive. It had seemed much easier for him to be detached and formal with her. On top of all the other problems, she was convinced now that their feelings for each other had no chance of surviving this confrontation and all the others that would follow.

Her buzzer sounded. "Mr. Bellini," Ruth said in a carefully ambiguous tone. Wynn wondered uneasily if the older woman suspected something.

"Thank you." She kept her own voice crisp and calm.

"Hello, baby." As always Wynn's pulses hammered at the sound of that rough, deep resonance on the line, the baritone so deep that he almost seemed to growl. "Rough day."

She answered breathlessly, "Yes. Very."

"But the weekend's coming up. In fact, as far as I'm concerned, it's here. What do you say I pick you up at your place and we head out of town?"

He sounded as eager and affectionate as before, and she marveled at his ability to ignore their ongoing professional situation. Obviously he expected them both to go on as if nothing had happened.

Trying to match his mood, she asked, "Where are we going?"

"Well, I'll just put this on the table for you to look over . . ." She could hear the smile in his voice. "I know a great little place on Long Island, a really nice inn where we could stay. And there's a theater nearby. We could catch the show, too, if you like.

Tomorrow maybe fool around by the water." He chuckled.

Suddenly she felt the familiar rush of warmth toward him. "I like the sound of that last item. I say yes . . . yes to the whole package."

"Now that's the way I like to negotiate." Everything was so good, so tender between them again that even that word held no terrors for her.

"When shall I pick you up? Your place, of course —I guess you'll need to put a few things together."

She laughed softly. "To put it mildly. Make it four-thirty."

"I'll be there. I can't wait, baby."

Neither could she. However it went next week, they would still have this, a glorious weekend together, totally alone.

"Another?" Duke's black eyes glinted as he held up his highball glass with a smiling side glance at Wynn.

"I think not." She smiled back, knowing that her answer was significant, that her tone said it was time for them to go upstairs.

He caught it, and a wide grin broke out over his tanned face. "I'm glad." He stood up at once, reaching in his trousers for his wallet.

She was already trembling with the thrill of his closeness. He stood behind her stool, very near, waiting for the check, and she could feel his own eager impatience.

Both of them were still riding high on the wave of giddy happiness that had buoyed them throughout the evening. They had arrived a little early for dinner and gone right to their room. With another private joke about a dinner they would not have together, they had made joyous love, lingering so long that they had had to rush to reach the theater in time. Afterward they had a late dinner at an elegant waterfront restaurant and drove back to the inn for a nightcap.

Now, as he followed her into their room, she was newly charmed by the immaculate, old-fashioned look and scent of the place, with its four-poster bed, candles in pewter holders and fresh flowers in pottery vases. Duke closed the door and took her in his arms.

Something possessed her that had never possessed her before, a wild new courage to do and say outrageous things to delight this man who had become her whole life's splendor.

She ran her small hands down his sides, feeling him shake with excitement; her fingers stroked his hard thighs, and his legs started to quiver. "Wynn, Wynn." His eyes blazed down at her in a stupefaction of pleasure. "What's gotten into you? I like it," he said hoarsely, pulling her closer.

"You're wearing too many clothes," she whispered against his chest, stroking him intimately again.

"You're a little devil . . . and an angel," he said in the same excited way.

Wynn touched him even more boldly.

"Oh, baby." His hands explored her body all over, through her thin wool crepe dress. "I never knew . . . I was afraid a woman like you wouldn't be . . . but you are! And you're so damned exciting. . . ." Duke's words trailed off. He made a sound deep in his throat and held her savagely, kissing her so deeply and so long that she weakened into water.

Her desire for him was burning, overwhelming,

but abruptly she loosed herself from his grasp. "Sit down. On the bed."

Surprised but still smiling with pleasure, he obeyed. She knelt down before him and grasped one of his feet.

"What are you doing?" he demanded softly.

"Undressing you. I'll be your geisha." She gave him a mock bow of the head.

"Oh, no you don't." Shocked, he held her hands.

"Oh, yes I do," she retorted stubbornly, tugging at his shoe. She pulled it off, then the other.

"Wynn . . ." he protested. But the protest was half-hearted.

"Admit it. You like this."

"Like it?" He grinned. "Nobody ever treated me like this in my life. I feel like one of those sheiks." He laughed with sheer enjoyment.

She looked up at him. He stared down into her eyes, wordless. Then he whispered, "You look . . . you look like a summer day, with your eyes and hair. You know, wherever you are, there's sunshine for me." He leaned forward and touched her hair with a wondering hand. "Now," he said briskly, "get up, sweetheart, and stop this masquerade."

"Not yet." She was determined, peeling off his socks, caressing his feet. She could feel him shaking, and his smile was shaky, too, his face dissolving into helpless longing. The light in his eyes was so bright that it dazzled her; their vivid blackness penetrated to her very core.

"Enough now, geisha," he ordered and took her hands in his, gently urging her upward. He held her loosely, unfastening her dress. It fell on the carpet and she stood before him in her lacy, pale blue teddy.

"How do you work this little thing?" he asked her, giving her another trembly smile.

For answer she undid the fragile undergarment and stepped out of it. He cried out at the sight of her naked body.

Then he was hastily undressing, throwing his clothes into a heap on the rug. She looked up at his massive nude body towering above her as he stood wide-legged and majestic, his torso tanned, his biceps enormous, his paler flanks narrow and lean, hard as whipcord.

He lifted her onto the bed and set her down. His hands began their eager search along her body from her shoulders to her breasts, her belly to her thighs. He drew her to him and their bodies were newly, intimately entwined, rocking in a maddened, blinded dance. She realized that they were becoming more and more fully one, that the wonderful mad dance had been transformed into the ultimate nearness, to the frenzied meeting of their eager flesh.

And there was nothing, nothing anymore but their bodies' meeting, the barbaric and forgetful thrusting rhythm, the taking and the giving of that fiery pleasure. There was no ceasing now, no turning back, and they moved together until the sharp, bright instant of her final, heart-bursting point of delight, the eddying waves of joy that circled outward from her dazzled, pulsing core, his outcry and his swaying. They fell together, spent.

Still locked in their embrace, they lay in a hush of wonder, trembling with the aftermath. At last, speechless but still trembling, they released each other a little and lay in a calm embrace.

"Wynn." He kissed her hair. "It's never been . . . quite like that before. Has it?"

"No. No, never." She could feel her warm breath

wafted back to her from his neck, where her face was buried. "But it will be, more and more, Duke. Better and better."

"If it is, I don't think I can stand it," he said with a soft chuckle.

"Oh, you will." She kissed his neck, and his arms went around her tightly again. She touched his body with great gentleness, amazed to feel him quickening so soon.

"As a matter of fact," he whispered, "I don't believe it."

"Believe it." She laughed softly, touching him with a bit less gentleness.

"I'm a wild beast."

"My favorite kind." She sat up.

"Where are you going?"

"Nowhere. Lie down," she ordered, smiling.

"But what . . . ? I don't get it." He was studying her, puzzled.

She giggled. "Oh, you'll get it, all right." She saw his dark eyes gleam and his look of astonished delight before she threw herself upon him brazenly. Hearing his outcry of gleeful wonder, she caressed him with greater boldness.

"But honey, you can't do that . . . you . . ."

And then he said no more, while she kissed his quaking body and went on with the wild caress that she had never before given him, that he had given her.

When at last she summoned a groaning cry that seemed to come from his very depths, and he shuddered beneath her lips with a titanic and almost agonizing frenzy, she knew that her love had reached its height. She had found the meaning of her existence, the center of her heart.

He could not move or speak for a long interval.

Then his strong hands found her, pulled her upward so he could hold her, kissing her and stroking her again and again. He said, breathless, "You love me that much."

"That much . . . and more, Duke. So much more."

He held her so closely then that their flesh kissed, saying solemnly, "I'd die for you, Wynn. I'd die for you."

She could find no answer to give except a gentle pressure of her hand on his face; she traced the fine lines of his classic features as he fell asleep. Still held close in his arms, Wynn began to drift into a slow, sweet drowsiness. Her last waking thought was that nothing could ever destroy this. Nothing.

All the next day and night they were still under the spell of that magical encounter. They slept very late, and after a leisurely brunch he suddenly insisted, "I've got to buy you something, Wynn Carson. Something special."

"But you already have," she protested, touching the antique brooch on the lapel of her gray blazer. The weather had turned chilly, and she was wearing matching gray slacks and an aqua sweater.

"Something else," he insisted. He seemed so determined and eager that she didn't protest further.

He was so intent on finding the perfect gift that they drove for miles. He rejected the jewelry stores in one town after another. "Looks like we'll have to go into Manhattan."

She laughed. "All right. Why not?"

They found themselves in the Forties before she knew it, in the midst of the jewelry district. At last, in an antique jewelry store, Duke found something "good enough"—a costly ring of flawless crystal with an intricate pattern of tiny diamonds. It was a perfect fit for the little finger of Wynn's right hand. She was dazzled by it.

Suddenly ravenous, they had a late lunch in the City, then drove back to Long Island. A misting rain had begun to fall. "Very good weather," Duke commented slyly, "for staying in."

They didn't leave their room until the next morning, making slow, tender love, drowsing, talking endlessly and watching television. They had a late dinner sent up to the room.

The sun was showing itself timidly by late the next morning when, after a light brunch, they took a walk on the beach.

Duke glanced at his watch. "I hate to say this, but we'd better be going back."

"So soon?" She looked up at him, bewildered. "But the traffic won't be heavy until much later. . . ."

"It's not the traffic, honey." He put his arm around her and slowed his steps to match hers. "I've . . . I've got a meeting with the guys this afternoon. I've got to make it. They were mad enough to begin with, wanted to make it yesterday. But I wasn't going to let anything interfere with our weekend." He bent down and kissed the top of her head.

"I didn't want to say anything before," he admitted. "I didn't want to . . . bring any of that up between us. Not these last two nights."

"I'm glad." She stood on her tiptoes; even in her midheel boots she was only as high as his heart.

He took her face between his hands and kissed her with a lingering tenderness. She leaned against him, clutching him to her, thinking that the world was closing in on them again.

\* \* \*

The Monday bargaining session strengthened that conviction. She went into the meeting with a feeling of uneasiness even greater than before. After that enchanted weekend, it was harder than ever to seem poised and calm, to hold on to the objectivity she needed to weather this.

But once again she saw how easy it appeared for Duke, playing his other role. Now that the initial proposals had been exchanged, and the niceties put aside, she realized that it was going to be a very stormy contest.

Furthermore, she had had a tough morning session of her own, with Noble and Jonathan Court. Court insisted that the money "just wasn't there" to accede to the union's demands. Wynn knew that it was, or should be, enough at least to cover the increases she had decided on. And she was damned well going to go over the books with Court that night and find it.

On top of that, both men had accused her of "caving in," and they seemed to be gathering support from her other key men. She was riding the horns of a dilemma: On the one hand, she was in danger of losing the respect she had to have from her staff to run Carson's. On the other, if the company took too unreasonable a stance, it could lead to a job action, even a strike. And there hadn't been a strike at Carson's for nearly twenty years. What a black eye it would give her if it happened during the first year of her leadership!

She saw Duke studying her from across the table. His black eyes looked as flat as slate; it was almost as if he didn't see her, certainly not as he had before, just a day ago.

They were still haggling about the hourly raise for

forklift operators and warehouse employees. It was common knowledge that the union started with a high bid, the company with a low one, each side aware that it would have to compromise until they met somewhere in the middle. But the 117 delegation showed no sign of backing down from its initial position.

"How about it, Miss Carson?" Bernie Halloran demanded. His air of false geniality was long gone. "I think you're playing with us here."

"Take it easy, Halloran." Duke's snappish tone made Halloran glance at him in surprise.

She couldn't help reacting when Duke came to her defense, couldn't stop the quick flush that she felt in her cheeks. Noble and Court were staring at her, and she felt the curious stares of Weinfeld and the union lawyers. They were studying both her and Duke Bellini.

She both regretted Duke's revealing outburst and was glad of it. He was human, after all; he couldn't let his man take that bullying tone with her. Wynn's heart thudded.

"The money isn't there," Court interjected. "I've stated that previously."

"Is that true, Miss Carson?" Duke asked her quietly.

"Just a moment, please," she said sharply. "This is not the time or place to go into that." She gave Court a repressive look, and he puffed up with indignation. It's going to be some fine evening, she considered darkly.

But she addressed Duke and the 117 delegation in the same quiet tone he had used to her. "The problem now is the warehouse rate. There's no way we can settle that without settling the question of how many men are required on the trucks as handlers."

"That's an operations, not a wage, matter, Miss Carson—which you would know,"—Weinfeld smiled nastily—"if you were fully conversant with the mechanics of negotiations."

Duke looked nettled again and seemed about to speak, but he apparently thought better of it and remained silent.

"I assure you, Mr. Weinfeld, that I am totally conversant with every aspect of negotiations," Wynn retorted in a steady tone. "I insist that in this case the two cannot be negotiated separately. Surely even you will concede that our budget must be computed on the basis of outlay, period. Let's be realistic here." She felt her temper slipping and took a deep breath.

"That's nonsense," Weinfeld protested. "Unprecedented."

"Oh, I don't think so, Aaron," Duke commented, smiling. "Big Mike demanded the same thing six years ago, remember. And it almost came to a walkout, if I recall." The soft threat in his voice was all too clear.

Wynn's back was going up. Noble remarked, "You're threatening us over this petty garbage?"

"This is hardly garbage, Jim!" Wynn sharply brought him back into line. "This is five figures." She glanced at her watch. "And it's five o'clock," she added tiredly. "Shall we wrap this up until tomorrow morning?"

The delegation from 117 looked uncertainly at each other. She knew that she *was* "caving in," caving in to weariness and dismay and still faced with the prospect of fighting it out with Court that night. The union men, she knew, were used to round-the-clock negotiations. And it might come to that, she concluded with gloom.

Reluctantly Duke nodded. "Okay. Nine o'clock tomorrow, Miss Carson?" She agreed.

This time the 117 delegation left without the usual amiable good-byes. Wynn watched Duke walk away ahead of his men, saw his tall figure disappear behind the doors of the closing elevator, and her heart sank into her shoes. He was another man now, in this contest of wills; the same eyes that had looked on her with love were now a stranger's.

She shook off the thought, sternly reminding herself of the business at hand.

"Jon, can I have a word with you . . . in my office?"

Court glanced pointedly at his watch. "It's been a very long day. But very well." His assent was grudging, hostile.

When they walked through the reception area, Wynn noticed that Ruth was still at her desk. "Miss Carson . . ."

"You didn't have to stay, Ruth. Why don't you go home now?"

"But, Miss Carson, there's something—"

Wynn cut her off. "I'm sorry, I can't stop now." She could feel Ruth's hurt surprise and regretted her sharpness. But she knew if she didn't jump right into this business with Court, her nerve might fail her. And she needed to go on while her confidence was still high, while her righteous indignation was still warm. She'd had a terrible suspicion about Court, and she was going to prove it either right or wrong. And soon.

"No calls, please," she said and, gesturing to Court to enter, closed her office door. With irritation, she noticed that a newspaper had been placed exactly in the center of her desk. That was not the spot for papers, and Ruth knew it. What was it doing there now, cluttering up her correspondence?

She sat down and shoved the paper aside without a glance. "Jon," she said abruptly, "I want to take a look at the bookkeeping records tonight."

"Tonight?" he repeated, annoyed. He was still standing. "All my people will have left by now."

"Oh? Why is that? I told you that everyone should be on call during negotiations." Now she was really irritated.

"They are," he retorted, "if I'm notified early enough. I run my department with a certain order." This was such a slam at her that she had to bite her tongue to prevent a nasty reply. He had her there.

"Sorry. You're right," she admitted. "Nevertheless, I plan to spend several hours here, going over the books. I'm afraid I'll have to ask you to get them ready for me."

"May I ask for what purpose? Surely I've given you very precise figures relating to what we can afford to concede to the union." Court looked belligerent.

"You did indeed. But there are certain . . . discrepancies that bother me," Wynn answered steadily, looking into Court's flinty gray eyes.

She was thinking of Big Mike's last directions to her; some had been precise and detailed, dictated at the beginning of his illness. Others, like the warning to "watch Court," had been written when his strength was failing, when words could not be wasted. It hadn't been clear whether Court was planning to undermine her position or whether it was something about the books. Wynn had a cold feeling it could be both.

"Such as?" Court demanded.

The buzzer on Wynn's desk sounded. Wynn answered impatiently. "I said no calls," she snapped.

"Sorry," Ruth said in quick apology, "but please look at the afternoon paper on your desk. It's important. I have it open to the place."

In the same impatient tone, Wynn answered, "All right." She added a belated "Thanks, Ruth. Why don't you go home now?"

"I will." The secretary hung up.

"Excuse me, Jon." Wynn turned to the paper. It was open at the page for Louis Fleishman's labor column. That would be it. Wynn scanned the article, catching her name and Duke Bellini's. She did a double take and read more carefully. "Word around town has it that there's an interesting new duo— Wynn Carson, president of Carson Trucking, and Local 117 Truckers' prexy Donato Bellini. Lots of observers are wondering if Cupid's darts will hit the upcoming agreement between Carson's and the union . . . if the pair's sweetheart arrangement (a dirty word in union-management circles) will extend to the truckers' pact."

Wynn muttered a low exclamation and put the paper down. Where had Fleishman gotten that? Perhaps he'd seen them together. But it probably wasn't that simple. Maybe Howard Bartley and Jonathan Court were the snakes in the grass.

"What is it?" Court asked. She looked up and noticed that his hard eyes had a strange, almost amused glint.

"This," she said bluntly. He'd certainly see it anyway, sooner or later. It might as well be now. She handed him the paper. He scanned the column without expression, then put the paper back on her desk.

"Frankly, Wynn, I suspected something like this was going on. And it doesn't look good for Carson's, does it? A sweetheart deal can work two ways—this could also mean that man has you in the palm of his hand. I'm afraid you've been very indiscreet."

His tone was so much like a reproachful schoolmaster's that Wynn exploded. "Don't instruct me on my personal life! Perhaps you'd be good enough to arrange the books for me."

He stared at her for a minute. She could almost read his expression—Who is this little snip to order me around? However, he answered calmly, "I'll do that. Excuse me."

When he'd left, Wynn leaned back in her chair. Her neck was stiff with tension, as were her shoulders and her upper back. She closed her eyes. Jonathan Court might be after her in more ways than one. Checking on her for the Honorable Howard. And maybe dipping into the treasury as well.

She heard him leave about a half hour later and went into Bookkeeping. Ledgers were neatly arranged on his desk. Wearily she opened one and began to go over it. Nothing there.

She repeated the process with a second and a third. It took her the best part of two hours to scour the place for duplicate books; there were such things. But then there was the computer area to cope with, and her education was sadly lacking there.

Only an auditor could really handle this, she decided. Quickly she dialed the auditor Carson's used and apologetically asked if he could come over that night.

It was six-fifteen before he arrived and nearly eight by the time he'd reached a very tentative conclusion.

"This is going to take a couple of days," he said.

"I'm really tied up tomorrow morning, but I can send one of my guys in at eight-thirty."

"No. No, don't do that," she said hastily. "This is a . . . delicate matter. I'd like to have the work done in the evening, if possible."

The auditor gave her a keen look. "I can understand that." He hesitated. "Okay, I guess I can take it on for you, then. I can start tomorrow night. Just tell me the time."

"Six is good. Naturally I'll be prepared to pay you a premium."

He waved his hand. "We'll talk about that later. I knew your father for a good long time," he said, smiling. "What we've got here is a real tangle. It's not going to be easy."

When he'd gone and Wynn was turning out the lights and locking up, she reflected. It *wasn't* going to be easy . . . any of it.


"Wait a minute. I want to get a paper," Weinfeld said.

Duke and Halloran paused outside the restaurant while Aaron Weinfeld bought an afternoon newspaper. Then the three of them walked into the hundred-year-old restaurant on Ninth Avenue, with its bustling taproom atmosphere, brass lamps and traditional paintings from the Hudson Valley school.

As they passed the bar, a beaming maître d' greeted Duke. "Good to see you." His smile included Halloran and Weinfeld. "This all right?"

"Fine, George," Duke answered absently and sat down on a banquette by the wall.

Halloran sighed. "Boy, can I use a steak tonight. And a drink." He smiled at George. "Right away, Mr. Halloran." The maître d' snapped his fingers, and a waiter appeared to take their drink orders.

"Excuse me." Weinfeld began to leaf through the paper. "Well, I'll be damned."

The waiter had already set their drinks before them. Duke took a sip of his bourbon. "What's up?"

"This." Weinfeld folded the paper and handed it to Duke, Louis Fleishman's column face up.

Duke Bellini's black glance flashed down the lines. His mouth tightened. "Stupid idiot. He sounds like a female gossipmonger."

"That so, Duke?" Halloran was regarding him over the rim of his highball glass. He sipped his drink and put the glass down. "I never heard of smoke without fire, and I've been around a long time."

"What's that supposed to mean?" Duke demanded. He met Halloran's hard blue eyes and looked at Weinfeld. The latter's stare was flat and accusing.

"You were pretty soft on that little broad today, Duke." Halloran's quiet voice was level, but full of overtones. "You never caved in like that to Margie Ball or Hester Glushein. But then"—Halloran's chuckle was unpleasant—"Margie weighs three hundred pounds, and Hester's old man is built like a redwood."

"If you've got something to say, Bernie, say it." Duke felt his hackles rise.

"You know what he's saying, Duke," Weinfeld intervened. "If you're gonna play around, why mix it with business? You've always had more sense than that. Has Lou got the straight story? Are you and this Carson dame . . . ?" He leered as he left the sentence hanging.

"Watch yourself." Duke brought his hands up on the table, and he could feel them balling into fists. "Wynn Carson's no 'dame.' "

"Hey, wait a minute!" Halloran spoke with dawning suspicion. Both men were staring at Duke. "Are you serious about this little . . . about this Carson woman?" he amended quickly, noticing Duke's expression.

"That's none of your damned business." Duke bit the words off.

"Anything that affects the union is our business, pal," Weinfeld retorted in a warlike tone.

"Don't call me 'pal,' pal. This column is a lot of garbage. This has nothing to do with bargaining. You should know me better than that by now. Since when have I ever given you or the guys anything but a fair shake? When?" Duke demanded.

"Okay, okay, Duke. Since never." Halloran's tone was pacific. "But all the same, we can't fool around with this. Listen, this da— this woman might be giving you the old one-three. You gotta think of that. She might be stringing you along to get a sweet deal for that company, Duke."

"You're nuts. You heard her at the initial talks, and you heard her at the other sessions. She's been completely reasonable. What the hell do you want— for her to offer more than we asked? Would that satisfy you?" Duke's voice was rising.

"Take it easy, Duke." Weinfeld glanced at the other tables. "They can hear you up to Central Park."

"What the hell difference does that make?" Duke retorted. "This garbage is already all over the papers. What do you want from me?"

"We want you to take it easy, Duke." Halloran spoke in a low, pleading voice. "We want you to think about it. What if this Carson woman is pulling a fast one? I just don't think you should work and play in the same place, that's all. Do you, Aaron?"

"Damned right I don't," Weinfeld agreed. "This doesn't look good for us, Duke. You've gotta know that."

Duke slid out of the banquette and stood up, glaring down at them. "I don't give a damn what looks good. Nobody's telling me how to run my personal life." Even as he spoke he regretted saying it. This wasn't helping, he knew. It wasn't helping at all. He should have held on to his temper. But it was too late now.

"Where're you going?"

"Out of here." Duke threw down a bill to cover his drink and stormed out past the surprised maître d' onto Ninth Avenue. A light drizzle had begun to fall. It felt good, cool on his anger-heated face. He strode to a public phone booth and, to his surprise, found that it hadn't been vandalized. He dialed Wynn's home number. There was no answer. He cursed. Retrieving his dime, he called her office.

He let it ring six times and was about to hang up when she answered.

"Hello, baby. How are you?"

"Not so good." Her voice sounded strained, tired.

"What's the matter? Is it that jerk's column? You saw it, I guess." That must be it, he thought. "Don't pay any attention to that garbage."

"It's not just that." Again he got the feeling there was something she was holding back.

"Come on, honey, tell me."

"I can't right now." He was sure of it. She sounded cold, confused.

"We've got to talk, sweetheart. Shall I come down there and get you? Meet you at your place?"

There was a long silence.

"Wynn?"

"No, Duke. Not tonight."

"But why, honey? I want to see you. We've got to talk about this thing. What's the matter, Wynn? You can tell me."

"No, I can't, Duke." She sounded more sure of herself, but colder than ever. It gave him the willies. "It's a lot of things," she went on. "The way you looked at me today . . . the whole situation. It's impossible. It can't work, Duke."

He grasped the receiver until he thought it would crack in his fist. "Don't say that, Wynn. That's crazy. We can make anything work." There was silence again. "Are you listening?"

"Yes." Her reply was distant, unwilling. She *wasn't* listening, he thought. She wasn't hearing him at all.

"Wynn, you've got to let me see you tonight. Didn't you mean anything you said this weekend? Don't you remember what happened? This is me, Duke Bellini."

"Oh yes, I know. I know that, all right." The irony in her tone stung him, and in spite of himself he grew more and more impatient.

"Well, is it yes or no?" he snapped before he could stop himself.

"No," she said curtly.

He was hurt and angry. "Okay, sweetheart, what we've got here is a lockout. Apparently that's the way you want it." Impulsively he slammed the receiver back on its hook. Then he thought, You dumb cluck! and scrambled in his pocket for another dime. By the time he found one and dialed he got no answer.

Without waiting for his dime, he slammed out of the booth and headed west on Fourteenth Street,

thinking, Damn all women. They're crazy, crazy.
But something deep in him was hurting—bad.

It was still raining the next morning when the talks
resumed at nine, a chilly, almost wintry rain that
made Duke feel lower than ever. He was aching to
talk to Wynn alone, desperate to apologize for his
idiotic rudeness. But it didn't look as if she was
going to give him any chance at all.

She looked very formal, but she also looked so
pretty that it was all he could do not to walk around
the table and take her in his arms. Everybody else in
the damned boardroom, he thought, looked like
they were going to a funeral. But there was no way
she couldn't look bright, with that sunny hair and
her orange-colored dress that seemed as warm as
fire. She'd never been more beautiful, reflected
Duke Bellini . . . or more unapproachable.

He couldn't help noticing that she wasn't wearing
his pin. But a glance at her right hand told him that
she was wearing the ring.

It was the first time in his career that Duke let
anything distract him from negotiations. He didn't
like the way his mind was wandering. He pulled
himself together and joined the fray.

Wynn was still adamant about the warehouse-
men's rates and numbers. They fought that out for
about an hour without resolving anything.

When she suggested they table that for the moment and go on to load weights, number of stops and
size and location of routes, Duke and the delegation
concurred. That seemed to go a little better, but
there were still plenty of knots to untangle. To make
it worse, Wynn seemed to be reversing herself from
her former liberal position.

Something was up, Duke thought, and he'd

damned well like to know what it was. This was like
driving an eighteen-wheeler in a peasoup fog; it
made him feel just about as secure. He intended to
get to the bottom of this. There was some internal
problem, he was certain. She would never be petty
enough to let their tiff intrude on this.

Or would she?

Duke stared at Wynn, almost willing her to catch
his eye, but she wouldn't. Then he realized that his
own men were checking him out and got down to
business.

They struck another snag. After a short lunch
break, they went back and stayed hard at it until
nearly six, but it looked like management wasn't
going to budge an inch. It seemed to Duke that the
old guy, Court, looked kind of funny, not like
himself at all. He and the rest of the management
team had been thrown off base. Evidently Wynn had
pulled something on them. Still, they had to be
feeling good about her tough new stand. Duke
almost smiled at the sight of his men's faces. This
was one reason why he'd always enjoyed bargaining
with women owners—they threw you a curve ball
every time, and it kept a guy hopping.

Wynn Carson was another kind of challenge, too.
Duke glanced at her covertly again. Her pretty face
was smooth as marble, with a blank, neutral expression. Damn it, Duke raged silently. Damn it all to
hell.

She seemed very sure of herself, very cool. There
was no question of any of her men speaking for her
now. They were there only as a backup to answer
questions or contribute specific information according to their individual specialties, just as his own
men were.

As he watched her bounce the verbal balls back to

the union, Duke's frustration grew. There were even moments when he felt an unaccustomed sense of uncertainty and got rougher than he had intended. But what the hell, he was running a union. This was no damned tea party.

By the end of the session, the two sides were practically at each other's throats.

The next day was the same, a real Ping-Pong number, back and forth. To make it worse for Duke Bellini, he'd called Wynn several times the night before, but she hadn't answered. He'd pictured her going out with another man. Or worse, staying at home with one, just ignoring the phone. But she wasn't like that, Duke told himself. She couldn't be.

Wynn was exhausted from the Wednesday session. But she couldn't think of going home. Tonight the auditor would give her the answer to what she was seeking.

When Ruth made a sympathetic comment about her working late again, Wynn gave her an evasive answer. After the secretary had gone, Wynn went out for a hasty dinner, which she ate without appetite, and hurried back.

It was seven o'clock before the auditor came in to her office with a grim look.

"I found it," he said curtly. "I'll have to give him left-handed credit. This was a slick operation. He sold bogus stock and diverted investment funds into two dummy corporations. The details are in this folder."

"What kind of shape does this leave us in?" she asked baldly.

"Not too great. Now, if he can be persuaded to make reparations—to avoid prosecution, for instance—you'll be back in business. May I advise you?"

"I wish you would," she urged him.

"I think you'll be a lot better off if this is handled quietly. It won't help Carson's to get a reputation for having shaky finances. Who have you got you can really count on?" the auditor demanded.

"Mostly lower echelon." Wynn named them.

"Promote them. Get rid of Noble. You can see from that"—he indicated his folder—"that he was in on this, too. Promise immunity from prosecution if you get full reparation. Revamp the whole book-keeping operation."

Wynn was so overwhelmed that she was afraid she was going to burst out crying. "In the middle of negotiations?"

The auditor shook his head. "It's rough. But you've got to do it."

Wynn let out a shaky sigh. "Okay. And thanks."

"Forget it. Let's say I owed Big Mike. If you need me, let me know."

Once he'd gone, Wynn sat motionless in her leather chair for a long moment. Then she straightened and dialed Jonathan Court's home number.

"I know it's an unusual hour," she told him crisply, "but I've got to come over. I've got to talk to you tonight."

Hanging up, she reflected, At least I'm getting started. She took the folder and went out.

# Chapter 8

WHEN THE ADVERSARIES SAT DOWN AGAIN ON THURSday morning, Duke Bellini discreetly checked out Wynn Carson. On the surface she was as lovely and well-groomed as always, but she looked like she'd been pulled through a wringer. There were deep shadows under her eyes, and her cheeks had a hollowness that was new.

He couldn't help wondering if she missed him as much as he missed her. He'd called again the night before and gotten no answer.

On top of that, Court and that lawyer Noble were missing in action. Duke was surprised to see a much younger lawyer in Noble's spot and Tommy Wilson, a guy who'd come up through the ranks and was smart as a whip, in Court's.

But what really threw a monkey wrench into the works was Wynn Carson's attitude. She was acting like she was going to squeeze every penny until

Lincoln yelled. And that was putting him, putting all the union men, into one hell of a position. What was she trying to pull? he puzzled.

Near the end of the session, it looked like there was only one way out.

Duke took a deep breath and said, "Miss Carson, if this is your final offer, we're going to have to walk."

He saw her exchange a worried look with Wilson and the young mouthpiece, What's-His-Name.

"We don't want a strike, Mr. Bellini," she answered in a trembling voice. There was no way in the world Duke couldn't feel sorry for her. She was so little, so . . . What was she doing in this war, anyway? She looked so helpless.

Duke laughed silently at himself. Helpless. About as helpless as a black belt in karate, when you considered how she'd handled herself in these talks, how she'd cut him off.

"I wish," she said in a steadier voice, "that you would consider taking this into mediation."

Duke stared into the shadowed blue eyes he loved so much. "Tell you what," he replied coolly. "Why don't you give us a while to talk this over? A half hour?"

"Take all the time you need." Her relief was so plain that Duke's heart turned over. "Gentlemen?" Wynn gave her fellow negotiators an uncertain smile, rose and led them from the boardroom.

As soon as the door closed, Halloran said flatly, "I say we ought to walk. It's the only thing with teeth in it, and you know it."

There was a mutter from the other men. Weinfeld said, in his sarcastic fashion, "You're such a fire-eater, Bernie. You know my stand: A strike's the last resort."

"Stuff it, Aaron," Halloran growled. "I say we oughta get the men in for a strike vote, ask for sanction today."

"Hold it, Bernie," Duke snapped. "I want to hear from all the guys." He polled the attorneys. They opted for mediation.

"That's it, Bernie." Duke grinned. "Five to one we mediate."

"You haven't heard the last of this, Duke, I'm warning you. The guys'll never ratify a contract like that." Halloran reddened with indignation.

"Are you nuts?" Duke demanded. "We don't have a contract yet, remember?"

Halloran reddened more deeply, embarrassed at his stupid mistake. "Sure, sure. What I mean is, the men want a standup union," he concluded weakly.

Weinfeld gave Halloran a look of contempt.

Duke stood up. "I'll bring them back in."

When he'd gone out, Halloran said to Weinfeld and the lawyers, "I'm telling you, we haven't heard the last of this. We're not going to get anything from a lousy mediator. I'm telling all of you, if Duke crosses the men, they'll bust him."

The other negotiators began to study Halloran with new eyes.


Duke looked through the Sunday papers without interest, thinking what a lousy weekend it had been. Friday and Saturday they'd had long, hard sessions with the mediator. Wynn Carson must have pulled some strings, he thought, to get him in that soon. No one had ever gotten such swift action before.

The mediator had shuffled back and forth between

the labor caucus room and the management caucus room; then Wynn and Duke had met with the mediator in *his* room. The result of Friday's talks had been zilch. Only the night before, Saturday night, had they begun to make some progress. The way it looked now, Monday might wrap it up. Duke Bellini was not too pleased with what 117 was getting. Still, he was sure Wynn wasn't pleased, either, with what Carson's was giving.

Duke smiled grimly. The same old drill, with the mediator telling him, "You know she's not going to go along with that two-man requirement on every truck. Carson's freight load doesn't require that. So if you bend on that issue, she'll probably go along with the rate."

And then the mediator would tell Wynn that if she conceded the rate, Duke would ease up on the two-man demand.

What a way to spend the weekend, Duke thought sourly. He remembered the last one, and the thought was like a punch in his gut. He hadn't had the nerve even to call her at home Friday night; she had looked so tired that he guessed she just fell into bed as soon as she got home. And then the night before there had been no answer at all. He couldn't take this much longer.

Damn it, he was going to see her if it was the last thing he ever did. He threw down the paper and looked out the window of his apartment. A light rain had begun to fall. He put on a poplin jacket and, hatless, went out.

He walked downtown quickly and crossed to Washington Square. It was full of the kind of characters who usually hung out in the rain. Why he'd expected to see Wynn there, he didn't know. She had too much sense to be among this crew—weird old guys playing chess at the concrete tables, right on through the drizzle; out-of-the-neighborhood types with transistors; way-out kids on roller skates; bored, resentful-looking cops.

Duke turned up his jacket collar and retraced his steps, heading west. Then he stopped. Damn it, I'm going to see her, he said to himself.

He turned around again, hearing the laughter of some girls who'd been staring at him. "Doesn't know if he's coming or going," he heard one of them say in a small, shrill voice.

"Boy, he could go with me *any* time," one of her companions remarked.

Duke strode east again, passing under the great Washington Arch, the famous landmark on all the postcards, the spot at the foot of Fifth Avenue where he'd played when he was a kid. He looked up the misty vastness of the avenue that stretched to the north, meeting with a vaulted, cathedral-like effect as the gray skyscrapers seemed to come together in the distance.

She made me see how beautiful the city is, he thought. His heart hammered against his ribs. The mews where she lived was just a few steps away. He was going there, and the hell with the consequences. It was crazy, it was stupid for them to be apart after all the things that had happened between them. She was his woman. He loved her.

With a resolute stride he crossed the street and stepped onto the sidewalk a few doors from the mews. Reaching the grilled gates, he cursed himself for a fool. They were locked, of course. There was no way he could get in.

But, not to be beaten, he determinedly sought out a public phone and called her number. He let it ring eight times, then let it ring some more. He'd make her answer this time.

The phone kept on ringing. Wynn put her hands to her ears to shut out the insistent call for an answer. She knew it was Duke. She just knew it.

She turned on the television set to drown out the shrill sound, but the ringing went on and on. Why hadn't she taken it off the hook? Then she would have been safe. He couldn't possibly get through the gate.

Pacing back and forth, she reflected how strange it was that she should think of being safe from him, when only a short time before he had become the center of her life. But everything had changed, she reminded herself grimly. After that enchanted weekend they had been catapulted into the deadly game of bargaining, the game in which so much was at stake for both of them. She had realized in one sickening flash, at the beginning of the last week, that they were antagonists, natural enemies. They would never be able to make it together.

She admitted to herself that one reason she had avoided answering his calls was that she was afraid— afraid he would cajole her into being with him again. He *could*, with his caressing mouth, his magical touch. Yes, he could talk her into it, and then they would have been exactly where they'd started, in that half-dream of love that they could never sustain.

Suddenly the phone stopped ringing.

Wynn turned off the TV and heard the sudden silence with relief, yet with a certain odd, gnawing sadness. Even Duke Bellini, the invincible Duke Bellini, had to give up after a while. The idea made her head ache.

She sighed and wandered into the living room.

She lay down on the couch, reviewing the hectic pattern of the last draining week—the proof of Court's wrongdoing and Noble's involvement; the scramble to reorganize, to replace them. Wrung out from each day's bargaining, she'd still had to stay late every night at the office, conferring with the auditors and what remained of the treasurer's staff, the attorneys, Tommy Wilson and other newly promoted executives. The upshot of it was that Carson's would be in a bit of trouble for a time, but Court and Noble had gladly accepted her offer of silence for full reparation. That, however, would take time in itself. Both Carson's and the men's individual finances were in an awful tangle.

Blessedly, though, no one had gotten wind of what had really happened within Carson's. The company would contrive to present a solid front to the financial world, with the cooperation of certain brokers and bankers who still remembered Big Mike with affection.

At least there was that, Wynn decided, closing her eyes. But *she* hadn't bounced back. After the harrowing sessions with the mediator Friday, she'd had to meet with her own people until ten Friday night. She'd taken a taxi home and fallen asleep in her clothes, sleeping until her alarm woke her at nine Saturday morning, with just enough time to shower, change and rush to the office for the ten o'clock resumption of talks.

Saturday night had been a repetition of Friday night. That morning she'd slept until noon. When she woke she was at least somewhat refreshed. And she realized with wonder that she'd been so rushed and harried and overwhelmed she'd hardly had time to think of Duke Bellini.

At the same time, she wondered if he'd called her

Friday or Saturday night. She'd been so exhausted that she probably wouldn't have heard the phone.

As if in answer to her thought, the phone began to ring again. She opened her eyes.

This time she'd answer. She'd be woman enough to tell him, once and for all, that it was over.

She went to the instrument and picked it up with trembling fingers.

"Wynn," his voice rushed over the line before she could even say hello. "Oh, Wynn. Talk to me," he pleaded.

"Yes, Duke." She tried to make her voice as steady as she could. "I'll talk to you. What is it?"

"What *is* it?" he repeated. "What *is* it?" His voice sounded choked and hollow. "I love you. That's what it is. Don't keep on doing this to us. Let me see you. Let me talk to you."

She took a deep breath, trying to find the words.

"Wynn," he said again, cajolingly. The deep voice struck her nerves and something within her melted. All her resolution dissolved in a second, like ice in fire. "Wynn, let me come over. I'm right here, at Fifth and Eighth Street."

"All right, Duke. Come over."

"I'm on my way," he exulted, and she heard him hang up, then listened to the open line.

I'll go down to meet him, she decided. I'll have to open the gate, anyway. She flung a raincoat on over her slacks and flowered tunic, took up her keys and went out, running down the stairs.

When she got outside, he was already standing at the barred gate to the mews, looking tall as a tree, his shoulders wide in his tan poplin jacket. She unlocked the gate, and he came through it with one immense stride, grabbed her in his arms and held her like a vise, his mouth caressing her mist-dampened hair.

"Wynn, oh, Wynn," he said over and over, holding her, caressing her, unconscious of the passing pedestrians, the steady flow of Sunday traffic.

She relaxed against him, feeling the familiar, beloved strength of his mighty arms, his breath warm on her head, the closeness of his tough, aroused body.

"Come on, baby." He released her suddenly, smiling down into her eyes. "Let's get you out of the rain."

She shut the gate, and they walked quickly together along the short private street to her apartment door. Neither of them said a word as they went upstairs, until they were inside and the door was closed against the world.

As soon as it was shut, Duke took her in his arms again and kissed her with a new savagery and desperation, deeper and stronger than anything that had come before. She felt her lips take fire, and all the rational arguments she had prepared against this meeting evaporated. All her reasons became only foolish words with no power to stem their tempestuous emotions. A gale-force wind of desire swept her forward in its wake, leaving her weakened, powerless.

When he raised his mouth from hers, still staring down into her upraised eyes, Duke demanded in a tender voice, "Why did you do this to us, darling? Why did you lock me out . . . out of your arms, your bed . . . out of everything I need and want in this world?"

"When you hold me like this, I hardly know," she admitted, caressing his face. "I thought we couldn't make it together. At the talks you were so . . . such

a stranger. And then that night on the phone . . ."
Her voice shook.

He held her near again, kissing the top of her
head. "Honey, honey, I'm sorry. I'm so sorry. I
don't know what got into me. I guess I was going a
little nuts from not being with you." His eager
breath was hot against her hair; she could feel her
whole body tremble and ignite.

"Duke, Duke." She raised her arms from around
his lean waist and put them around his neck, urging
his face downward to hers again for another fever-
ish, hungry kiss.

She was aware of his strong excitement, conscious
that her own wild needs were answering his. She felt
something stir in her as his steely arms pressed her
close again. That fluid excitement strengthened
when he stroked her breasts and waist, her softly
blooming hips.

He gently took her coat off, laying it on a chair,
then knelt down before her, kissing her again and
again, a caressing that almost burned her skin
through the thin, sliding jersey of her trousers. She
was wearing next to nothing underneath her clothes,
and she trembled at the heat of his mouth and his
breath through the light fabric.

Only dimly aware of what she was doing, Wynn
leaned suddenly closer to him and kissed his thick
black hair, her hands stroking his sinewy neck above
his open collar. He gave a kind of moaning cry, and
his hold on her tightened. Still leaning on him, Wynn
cried out in answer, the sound muffled in his clean,
spice-scented, onyx hair.

She was in his power again; she belonged to Duke
Bellini, as she had from the first time she'd looked
into his eyes.

She could find no words to say when he looked up

at her again with the black coal glinting of his eyes. He, too, was silent as he rose and, still fixing her with his magnetic stare, picked her up and strode into the bedroom with her in his arms.

He held her close as he walked. She was breathless in that bruising grasp, melting against the demanding hardness of his chest and arms. She felt herself go fluid everywhere; she seemed to be flowing into him, around him.

In the dimly lit room, with its drawn curtains, he set her on the bed. Then he lowered himself to her, and she felt him shaking as his mouth parted over hers.

We can't let each other go, she thought with abandoned joy. She felt his hands unfastening her tunic, pulling it over her head, drawing her soft trousers over her legs until she lay bared and vibrant, waiting.

She looked at him while he flung off his own clothes, feasting her sight on his massive naked body. More than ever he looked like a Roman warrior, a beautiful statue in a museum. In the dim golden light, the breadth of his shoulders had an awesome power; his muscular arms were even more beautiful than she remembered. He stood there staring, staring, and his black gaze seemed to stroke her face and body like loving hands.

Her whole self was open to him; it was like a sudden flood of sunlight for someone who had been shut up in the darkness. He kneeled down on the bed; she saw his dark head lower and then felt the rhythmic beginning of that caress that was so poignant at first it seemed almost pain. But then, as it had before, that strange sensation became a point of burning light within her, narrowing to a miniscule sliver of pleasure so acute that she cried out to him for happiness. She heard her own voice with a kind of wonder, as if the sound had come from someone else, a wild, abandoned woman knowing nothing beyond the instant's joy.

In the storm of shuddering wonder, the dim thought came, If I feel any more such pleasure, I'll die. But he wasn't done, and in the imminent and closer meeting of their bodies, she was to find an even greater revelation.

Never, never before, her mind sang silently to her vibrating body, had their love been this overpowering, this sweet. Where there had been a throbbing hollowness, she was fulfilled. Their bodies danced, and when the broken light began to darken through her dazzled lids, the inner fires were lit again and spread, this time with even greater stunning power, into a wide and wheeling blaze of broken light.

Through her closed lids Wynn saw pinwheels of scarlet on a sky of night, and dazzled stars and lightning threads. She heard Duke's triumphant cry.

They moved closer into each other's arms, subsiding, and she felt the gladness of a wanderer returning home.

Both of them drowsed a little; she had the feeling that he was almost as tired and sleep-deprived as she.

She awoke first and rose on her elbow, watching him sleep. She stole out of bed quietly, showered and came back freshly scented, wearing the bronze satin robe, her hair newly washed and blown dry, a soft golden glory around her shoulders.

"Beautiful. So beautiful." He was propped up on pillows in the bed, regarding her through the haze of a cigarette, absolute worship in his eyes.

She came to him, and he held her against him,

kissing her repeatedly. Then at last he got up to shower and dress again.

He asked her, smiling, if she thought they could manage to have an actual dinner, and she said she thought they might. They decided to make it up to Enrico for their earlier lack of appetite and settled on Fedora's. She dressed casually, to match him, and they had a pleasant walk west in the clearing air to the relaxed restaurant.

Later Wynn urged him to stay. He said, raising an eyebrow, "You couldn't have gotten rid of me, anyway." They had a close and lazy evening watching television and fell asleep early.

He planned to leave her in the morning to get back to his place, to change and to repeat that earlier charade of arriving separately at Carson's.

When he kissed her lingeringly in the morning and left, Wynn's heart sank again, despite the glowing aftermath of their night together. It was exactly as she'd predicted: They were right back where they'd started from, except that this time it was more difficult than ever. She knew now, with deep certainty, how impossible it would be to say a lasting good-bye to him, as she had tried to do before.

The Monday sessions with the mediator lasted a grueling twenty hours without an agreement being reached. Duke managed to find a second alone with Wynn and, noticing her exhausted look, said softly, "Go home and get some rest, baby. I'll see you tomorrow."

She was touched by his protective manner, his understanding. She'd confided in him the night before about the disastrous situation at Carson's, so he knew the work that faced her. She felt totally overwhelmed by the prospect of what lay ahead for them both. If and when an agreement was reached,

Duke would have his hands full with matters relating to the contract and its ratification by the membership. And she knew that this would not be the finest contract ever obtained by Local 117.

She herself, as soon as this killing interval was over, would have to rush on without a break to the reorganization, to cope with the company's financial squeeze. They'd have to tighten their belts for a while.

Through everything she would be faced with a serious, lifetime decision—what was she going to do about Duke Bellini? He wasn't the kind of man to be content with a continuing affair, any more than she would be. They were coming nearer to a permanent commitment, but how could she make the right decision with her judgment warped by exhaustion and distraction?

The next day did not improve matters. There were still thorny problems with the talks. The two sides had not yet reached an agreement.

And now, in addition to the grind of negotiations and the never-ceasing daily routine of Carson's, Wynn felt another burden: Duke. It was horrible to think of him like that when he had brought her the greatest happiness of her life, but she couldn't help feeling haunted by their other deep commitments. In their intimate conversations Duke had scoffed at the contemporary liking for noncommitment. "If you're not committed, you're dead. A cipher," he'd told her.

They needed to be openly together. He wanted to meet her family; she wanted to know his. But how could they ever marry, when the union was his very life and Carson's her irrevocable responsibility? They'd have a conflict of interest forever, she reflected with bitter humor, in more ways than one. He might even have to give up his presidency if his own wife was a trucking boss. He couldn't. And she couldn't quit Carson's.

On Wednesday Carson's and the union reached an agreement. A subdued union delegation left at seven. Wynn sat at her desk, gathering her strength for the journey home. She'd put Duke off, and he'd studied her with anxious, speculative eyes.

Her private phone rang. It was Dolores, her sister-in-law. Dolores had called a few times recently to check on her, but Wynn had had little leisure for other conversation.

"Is it over?" Dolores asked in her soothing, husky voice.

"Yes. At last."

"You sound awful. So tired. I hope I'm not keeping you from going home or anything."

"No, no," Wynn assured her. "I was just . . . getting my breath. I'm glad you called. How's everybody?" she asked belatedly.

"Great. I just wanted to remind you of Greg's concert, Wynn. Next Thursday, Town Hall."

"Oh heavens!" Wynn gasped. "So soon?"

"So soon?" Dolores chuckled. "Shame on you, lady. He's been looking forward to this for months. Have you forgotten?"

"I've had a few things on my mind," Wynn snapped. Then she hastily apologized and filled Dolores in on the tough bargaining. She couldn't reveal the rest. Not yet.

"Oh, Wynn. You poor kid." Dolores sounded conscience-stricken. "I shouldn't have pressed you. Forgive me."

"There's nothing at all to forgive," Wynn asserted. "I'm just . . . beat at the moment. Of course I'll be at the concert. You know I will. I wouldn't miss it for all the trucks in America," she concluded with a dismal attempt at humor.

Just as she was leaving the office, her private phone rang again. It was Duke.

"How are you, honey? You seemed beat when we wrapped it up."

"I am. And you?" She could imagine how he must be feeling. Added to his own exhaustion, she suspected, was probably a sense of having failed his people.

"Still here." He sounded as weary as she felt. "About tonight . . . I know you need to get some rest, but I wish I could come by for just a little while."

"Of course you can," she said warmly, shutting her eyes and rubbing them. They felt gritty from tiredness.

"I think I may have a big problem." She waited. He sounded so woebegone that she wished she could take him in her arms at that very instant. "I've got to go to Detroit. A royal summons from the Old Man himself, the national president. Listen, honey, I've got to go. There are a hundred things hanging fire here right now. Can I come over about ten? I'll use the key you gave me."

"Of course, Duke." She was afraid that some of her reluctance, based on her grinding exhaustion, must have been revealed in her voice.

"Thank you, honey. So much. I really need you now."

Wynn left the office and took a cab home, afraid to trust her driving. With relief, she realized that she could squeeze in a nap before he came. Too bone-tired even to shower, she undressed, put on a robe and fell on the bed.

The doorbell roused her. Fuzzy with sleep, hoping

she looked all right, she stumbled to the door. He had keys to all the doors, but he didn't use them unless he mentioned it first, and she liked that courteous little gesture.

When he came in his face looked hollowed out; his eyes were darkly shadowed. "What a day." However, his black eyes gleamed when he looked at her, and he took her in his arms at once, kissing her hair.

"Even when you're absolutely knocked out, you're gorgeous." He grinned.

"Sit down," she urged him. "Can I get you a drink? I'm going to have coffee myself."

He sank down on the couch and leaned back gratefully. "Honey, a drink would knock me right on my . . . heels. Coffee would be wonderful. But I don't want you to wait on me when you're so tired."

"Please . . . I've had a nap, which is more than you've had." She caressed his hair and went into the kitchen, returning shortly with a tray containing a coffeepot, cream and sugar, cups and saucers.

He got to his feet, taking the tray from her. "Hey, let me do this," he ordered. "Where do you want it?"

She indicated the coffee table, saying, "Thank you, sir." A warm tenderness flooded her; he was always so considerate and caring. "You're so sweet to me," she said, and kissed him.

"Oh, Wynn, how could I not be?" He looked up at her. "Sit down here."

She complied and poured out coffee for both of them. He took a sip and sighed. "Wonderful."

"Duke," she said gently, "what is this about Detroit? Tell me."

He set his cup down, looking grim. "The Old Man's gotten wind of that jerk's gossip column, of course. I got a telegram tonight"—he smiled crookedly—"telling me that he'd 'appreciate' seeing me at the main office a week from tomorrow."

"A week from tomorrow," she repeated. "Thursday."

"Yeah. Is there something special about that?"

It was the night of Greg's concert. Wynn had half hoped to ask Duke to go with her, no matter how indiscreet that was. But now . . .

"No," she lied. "No, nothing special. I was just thinking that . . . that's a long time to be kept in suspense."

He put his arm around her and drew her head down onto his shoulder. "You've got that right." He kissed her eyebrow and cheek and hair, and she melted at his touch. What a tangle it had all become. Now his very career might be jeopardized.

"What are you thinking?" he asked her gently.

"About Detroit, of course. Do you expect . . . Duke, I'm the one who's caused this problem. Isn't that true?"

He squeezed her to him. "If this is a problem, lady, load me up with problems."

She said soberly, "That's not exactly an answer, is it?"

Duke leaned back and looked into her face. He took her shoulders in his big hands, and she trembled at the touch of them. "Well, honey, sure. That column is causing a hassle. We both know that. But it's not your fault. None of this is."

She felt tears gathering in her eyes. "But it's because of us, Duke, don't you see?"

He took her to him again. "Honey, please . . . please don't cry. I can't take that. Please. Look, it's not just that stupid nonsense. I think there's more to it. I have a nasty feeling that somebody in 117 is out to get me."

She remembered Halloran's conversation with Weinfeld. And then she thought of her own position at Carson's. "Welcome to the club," she said with bitter humor.

"Yeah. We're both in the same boat in a way. But I'm glad you caught on to Court and Noble. I think maybe my trouble will be with Bernie Halloran."

"What makes you think that?"

"Partly the stuff you heard at the art show, but mostly a lot of other things. He was the one who wanted to walk, more than the rest of us. Accused me of not being a standup president."

"That's ridiculous." She was indignant. "That's not what my father said . . . and I think he was a pretty good judge of people."

Duke grinned, looking cheerful for the first time since he'd arrived. "So do I."

Wynn poured out some more coffee for them. "Duke?"

He nodded his thanks. "Yes, honey? What?"

"Oh, Duke. I'm afraid." She put down her cup. So did he. He took her hands in his.

"Of what, Wynn? Tell me."

"I'm afraid they're not going to let us be together." Tears were perilously near the surface again, and she blinked them angrily away.

"'They' don't have a damned thing to do with anything," he said calmly. "You and I are going to be together, lady, make no mistake. Come what may."

"I wish I had your confidence." She tried to smile.

"You're just worn out, that's all. When we get this mess straightened out, we'll take some real time together. Won't we?"

"Oh yes. Yes, I'd love that." Her eyelids were beginning to droop again.

"Somebody's mighty sleepy," he said tenderly. "Maybe I'd better go."

"Go!" She grabbed his hand and held it tightly. "No. Oh no."

"You don't think I want to, do you?" he reproached her softly. "But maybe you need tonight to yourself."

She put her arms around his neck. "I never need to be away from you," she protested. He hugged her close.

"I guess that settles it." He kissed her nose and forehead, her cheeks and chin, finally her mouth very gently. "You won't believe this in a million years, but all I really want tonight is just to hold you. To literally sleep with you." He grinned.

"That sounds heavenly."

That was just what it had been, Duke thought as he strode into his office the following Wednesday morning. As for the rest of it, there was hell to pay. He needed to be three people right now. Last weekend he and Wynn hadn't been able to spend much time together, what with all they had to handle. What time there was had been just great, though. So great.

He sat down at his desk and looked at the morning mail with a peculiar distaste. Usually he jumped right in, but this particular morning he had a nagging, anxious feeling that had never bothered him before. The summons from the Old Man didn't help, of course. But things didn't feel right at the office either.

Duke hit his secretary's buzzer. "Margaret, is Bernie in yet?"

"He won't be in this morning, Mr. Bellini. He said he was going to the sites with the agents."

That was funny, Duke reflected. "Thanks."

Now why in hell was Bernie Halloran visiting the terminals with the business agents? That had never been his job. It was common practice for the reps to go to the sites after a tentative pact had been concluded to tell the men what had happened, to explain new contract provisions. But union officers didn't usually get involved in that—unless there was some kind of trouble.

Duke had a strong suspicion that if there was to be trouble, Bernie was going to cause it, not try to smooth it over. He wondered if Halloran was trying to undermine him with the guys. It was possible. He'd been "agin" everything Duke had tried to do for the past couple of years, and under that genial mask Duke sensed a far from genial attitude.

Hell, I'm getting paranoid, Duke scoffed at himself.

He put the mail aside for a moment and dialed Wynn's private number. He heard her sweet voice right away.

"How's it going, baby?"

"Not bad." He could see her smiling, and it made him feel better. "Are you getting squared away for the trip?"

He laughed. "Procrastinating at the moment. See you tonight?"

"Of course. Why don't you reconsider. Let *me* drive you to the airport in the morning?"

"Not on your life. It's too damned early," he protested. "But listen, I'll make it a point to wrap things up so we can have dinner tonight for sure."

They talked for a few more minutes. Then he hung up with a renewed optimism and attacked the stuff on his desk.

When his secretary came in to take dictation and

pick up the mail for distribution, Duke said, "Would you tell Bernie I'd like to see him as soon as he comes in?"

"Certainly. He did say that wouldn't be until about three."

"Whenever." Duke handed her the mail.

"While you're gone, should I give your mail to Mr. Halloran, like always?" Margaret asked matter-of-factly.

Duke hesitated. "No." He noticed her look of faint surprise. "Aaron Weinfeld will handle it this time."

She nodded and went out. Duke wondered what instinct had made him give those directions.

That afternoon he was to find out.

Halloran sauntered into his office at about three-fifteen with a genially blank look, but his hard blue eyes were wary. "You wanted to see me, Duke?"

"Yeah. Sit down, Bernie. Take a load off your feet." Duke made his voice as neutral as he could. Halloran sat.

"What's this about your going to the sites, Bernie? What's up?"

Duke Bellini, like his father before him, was a skillful interpreter of expressions. Now he noticed Bernie Halloran's. The man's face was a little too blank, his answer a little too easy. His smile never quite reached his eyes. Duke could almost see him mentally shifting gears.

"Just giving the guys a hand, Duke. That's all. This is going to be a tough pact to sell. And Hamer's new. I thought he'd need some help interpreting the new provisions."

"You were with Hamer all day?" Duke asked casually. "He's always back here at noon."

That hit home. Halloran's careful blandness seemed to slip a little.

"Well, not all day. I went around with some of the other reps, too. They seemed to be having some trouble at the warehouses, and I wanted to nip it in the bud."

"What kind of trouble?" Duke demanded.

"I told you, Duke. This is going to be a hell of a hard package to sell to the men." Halloran looked nettled.

"Is that what you've been telling the agents?"

"Sure. We're always up-front with them, aren't we? What's gotten into you, Duke?"

Duke put his hands flat on the desk, leaning forward. *"You've* gotten into me, Bernie," he retorted. "You know that contract is the best we could get with the way things are."

"Was it, Duke? Are you sure you didn't make a little deal on the side with that Carson wo—with Carson's?" Halloran smiled, and it wasn't a pleasant smile.

"What the hell did you say?" Duke felt his rage building.

"You heard me. How do we know she didn't pay you off?"

Duke stared at him, speechless with anger. He was afraid he was going to flatten the man at any minute. And if he did that, he would hurt him bad, very bad. Halloran was twenty years older and soft as dough. Duke took a deep breath and got himself under control.

"Tell you what, Bernie. I'm going to pretend I didn't even hear that. Otherwise, I'd be very tempted to knock you out of that chair." Halloran reddened. "And while we're on the subject, I'm going to say something I've never said to you. This is one hell of a way to repay my father . . . and me."

"You'll never let me live that down, will you, Duke? That little trouble that—"

"That 'little trouble' nearly cost my dad his life! You were drunk and you were driving and we covered up for you, remember?" Duke's voice was shaking.

"Yeah," Halloran replied sullenly. "You and your old man did me a little favor, and the rest of my life I'm supposed to kowtow to you. The great Bellinis. The bullheaded old man and his softheaded son."

Duke was once again within an inch of hitting Bernie Halloran, but he held on somehow. "Have you been in touch with Detroit, Bernie?" he asked with perilous softness.

"I didn't have to be, Duke. Everybody in a rig knows you sold out. And you also know Detroit doesn't sit still for that. The Old Man can read, you know. He read the papers. Why try to hang it on me?" Halloran was looking at him now with naked dislike.

"Get out of here, Bernie. We'll take this up again when I come back." If Bernie didn't get out, Duke thought, there was going to be real trouble.

Halloran must have sensed that, because he got up right away. "Sure, Duke. I'll mind the store while you're in Detroit. Don't worry about a thing." He walked out. Duke heard him make an amiable, joking comment to Margaret.

Duke was so mad that he was seeing pure red. That bastard! That ungrateful, maneuvering bastard! Now he was sure why the top man had sent for him. Duke had put up with Halloran for a long time out of sheer sentimentality—the man had started out with Duke's father; he had some good things about him. But now he'd shown his true colors, and feeling sorry for Bernie Halloran was a thing of the past.

Duke could almost hear Halloran's phone conversation with the area director, who would have been the one to contact Detroit. That was the way it must have been. Halloran saying something in his sly way about being "worried about him . . . like a son to me . . . I think the kid needs guidance."

It had happened before, and Duke had let it go. Well, no more. Bernie wasn't going to make a monkey out of Duke Bellini. Not this time.

# Chapter 9

APPLAUDING WILDLY, WYNN ROSE WITH THE OTHERS from their front-row seats at Town Hall. Through the blur of emotional tears she watched her tall, gaunt brother bow, beaming, the stagelights shining on his bright blond hair that was so like her own.

"Bravo!" a man behind her called out. "Bravo!"

The applause went on. Wynn glanced aside at her sister-in-law. Dolores's eyes looked wet as she and Greg smiled at each other. The dazzled children were jumping up and down. Wynn smiled through her tears. She was hypersensitive for so many reasons: lack of sleep, since she'd persuaded Duke to let her go to the airport with him at six that morning; a positive ache of loneliness; a fervent wish that Big Mike could have been there with them. All those feelings mingled with her happiness for Greg and his family and a strong reaction to the beauty of the music.

Greg had finished the concert with the same Mozart concerto Wynn and Duke had listened to the first night he had come to her apartment. She kept remembering how Duke had compared the flute to birds . . . remembering everything he'd said to her, so new and wonderful.

She was sensitized by worry, as well. Duke had been gloomy on the phone that afternoon. The president had been faced with an unexpected crisis and wouldn't be able to see Duke until the next day. His suspense wouldn't end until then.

With all that on her mind, it was no wonder she was feeling weepy. But she felt Dolores's eyes on her and turned to her sister-in-law with a brilliant, false smile.

Soon they were making their way backstage, through the crowds, and Wynn could hear enthusiastic comments all around them. "Another Rampal," she caught. "Glorious." "Magnificent."

From there they went to the famous Russian Tea Room, a treat Greg had promised the children, who were being allowed to stay up long after their usual bedtime.

Wynn thought how wonderful it would have been if Duke were there, if she herself were like the glamorous and carefree-seeming woman in this exciting place.

She tried to put the other problems from her mind. She *was* happy for Greg, happy for all of them. He ordered huge meals for Dolores and himself. They were both ravenous, having had little appetite before the concert. She heard him listing chopped eggplant, cold borscht, Karsky shashlik and *cotelette à la Kiev*. Just hearing his recitation took away what was left of Wynn's appetite. She had chosen only a dish of *sirniki* pancakes as the lightest of all the items.

While Greg was hopping from one table to another, excitedly greeting acquaintances, Dolores settled the children down to tiny meat-stuffed pastries and observed Wynn. "This is the first minute I've had a chance to think . . . or ask you." She smiled. "How are you? Have you really recuperated from those horrible negotiations? I think you've lost a little weight."

Her soft dark gaze lingered on Wynn's face, then flicked downward to her fragile neck, pale between the cascading ruffles of her dress. Wynn had purposely worn the dress to hide her new thinness; its ruffled cap sleeves and stretch waist added a little roundness to her figure. It was navy georgette with a windowpane check in pastels, and she regretted the color now. Maybe it made her look too pale. "A little, I guess," Wynn admitted. "That was quite a schedule."

Wynn felt Dolores's keen look as she glanced away. She wasn't going to tell Greg about Court until tomorrow or the next day. She hadn't wanted to upset him before the big night.

"What is it, Wynn?" Dolores persisted gently. "There's something going on with you. We've lost touch a bit, and I hate that . . . although these last few weeks I know it's been unavoidable. We've been as frantic as you, with good reason." Dolores grinned, looking fondly at Greg, who was coming back to attack his shashlik.

The conversation turned again to the concert and other matters. When the children were nodding with sleepiness over their jellied fruit desserts, Dolores decided it was time to "pack them up."

"Come home with us," Dolores urged Wynn. "Please. When I get rid of these three"—she grinned at the children and at Greg, who seemed as tired as they were after the excitement of the evening—"we can have the talk we've been missing."

Wynn hesitated. She was almost asleep on her feet, but she yearned for the motherly presence of her sister-in-law and thought how great it would be to talk everything over with her. That had always helped before, and maybe it would again.

"All right, I'd love it."

Later, in the big, comfortable living room of the apartment near Lincoln Center, Wynn sighed with content and curled her stockinged feet underneath her body as she waited for Dolores to come out of the children's bedroom.

Dolores emerged in a russet lounging robe and bare feet. "Like I always say," she grinned, "I adore them all, but it's so nice when they're asleep."

"Greg, too?" Wynn smiled.

"Oh yes. He's worked so hard. He's napping, he says, but I have a feeling he'll nap till morning. Or at least until the first review comes out." Dolores walked to the bar at the other end of the room. "What'll you have?"

"Nothing. I'll go to sleep on your couch if I have a drink."

"Let me get you some coffee. I've got some on the stove." Dolores started out of the room.

"No. No, please." Wynn looked at her. "Just sit and talk to me."

"Okay. I won't argue with *that*. It's been quite a night." She joined Wynn on the tweed couch, stretching out her legs like a contented cat.

"You know," she continued, looking at Wynn, "I've been so involved with Greg and the kids and us in general that I feel like I've neglected you." Wynn shook her head, but Dolores ignored her denial. "Yes, really. Now tell me," Dolores urged her, taking Wynn's hand. "What's up?"

Wynn said slowly, "Well, first of all, there's something I haven't wanted to bother Greg with yet." Carefully, she told Dolores about James Noble and Jonathan Court.

"Oh, my lord." Dolores's dark eyes were wide with shock. She leaned over then and kissed Wynn. "Thank you. Thank you for not coming to Greg. But it was quite a load to carry by yourself. You know, you're some fine lady."

Wynn felt tears start and blinked them back. She felt overwhelmed with love and gratitude, the emotions more acute than ever in her weary, highly emotional state.

"And I have a feeling there's something else," the canny Dolores remarked in a gentle tone.

"Oh yes." Wynn began then to tell her about Duke, everything from the very first.

At the end of her recital, Dolores said softly, "I see. Yes, I see a lot of things now. Do you love him? Are you sure?"

"Very sure," Wynn said steadily. "But I'm just as sure that if I marry him, it'll ruin his life."

"Nonsense. You'll ruin it if you don't, from the sound of things." The brown gaze dropped to the crystal and diamond ring on Wynn's little finger. "A man doesn't give a thing like that to someone he's taking lightly . . . doesn't act the way this man has acted, according to what you've told me."

"But how can we ever make it?" Wynn demanded, afraid she was going to start crying.

"You'll find a way."

Looking into her sister-in-law's dark, kind eyes,

Wynn was reminded sharply of Duke Bellini's eyes, the confidence he seemed to have in common with Dolores.

Once again she wished she could share their optimism.

Wynn caught up on her sleep that night to such an extent that she didn't get to the office until ten.

"About time," Ruth Wiley remarked with a twinkle.

"That I came in?" Wynn asked her, grinning. She had to confess that she felt a lot better for the sleep.

"No, that you slept a little for once." Wynn looked at her loyal secretary, thinking, I've shut her out of my life as I never have before, and yet she's still as warm and caring as ever.

"I'm a lucky woman to have you here," Wynn commented. "And that's a terrific dress."

"Thanks." Ruth beamed, glancing down at her red-and-white striped shirtwaist dress, fresh and cheerful as a big peppermint stick.

In her office Wynn glanced at her watch. It might be hours before she knew what had happened in Detroit. She decided to stay very busy and keep her mind off that for as long as she could. She plunged into the day's mail and problems so intently that it was nearly noon before she knew it.

When she returned from lunch, Ruth was in her office, putting the afternoon mail on her desk.

"I must say, there's been one big improvement around here," Ruth declared, putting Wynn's messages on top of the letters.

"What's that?" Wynn asked absently, glancing through the messages.

Ruth laughed. "The conspicuous absence of the Honorable Howard."

Wynn chuckled. "How right you are." She could hear the implied question in Ruth's comment. "I think he's finally conceded," she said lightly. She couldn't go into all of it—Howard's being a relative of Court's and all that. But she realized with surprise that she hadn't given him a thought in weeks.

Jonathan's resignation had seemed to settle the problem of Howard, she concluded in silent satisfaction. So much the better.

Just before Ruth walked out, the interoffice buzzer sounded. Ruth answered it.

She turned to Wynn with a questioning look. "Mr. Halloran of 117 is here, asking to see you."

"Halloran?" Wynn was mystified. "Okay. Shoot him in."

She was still puzzled. When Halloran came in, however, she smiled at him cordially.

"Mr. Halloran, what can I do for you? Sit down. Is it something about the contract?" She hated the looks of the man. There was a slyness about his face, and his geniality always seemed so phony.

"I'm afraid not, Miss Carson." The smile he gave her didn't reach his eyes. He sat down, facing her.

"Could I get you some coffee?" Wynn asked politely.

"No, thanks." His hard blue glance flicked up and down, taking in her smoothly rolled hair, her businesslike clothes, lingering on her face.

"Is there something I can do for you," she prompted, "while Mr. Bellini's—" She stopped. She had been about to say, "while Mr. Bellini's out of town."

Halloran's hard eyes glinted. "While the boss is away?" He grinned.

Wynn quickly recovered. "He mentioned something about being out of town," she said calmly, "and that I should call you or Mr. Weinfeld if there are any problems."

Immediately she saw her mistake. Duke had said he was suspicious of Bernie Halloran. What a stupid blunder. She saw it mirrored in Halloran's smile.

"He said that, did he? Well, he's right. We hold down the fort when our peerless leader's away."

His attempt at lightness fell flat. She hated the implied sarcasm. Her face felt hot; she hoped it didn't show.

"No, Miss Carson, I've come about a personal matter."

"A personal matter?" Now she was really surprised and couldn't help sounding it.

"Forgive me. About you, Miss Carson, and Duke Bellini." Halloran stared at her.

She knew that her cheeks must be as red as fire. "I'm afraid I don't follow you, Mr. Halloran."

He shook his head and answered in an ironic tone, "Come now, Miss Carson. We all read the papers, don't we?" His inflection infuriated her, but she resolved to keep cool. "We all know what folks are saying, don't we?"

"Why don't you tell me, Mr. Halloran? I don't know what 'folks are saying,'" she snapped.

"That Duke has sold out."

Wynn was stricken silent.

"Oh yes," Halloran went on in a soft, oily voice. "And, Miss Carson, this hurts me. That boy is like a son to me, whether you know it or not. I worked with his father before him. I think the world of that boy. And I'm here to tell you frankly that his association with you is going to ruin that boy . . . *ruin* him."

She was so dumbfounded that she couldn't answer

for a moment. Then she gathered her wits and said deliberately, "You're out of line, Mr. Halloran. Way out of line. In the first place, if an 'association' exists between me and Duke Bellini—and I'm not saying it does—don't you think that concerns *us,* not you?"

"Wrong, Miss Carson. If our union's national president thinks our local president is on the take, it's everyone's concern. Get that straight right now." Halloran was no longer amiable; his tone was as hard as steel. "I'm asking you to leave him alone. Get him out of your life. For his sake and ours. That's all I came to say. If you care about him, you won't destroy him. Am I right?"

"I think you had better leave, Mr. Halloran." Her voice was shaky, and she couldn't control it. She thought, I'll scream if I start crying in front of this man.

To her relief he said, "I'm going. But I ask you one more time—please stay away from Duke Bellini."

He stalked out of the office, leaving Wynn staring after her. How dare he! she raged silently. How dare he come here and talk to her like that! The very man Duke mistrusted so. Didn't the fool know she'd tell Duke?

Then the answer came to her in a flash. She wouldn't. And the wily creep would count on that. She knew Duke's hair-trigger temper by now, from all he'd told her about himself; she'd experienced it firsthand that night he blew up on the phone.

Halloran had counted on her knowing that about Duke Bellini, assumed rightly that she would be hesitant to create such an explosive situation that Duke would assault Bernie Halloran, maybe be arrested for it. She didn't have to picture Duke's reaction. She knew exactly what it would be. Those fists could smash the older man to pulp if Duke should get mad enough.

Bernie Halloran was a twister, all right. If she could only find a way to let Duke know without telling him the whole story, but at the moment she couldn't.

The one thing that echoed in her mind above all the others was Halloran's warning: "You'll ruin him."

True, Halloran was a manipulator; most likely he'd do anything in his power to trip Duke up. But in that one thing, she admitted with dark reluctance, he was right on target. If they went on together, Wynn Carson could in truth ruin the life of Duke Bellini. That realization was like a cold blade in her heart.

Duke called from Detroit before Wynn had recovered from Halloran's visit.

"How did it go?" she asked him anxiously.

His voice came to her faintly over the crackling of a bad connection. "Not well." Her heart sank. "Wynn?"

"Yes. I can hardly hear you."

"I know," he said more loudly. "It's bad here, too. In every way. You might say I'm on probation with the national office." He sounded angry and gloomy.

"Oh, Duke, I'm sorry. I'm sorry."

"You sound strange, baby. Is everything all right there?"

"Of course," she lied, trying to sound cheerful and matter-of-fact. "I just . . . miss you, that's all."

"I miss *you*. I'm flying back tonight."

She asked him what time, saying she'd meet him. Then she hung up, wondering how she was ever going to tell him her decision.

That evening, when she saw him striding eagerly toward her, she was afraid she'd never have the courage, not then, anyway, not while he looked so strained, so needy. And not while she herself was so overcome with tender desire that her insides shook as he came nearer.

He let his bag fall on the asphalt with a thud and grabbed her in his arms. Oblivious of everyone, he kissed her as if they had been parted for months, not days. Then, releasing her, he picked up his bag and put his arm around her waist so tightly that they had to walk as slowly as dancers into the waiting room. Just the way, she thought, they had walked together on that first magical night along the mews.

Neither one said anything until they reached her car. He tossed his bag in, and when they were inside, he whispered, "Wynn, Wynn." They came together for another long and starved embrace. Her heartbeat fluttered like the wings of a captured bird; her whole self melted in his urgent, strong clasp.

Finally he said, "Let's get out of here. Your place?"

"Yes." She nodded eagerly.

As they sped through the night, he told her about everything that had happened in Detroit. "It seems," he concluded darkly, "that they're going to 'investigate' my case. They'll be keeping an eye on me."

Her hands tightened on the wheel. She took a deep breath and ventured, "Should we . . . should we stop seeing each other for a little while, Duke? What if—"

"What?" He sounded stupefied. "What did you say?"

"I said . . . maybe it would jeopardize things for you if we keep seeing each other now." She could feel him stare as she kept her eyes on the road before them.

"You can't mean that. This thing could go on for weeks . . . months. Wynn, I can't believe I'm hearing this." He sounded so disturbed that she decided not to pursue it further. At least not right then.

"I'm sorry, Duke. It's just that I don't want to make things harder for you than they already are."

"The only way you can make things harder is not to see me, Wynn Carson. I thought we'd already decided that." He put his hand on her thigh, and she trembled at the touch of his fingers.

When she remained silent, he said, "Haven't we?"

"Yes," she admitted weakly. "Yes, Duke." She was getting in deeper and deeper; every moment they spent together would make it harder to tell him what she was really thinking—that it could never work for them. That they'd been living in a dream, while reality was out there waiting to pounce on them and destroy this warm, inimitable magic.

They drove on through the night, his hard thigh pressed close to hers, and as she fell under his spell again, Wynn began to doubt her doubt.

When they reached the gate, he jumped out to unlock it. Both of them seemed possessed of the same breathless expectancy as she parked in her garage and they walked through the mews and up the familiar stairs.

Inside he tossed his bag in a corner and drew her close to his tall, steely frame. "I can never believe the things you do to time." He smiled down at her. "You make days into weeks for me, Wynn Carson. And then, when we're together, you make a whole night seem like a minute."

She gazed up into his face, wondering how this could be wrong. Everything . . . everything with them was so inevitably right, so true.

But words were futile in the renewing marvel of his kiss, and even thoughts seemed cold. Duke stroked her body all over, his hands learning again the contours of her slender neck, her shoulders and her throbbing breasts, tracing the shape of her hips, pulling her body closer to his until she was aware of the fullness of his need.

Thoughtless, uncaring and with a desperate new boldness, she moved against him until he moaned some soft and incomprehensible words, melodious and strange, his breath hot on the softness of her tumbled hair. His strong hands drew her closer and closer to him as he unzipped the back of her thin, lilac-colored dress. She felt it sliding down over her shoulders, slipping over her hips to fall in a flower-like circle on the carpet.

Murmuring, trembling, he knelt down and re-moved her delicate shoes, first one and then the other. She shook all over and emitted a small, catlike cry of yearning. He reached up then and held her with one massive hand while, slowly and gently, he pulled her fragile lace panties away and tossed them aside as he lifted one submissive knee and then the other. Then he rid her of her transparent bra to free her breasts. Moaning with desire, she sank back onto the carpet, watching him remove his clothes until his magnificent body was bare.

He moved over her, his darting tongue on the leaping hollow under her ear, caressing, playing on her skin until she shivered and cried out with deeper pleasure than she had ever imagined before. She felt the thrilling touch descending to her hard-nippled breasts. His mouth encircled each one, drawing from her another low and wordless cry. Then his steel-fingered hands parted her shuddering knees to launch a wondrous and maddening assault on her willing center, and she gave herself up to an ecstasy beyond all reason. The universe narrowed and tele-scoped into a single flame; then it widened as she gave a last, choked, sobbing outcry, her very bones turning to water.

Shakily he raised his lean body and entered her, and in that sudden fullness, that mighty coming together, her astonished flesh began to pound with even more titanic pleasure. They climbed together to the last delight and afterward lay wordless, almost without breath, in each other's arms, still on the carpeted floor.

After a time, as they lay silent and wondering in the half-dark, their longing came to them again. He lifted her into his cradling arms and strode with her to the waiting bed. That time she was the aggressor, making love to him, glorying in the sight of his dazzled face. Afterward they fell into a heavy sleep, but once again, sometime when the dark was paling to morning light, they half woke and slowly began to love one another to that perfect joy.

Parting reluctantly from her the next morning, Duke smiled and said, "It *is* decided, isn't it?"

She could only nod helplessly. No matter what else happened, she reflected, they had to keep this; they must not surrender this happiness, even if it had to go on in secret.

Their weekend was interrupted by his commit-ments and hers, but they spent almost all of the following weeknights together.

On Thursday night they walked back to the mews

after dinner. The streetlights were golden in the soft May night; they could feel the breath of summer.

As they strolled through the Washington Arch and crossed the street, Duke said abruptly, "We've got to talk."

She smiled up at him. "We're always talking. What about?"

He looked solemn, not returning her smile. "When this is over, you're going to marry me. Aren't you?"

There it was, the question she had both longed for and dreaded. "That's not a very romantic proposal," she teased, trying to keep her tone light.

The brightness of a streetlamp fell over them. He stopped and she could feel his penetrating stare. She was afraid that her doubts were clear on her face. She'd never been able to hide things, especially from him.

He took her by the shoulders and turned her to face him. Then he tilted her face up to his. "Wynn, don't play with me like that. That's not an answer. You've got to tell me. Now. It means the world to me. You know that."

She looked into his dark, pleading eyes, and her gaze dropped.

"What's the matter?" he asked her anxiously. "You've got to tell me." His fingers bit into her arms.

"You're hurting me," she protested.

"I'm sorry, honey. I'm sorry." He loosened his hold, but he persisted. "What are you trying to do? Are you trying to tell me you don't want us to get married?"

"Please, Duke. We can't discuss it here. Let's go to the apartment."

They walked the rest of the way in tense silence. Neither spoke as he unlocked the gate and they went upstairs.

"Let's sit down," she said nervously. He was still staring at her with his heart in his eyes.

"I can't sit down until you answer me," he replied tightly.

"Duke . . ." She took a deep breath and then plunged ahead. "I don't see how we can."

He was thunderstruck. "Don't see how we *can*," he repeated numbly. "I don't see how we *can't*. Didn't you mean anything you've said? Hasn't all this . . . all that's happened meant marriage to you? I can't believe I'm hearing this, Wynn."

"Please, Duke. Please." She took his hand, urging him to sit down on the couch beside her. Reluctantly he did so, holding her hand in a bruising grasp. "Duke . . . you know how I feel. You know I love you more than I've ever loved anyone or anything in my whole life. But if we get married, it could ruin everything for you . . . destroy everything you and your father worked so hard to build. Why can't we go on as we are? I won't ruin things for you. I won't . . . I can't." Her voice broke.

"Ruin things for me? How can you say that, Wynn? My God, you sound like Bernie Halloran."

Like Halloran. Involuntarily she winced. She was sure that her face had given her away, because Duke was studying her keenly.

"Wynn, what is it? Why did you look like that when I mentioned his name?"

What's the use? she thought gloomily. I can't lie to him. I never could. And it's not fair.

"Because," she answered in a low voice, "he came to see me. And he told me just what I'm telling you."

She could see bright anger flicker in his black eyes, and she was sorry she'd ever spoken.

"You've got to promise me," she said tensely, "that you won't . . ."

"Won't what?" he asked coldly.

"Won't do anything to him. You've got enough trouble now."

"Halloran," he said, as if he hadn't heard her. "Bernie Halloran. Do you mean to tell me you listened to that . . . you listened to the man who's out to get me? You're making no sense at all." Duke looked at her with bitter eyes.

"Not to him," she protested. "But to what he said. He's right. I'm no good for you, Duke."

He got up and stared down at her. "I can't believe this. It's too crazy, too . . . I think there must be another reason. Maybe you're just tired of me. Maybe you don't want to marry a mug like me, Wynn. Why don't you just say so and not give me all this . . . ?" He let his voice trail off, his hands balled into impotent fists.

"How can you talk to me like that?" she flared.

"It's not easy, baby. Not half as easy as it is for you to shaft me. What a jerk I've been. All along I thought you really cared, and now you let a little thing like this get in our way."

"A little thing?" she cried. "Your work . . . our situation . . . are little things?"

"They would be, if you loved me. Nothing would matter if you really loved me, Wynn. I thought you were a really gutsy lady. Now I'm not so sure. And now I know you don't care very much."

She thought she would scream with sheer frustration. "Don't care!" she cried out. "I never cared so much! Never!"

"Well, I can't go along with your way of caring."

He gave her one long, pained look and then reached into his pocket. He took out her keys and put them on the table.

Her whole body turned cold. She wanted to plead with him not to go, wanted to beg his forgiveness. But somehow she couldn't. She knew she couldn't break through that wall of stubbornness he'd built. Besides, Wynn Carson was too proud to beg.

She sat there silently, watching him walk out. When his footsteps faded on the stairs, she burst into wild, abandoned weeping.

It was a very long night; she barely slept at all. The next morning was worse; she remembered other mornings, waking with him. When she got to the office, she kept listening for her private phone, but it didn't ring all day. She wondered how she was going to get through the weekend. Inevitably she thought of the weekends they had spent together.

She was half tempted to call him, to apologize. Then she asked herself, apologize for what? He was the one who'd walked out. But not, she answered herself, until she'd told him that she'd listened to Halloran. That had really been the last straw for Duke Bellini, and she knew it.

She couldn't call him.

On Friday night and Saturday she kept frantically busy doing things around the house, shopping—anything to keep from thinking, to try to ease the empty ache within her. And then on Sunday she read an item in Fleishman's labor column that started everything again, the pain and the regret.

"Bad Boy Duke Bellini makes news again," Fleishman wrote. "He's fired Giorgio Bellini's right-hand man of many years, Bernard X. Halloran, just four months short of Halloran's retirement date, thereby knocking Bernie out of his full and hard-earned Truckers' pension. What's with you, Donato?"

Wynn stared at the column. Granted, Halloran might have tried to do Duke a bad turn, but doing the man out of a large portion of his pension seemed excessive. At least, Wynn reflected gloomily, Duke hadn't turned physical and ended up in jail for assault and battery.

She was vastly relieved when Monday came, gratified that there was still a great deal of work to do. She threw herself into it with a kind of frenzy.

In fact, she worked such long hours and accomplished so much that when she held a meeting with her new staff the next Friday, she found that things were really getting organized. And the auditor reported to her that if all went well, their finances would be capable of meeting the terms of the new contract with 117.

All was not lost, she decided, after the men had left the conference area. She looked up at the portrait of Big Mike. At least she still had this, whatever else she had lost. She was keeping Carson's on the road, just the way her father had.

"I don't know how you've done it, sis, but you've done it. And I think you're just terrific." Greg Carson smiled at her across their table at Windows on the World, the spectacular restaurant on the 107th floor of the World Trade Center.

The place afforded diners an incomparable view of the city; the restaurant was arranged on tiers, for maximum viewing. Wynn's and Greg's table faced north, letting them see the best panorama offered.

"Thanks." Wynn smiled at her brother. "I don't know how I did it, either." I don't know how I've survived this week, as far as that goes, she reflected darkly. But somehow I'm learning to live without Duke Bellini. And I'll go on doing that.

"You could use a vacation, though," Greg remarked, studying her. She knew she looked a bit done in. There were new hollows under her cheekbones, and despite her careful use of makeup, she was aware that she looked pale, her eyes shadowed. Her pink dress gave her some color, but she'd never been able to fool Greg or Dolores for long. "You're not exactly eager for food, either," Greg commented, glancing down at her croustade of chicken livers, still almost untouched.

"When was I ever?" she retorted lightly. "I don't know where you put it all, brother." Wynn ran an affectionate eye over his gaunt frame. It was a long-standing joke between them. Dolores always said that if she so much as smelled all the food Greg put away, she'd weigh a ton.

"Don't change the subject," he ordered, taking a sip of chablis. "How's your love life?"

She could feel the uneasy heat rush into her cheeks. "Nonexistent," she said in a flippant tone. "Who's got time?"

"Anybody in his right mind," Greg retorted. "Dolores told me, Wynn. You must have known she would. We tell each other everything, of course."

Of course. Wynn's throat ached. Greg and Dolores had what she had once dreamed of having with Duke Bellini. Well, that was all it had been—a beautiful dream, a magical interval. But the world was real, and that was where they both had to live. The sooner she accepted that, the sooner she could go on with her life again and forget.

"What happened, honey?" Greg's question was gentle, caring. "Do you want to talk about it?"

Wynn took a swallow of her own wine before she answered. "Not desperately," she admitted, trying to keep her voice from shaking. Greg put out his hand and took hers. "I guess what happened was that we couldn't make it."

"Why not?"

"A truckers' union and a trucking company can't merge too well," she commented dryly.

"But that's not what it is," Greg objected. "You're also talking about a man and a woman."

"A man attached to a truckers' union and a woman who's a trucking company," she retorted stubbornly.

"I can see why you handled the Court catastrophe so well." Greg chuckled. "You're a very bullheaded girl."

"So is Duke Bellini." She wished she hadn't said his name. Somehow it hurt less when she didn't. The very saying of his name conjured up his exciting darkness, his tall strength. If ever a man looked like his name, Duke Bellini did.

"Someone's got to give," Greg remarked. "I've never seen you look so unhappy, Wynn."

When she didn't answer, he asked, "Are you going to finish that lunch or not? I can have the waiter take it away. You want some coffee? I know better than to ask you about dessert."

She nodded indifferently. "Coffee. Sure."

When the waiter came the ever-hungry Greg ordered two coffees and a chocolate pastry cake for himself. They said nothing for a moment or two. When the waiter had brought the order, Greg resumed speaking. "You remember Dolores's father."

A little puzzled at this seemingly irrelevant comment, Wynn said, "Vaguely."

"A real Spanish grandee," Greg said. "There was

no way in the world he was going to let his daughter
marry a *gringo* flutist of such humble origins. You do
remember that?"

"Oh yes." Wynn smiled at the memory. "But . . .
here you are. Is that what you're trying to tell me?"

"That's just what I'm trying to tell you." Greg
looked at her with serious blue eyes so much like her
own that it was like staring into a mirror. Maybe,
Wynn mused, that was why they'd always been so
close. "We had plenty to fight, but we fought it.
Because it was worth it . . . oh, was it worth it. Is it
worth it to you?" he demanded.

"I don't know. I don't know any longer." But she
could hear her own uncertainty. Maybe she did
know and was only fooling herself by saying she
didn't.

"I wonder." Greg kept studying her. "Honey, I'm
not bringing this up just to be a headache to you, but
I think you may be making a big mistake, maybe the
biggest one of your life. You don't know how
different you look now from the way you looked . . .
before," he concluded in a delicate way.

"When I was seeing Duke, you mean," she inter-
preted flatly.

"Yes. Wynn, don't throw it all away. I'm here to
tell you, as much as my music means to me—and you
know it's been my life—if I had to choose, I'd take
Dolores, even if it meant I never played another
note."

Wynn looked at her earnest brother. He was really
serious.

She wondered if perhaps she had made the biggest
mistake she'd ever made, staying away from the one
man who had opened up another world to her.

# Chapter 10

THAT NIGHT, HOWEVER, WYNN DECIDED IT WAS FRUIT-
less to keep asking herself that question. She accepted an invitation to a party, stayed late and made
herself respond to several attractive men. She even
made a date with one for Sunday evening. Then she
found that he attracted her no more than Howard
had and refused his eager invitation for another
encounter.

As always, Monday was better. She could feel
herself getting back into stride, but she was exasperated that she couldn't fool Ruth any more easily
than she had fooled Greg. The incorrigible secretary
made several remarks about her loss of weight.

One morning Ruth went a little too far, and Wynn
snapped at her.

"You know, Wynn, I've had it," Ruth blurted.
"I've worked in this darned place for twenty years;

I've seen you grow from a little shrimp in rompers to a little shrimp executive. Everybody at Carson's knows what happened with Scrooge and Noble, yet you've never really talked to me about it. I'm beginning to feel like a temporary file clerk. I thought we were friends."

Remorseful, Wynn studied the loyal woman. She'd shut her out for too long. "You're absolutely right," she said gently. "Sit down. Let's talk."

They had a long, detailed conversation about the new order of things at Carson's. Wynn told Ruth everything about the trouble with Court. Yet she still couldn't bring herself to tell Ruth about Duke Bellini. It still hurt too much. It was best to leave it buried, where it belonged.

Ruth got up at last, looking down at Wynn with gratitude and affection. "Thanks. Now I feel I belong here again." As she started out, one of the other secretaries came in with a yellow envelope. "Telegram for Miss Carson."

Wynn ripped it open, skimmed the message and smothered an exclamation.

"Trouble?" Ruth asked with concern.

"No. No trouble." She couldn't meet Ruth's eyes. The wire was from Duke Bellini.

It read, "Congratulations. You've kept 'em rolling."

Wynn had a hard time controlling herself until Ruth left. Then she read the telegram again, clenching her hands until her nails bit into her palms.

How did Duke Bellni know she'd "kept 'em rolling" at Carson's? But more important than that, why should he bother to send such a message, unless . . . unless he still cared for her? It was too much. Too much.

Wynn felt like crying, but desperately controlled

herself. She fled to lunch early, telling Ruth she had an appointment beforehand.

It wasn't until late afternoon that she had the answer to one of her own questions.

Ruth came in smiling to say goodnight and remarked, "By the way, I told Sam I stole that picture of his you bought. He was tickled. And he said to tell you somebody was asking for you."

"Who was that?" Wynn asked inattentively, putting away some correspondence that she would handle the next day.

"Duke Bellini," Ruth answered. Wynn, looking down at her letters, could feel the secretary's friendly, curious regard. She managed a calm, vague reply, and Ruth went out.

Then she took the telegram from her purse, where she had been keeping it all day. Sam Sposato, she thought with affection. Big Mike Carson's long-time friend and right-hand man. Sam had told Duke about the job Wynn had done.

In the empty office Wynn found solace at last by giving way to her tears.

She cried for a long, long time. Feeling obscurely better for it, she got up and washed her face. Somehow the tears had exorcised that gnawing grief. She felt strangely light, with an odd sensation of freedom and emptiness.

Maybe it was over at long last.

On impulse she decided to take her postponed time off in June. She'd go to her travel agent and talk it over. She'd find the most fabulous place she could; then she'd buy a lot of wonderful new clothes and take off. And by heaven, she'd really enjoy herself. She'd forget Duke Bellini once and for all.

Her visit to the travel agent led to an embarrassment of riches. There was almost no place she didn't want to go, and she certainly couldn't shop for clothes until she'd decided that.

She compromised by loading herself down with travel folders.

Duke Bellini parked his dark-red Porsche in front of the Ceebee, got out and strolled into the diner.

Several men at the counter looked up when he came in. He thought they wore peculiar expressions.

"Hiya, Duke," one said, and another nodded.

It sure as hell was different from two months ago, Duke reflected. He took one of the stools and ordered coffee.

"Hot as blazes," he said casually to the first man who had greeted him.

"Yeah . . . well, it is June," the man said uncomfortably. One of the others shuffled his feet and made a motion to get up.

The first man fumbled in his pocket for change. "Well, gotta go. See you, Duke."

"Yeah. See you at the ratification meeting, right?"

"Sure, Duke. Sure."

The men went out, still looking ill at ease.

"Brrrr . . . it's sure not hot in here." The raddled, weary-looking redhead behind the counter grinned at Duke.

"No, you've got the best air-conditioning around, Polly." Duke tried to sound cheerful.

"I'm not talking about air-conditioning, Duke." Polly gave him a significant glance while she washed cups and saucers. They'd known each other for a long time, and she heard a lot of things at that counter, Duke thought. "What's up with this ratification, honey?"

The "honey" was purely maternal—she was old enough to be his mother.

"You've been hearing things, Big Ears," he joshed her.

"Have I ever." She dried the cups and saucers and hoisted a heavy coffeemaker to empty it. As she washed and rinsed it, she commented over the rush of water, "The guys were really going on about Halloran."

Duke flushed.

"I know, I know. I'm a nosy old dame. But I've known all you boys too long not to be interested. I read the papers, too, you know." She grinned crookedly, setting the coffeemaker upright under the tap to run more water into it.

"So who appointed you my mother?" Duke asked her with mock toughness.

"Me," she retorted, plugging in the coffeemaker. She laughed.

"You've got the . . . you're wise as a brass monkey," he said.

"You don't gotta be fancy with me, *ragazzo*. I've heard it all, and you know it."

"Okay, okay. Get off my back." Duke took a swallow of his coffee. "I want another cup of that when it's through." After a moment, he added, "For your information, I fixed it about Bernie's pension."

"I'm glad, Duke. That's really nice." She reached out and patted his hand with her chapped fingers. He marveled at how much she'd come to know and how friendly he'd gotten with her over the years.

It was good, he thought, to be touched by a woman. Even Polly. Women had a touch about them. His mother had had that touch. And Wynn.

Wynn. Suddenly he missed her so much and it hurt so bad that it felt like he'd taken a solid haymaker on the jaw. He let out a ragged sigh.

"It's okay, honey," Polly said consolingly. "The

guys'll stand by you. They'll vote that contract in all right."

"I wish it was just the contract," he said rashly.

"Uh-huh. Woman trouble. Am I right or am I right?"

"You're both," he admitted, grinning ruefully.

Polly wiped off the counter, glancing to the other end. There were only two other customers left, a couple, probably from the neighborhood, Duke judged swiftly. The guy was sure no trucker.

Nevertheless, Polly lowered her voice discreetly. "It wouldn't be that little blonde, would it, the one in the black foreign job that day? She was really something."

Duke studied her for a minute, then admitted, "It would. And she *is* really something."

"So what's the problem? She go for somebody else?" Polly's face was full of sympathy.

"No. But you see, she's . . ." Duke stopped. He'd never talked this confidentially to Polly in the nine years he'd been hanging around the Ceebee. Then he decided, why not? Polly had the reputation of having a small mouth and big ears—she heard a lot but never talked. What she learned at her counter had always been as tightly guarded as matters brought to a bartender or priest, Duke knew. In fact, he was flattered and amazed that she had told him what she had about the men's conversation earlier.

"She's a boss," he said flatly. "And I'm a union guy."

"Oh boy." Polly shook her hennaed head. "That's a poser, that one."

"Tell me about it," Duke retorted.

"You really go for this girl. Right?"

"Yeah. Oh yeah." Duke felt that stabbing pain in his gut again.

"And she goes for you?"

"I thought so. I think so. But she says we can't make it, being what we are," he said.

"Well . . ." Polly leaned on the counter, her chin on her work-roughened hand. "So maybe one of you could go into another line of work?"

She poured him another cup of strong, dark coffee.

"Funny you should mention that," he quipped. "My old man always said I should have had more sense than to go into union work."

"Man, he got that right," she agreed in a fervent way. "It beats me how you guys live through all that stuff. I never did want to work twenty-six hours a day and then take all that grief on top of it."

"You've got the picture, I guess, after all this time." He felt warmer than ever toward her, grateful. He took a sip of his fresh coffee and added, "Yeah. My dad always wanted me to go into labor law, I guess. But the union got in my blood."

"Well, think it over," she said pertly. "Winter's gonna come and those union guys aren't going to warm your feet for you, sonny." She gave her bawdy, earthy laugh. "Boy, if I was twenty years younger . . ."

". . . I wouldn't be talking to you about another woman." He chuckled. He finished his coffee and got up. He put two dollars on the counter.

"What's this, Duke? Whaddaya think this is, the Waldorf?"

"That's for the psychoanalysis. Thanks, Polly. Thanks." He leaned across the counter and, to her delighted amazement, kissed her on the cheek.

"Well." She beamed. "You think about what I said. Right?"

"Right." He gave her another grateful look and strode out of the Ceebee.

He got into his car and drove uptown to his apartment, keeping away from the central avenues. He couldn't take it right now if he saw Wynn, maybe with another guy.

Back in his apartment, undressing to take a shower, he had a sudden picture of himself and Wynn naked in her bed, and suddenly he felt like his skin had caught on fire.

"I can't take it," he said aloud.

Quickly he got into the shower and turned the cold water on, wincing under the frigid stream.

On a warm evening in mid-June, Wynn put on a long, loose robe and wandered into her living room. She was in an unhappy state of tiredness, too restless for sleep, too debilitated for activity. The travel folders lay fanned out on the coffee table, awaiting her decision. She cast a weary eye on them. On the cover of one was a couple in bathing suits lying on a white beach.

The whole world was paired off, she thought with gloom.

What good was traveling alone? She'd be a fifth wheel everywhere. What good were the Bahamas to a woman with no talent for lighthearted encounters? She'd promised herself a trip, a rest when the negotiations were over. But now there just wasn't any place she really wanted to go. Not alone. Not without Duke.

There, she'd admitted it at last, the idea she'd been stifling for weeks. She missed him horribly, desperately.

Wynn sighed, hearing the murmur of the TV in the bedroom. She'd turned it on for company. Listening to music was no good; most of it reminded her of Duke. Over the hum of the air conditioners it was hard to make out what the news announcer was saying. Not that it mattered.

She flung herself on the couch and looked around the lovely room, now ready for the warmer weather with touches of white replacing the spring's yellow— white candles in silver holders, masses of white flowers, pale lilac and white pillows interspersed with blue and magenta on the couch and some of the chairs. So beautiful, she reflected, so refreshing and cool. And Duke hadn't even seen it yet.

Wynn gave herself a mental shake, telling herself to stop mooning around over a man who'd probably forgotten her. She decided to go and watch the news. At least it would give her something else to think about. As she went into the bedroom, she heard something about "Local 117" and then the name "Bellini." Her heart thudded in her throat. She'd made herself forget, but now she remembered: This was ratification night. If the men ratified the contract Duke had presented to them, it would be a vote of confidence in him, squelching any dissidents seeking to unseat him as president of 117.

Wynn sat down on the bed and watched the taped interview. Answering the reporter's questions, Duke looked handsomer than ever in a short-sleeved t-shirt emphasizing his immense shoulders, exposing his powerful biceps, pointing up his lean waist. He was thinner than before, she noticed. There was a gaunt look to his face, and his eyes were deeply circled.

She trembled, recalling the touch of those arms around her, those hands on her naked flesh. And she remembered how that mouth, now so grim and unsmiling, had felt on hers.

Duke Bellini was like a man who'd been sent off to war without an encouraging word. She felt a pang of guilt and shame, thinking, I could have wished him luck. In spite of their alienation, he had sent that telegram to her, that greeting she still treasured.

She knew from Duke's descriptions how harrowing this situation was: fourteen-hour-a-day schedules; constant visits to the terminals; the perpetual pressure of often unreasonable members' demands. Some took full advantage of a squeeze like this, breaking the union official's backs with wild and extraneous requests. On the screen Duke looked exhausted.

Suddenly she wanted to go to him more than anything in the world, to hold him in her arms. But that was absurd, impossible. She couldn't.

It was a relief to hear the phone. A little while before she hadn't wanted to talk to anybody, but now she felt that anybody would do. She hurried to answer.

Dolores asked in a calm, husky voice, "Watching the interview?" Wynn could hear the same TV station she was tuned into echoing in the background.

"Yes," she admitted weakly.

"You don't sound good." Wynn couldn't pretend otherwise, so she didn't attempt to protest. "Wynn? How long are you going to punish yourself like this?"

"What do you expect me to do?" Wynn demanded, hurt. "Go to the union hall?" It was such a wild suggestion that she waited for Dolores's laughing disclaimer.

To her amazement Dolores answered steadily, "Yes."

"The boss-lady of Carson's showing up at the union? I think you've got the heat crazies. If there's any way to alienate the members even more, to really convince them that we have a sweetheart deal, it would be that. Surely you know that."

"Nobody said the *boss-lady* has to go, Wynn."

"What on earth does that mean?" Wynn protested. "I'm in no mood for riddles."

"I can tell that, all right. From the sound of you, you're dying to be with him right now. Am I correct?"

Wynn hesitated for a long, painful moment, then confessed in a trembling voice, "Yes. Oh yes, I am."

"Then go, darling. Listen, once I had to pose as a blonde in a situation between my father and Greg . . ."

"What?"

"It's too long a story to tell now. Use your imagination. Go as someone else, but go. Are there any lady truck drivers?" Dolores chuckled.

"Very few." Wynn's thoughts were racing. Maybe Dolores had something, after all. "But there are other things," she said in a more animated, hopeful tone.

"Now you're cookin'." Dolores sounded approving. Then, in a more serious way, she added, "I've been worried about you, Wynn. You've looked so miserable. I like that man. I approve of him. I think you two are right for each other. Go up there and apologize. I want you to be happy, lady."

"I want that, too," Wynn admitted. "Thanks. I'll think about it."

"Don't think about it too long. *Do* it," Dolores

advised and hung up. Wynn held the receiver in her hand for a moment, smiling and shaking her head. Her sister-in-law was something else.

She replaced the phone, thinking hard. Could she get away with it? Did she want to get away with it? What would she do if he received her with cold politeness? She'd die. She'd just die.

"Come on, Wynn Carson." She gave herself the order aloud. "You've never been afraid of anything before." Well, she hadn't. She hadn't turned back from the company presidency; she hadn't wilted in negotiations, hadn't given up with the board. And she'd had the courage all along to love her competitor, Duke Bellini. This was no different.

She went back to the bedroom to catch the rest of the interview. The woman reporter's expression revealed that she was very attracted to Duke Bellini. I don't wonder, Wynn thought dryly. Woman reporter . . .

Of course. She could pose as a reporter for one of those way-out Village papers.

She stripped off her robe and went to the closet, taking out a pair of gray jean-cut pants. She chose a yellow t-shirt with a deep vee neck. After emptying her pretty straw bag she put the contents into a rather battered saddle-colored shoulder bag she used for running around the Village on chores and slipped on old leather sandals. Reaching onto a back shelf of the closet, she found a straw fedora hat. She went to the mirror and stuffed her hair into the hat. With dark glasses and her hair hidden, she looked like a different person. In fact, the glasses were so big that practically all you could see was her mouth. She laughed at her reflection. Nobody would take this woman for Wynn Carson.

She slung a camera over her shoulder beside the

bag, turned off the TV set and went out. Thank heavens it was sunny; with Daylight Savings Time the evenings were very long. With the still-present sun, the glasses didn't look too bizarre.

Wynn flagged a cab heading south on Fifth Avenue and gave him the Eighteenth Street address of the union hall. Traffic was a little lighter at this hour, and it seemed no time at all before the taxi pulled up in front of the plain concrete building with its double glass doors. She'd never been here, of course, but Duke had driven her by once on a weekend to show it to her.

She looked up at the familiar wheel that hung above the door, a giant version of the one Duke wore in his buttonhole and that was part of the print of his Truckers' tie. Her heart was thudding so loudly that she was afraid the beating rhythm of it would sap her breath.

She took a deep breath and opened one of the heavy glass doors. She stepped into a dimly lit carpeted hall and heard loud male voices, laughter and excited comments from a room down the corridor. Duke had mentioned that the big meeting room was on the first floor. That was where the balloting was being held, of course.

Wynn started timidly forward. Then she remembered that it wouldn't do for a reporter to look timid and marched toward the door of the large meeting room. She glimpsed a crowd of big, laughing, jostling, shouting men, scenting the aromas of sweat and smoke and beer. The smoke from cigarettes and cigars was thick as a fog, but she could make out TV cameras in the chaos. Her fear returned.

It had seemed like an adventure before, but now it was deadly serious. What if some of the men from Carson's recognized her? That alone could kill

Duke's chances for good. But she was there now, and she had to make the best of it.

She noticed a TV man standing by the door, taking deep breaths of the clearer air in the hall. Maybe she wouldn't have to risk going in. Perhaps this man could tell her where Duke was; she hadn't seen him in the crowd.

She was uncomfortably aware that some of the members near the door were staring. A woman was a rare sight at a Truckers' gathering, she knew, and her vee-necked shirt was very sexy, the pants as tight as if they'd been painted on. A couple of the men whistled and one stamped his feet.

"Hello, hello, *hello*," the TV man said, grinning. He sounded slightly tipsy. She glanced at his identifying name tag and made her voice as crisp and curt as she could. "Excuse me, is Bellini in there? I'm trying to get a line on him."

"What's your paper, doll?"

She named a Village weekly.

"Sure thing." The man caught a signal from one of his coworkers and said, "I gotta go." He called back over his shoulder to Wynn, "I think he's up on five, in his office."

Her thanks were lost in the roar of the men's voices. The elevator was just to her right. She got on with relief, glad it was automatic and that she wouldn't have to say anything to an operator. A group of women clerks got on when the elevator reached three, but they barely gave her a glance. They were too busy complaining about working overtime and discussing what they'd order for dinner.

The women got off on four and some men got on, to Wynn's dismay. One of them punched Six, and she had to repress a sigh of relief. She was amusedly conscious that they didn't give her face a glance, too intent on studying the t-shirt and jeans. She'd been wise to wear that outfit, after all.

When she got out on the fifth floor, she imagined that they gave her a curious look, but she was too elated to care. She heard men's voices from somewhere out of sight and then heavy footsteps approaching the empty reception hall. Wynn looked around desperately and sighted a door marked "Women." She scurried through it and stood with an ear against the door, blessing the fact that no other woman was in the room at the moment. When the footsteps faded and she heard the elevator door open and close, Wynn stole out.

The men's voices had come from the left, down another hall. Maybe that was the location of Duke's office—he'd once mentioned that it faced Eighteenth Street. Wynn's rubber-soled sandals made no sound at all as she hurried down the corridor.

She saw a secretary's area and an open door from which brighter light streamed out. Going nearer, all she could see were two man-sized feet in desert boots, propped on a desk. She stuck her head around the corner of the open door.

Duke Bellini was lying back in a leather chair with his eyes closed. He seemed to be lightly asleep. The shadows under his eyes, his long lashes, tugged at Wynn's heart.

"Duke," she called softly.

He jumped. His eyes flicked open.

He stared at her, too surprised to move, the black eyes feasting on her hungrily, taking in her snug jeans, the thin yellow t-shirt, glasses and hat.

"Wynn." He swung his legs down from the desk, staring. "Come in. Shut the door." She obeyed and he got to his feet, still staring.

"What's all this? A disguise?" He grinned.

"Yes." She stood there looking up at him, longing to touch him, and she could feel him yearning toward her. "This was the only way I could safely come. I'm supposed to be a reporter." She tried to steady her voice. "You looked so . . . tired on television, Duke. I couldn't stay away any longer."

With gentle fingers he took off her hat, then her glasses. He cupped her face in his hands, leaning down slowly. When they kissed it was as if no time had passed at all, as if they'd never been away from each other. Her hair slipped from its hasty arrangement and tumbled around her shoulders.

Their ravenous mouths couldn't seem to part; she trembled all over to feel the hard firmness of him again, so longed for, so familiar, the demanding hold of his arms, the contours of those lips.

When he let her go, she whispered, "I feel like we've always been together, ever since I can remember. That we never went away."

"We didn't, not really, darling." His big hands kneaded her head, stroked her hair as he drew her tightly to him. She felt warm and blessed and safe again at that touch. "Honey, you said there's no way we can get married. Wynn, there's no way we *can't*. I can't make it without you."

She leaned against his chest, sensing the waking hardness of his strong body, nestling into the arms that spelled home.

"I can't either," she admitted. "Oh, Duke, I can't make it either."

Suddenly she heard a rising wave, a roar of cheering all the way from the first floor, through the open window. "That's it, baby." Duke sounded triumphant. Still holding her, he said, "That's it. The guys told me it was going to happen. They must have voted in the contract. They've finished counting the ballots."

She heard men yelling, "Duke! Duke!"

"I'm being paged." He leaned back and grinned down at her. "The ratification means that Duke Bellini's still in." His black eyes were shining. "They believe in me; they know I won't let them down. They believe in me, Wynn, the way I believe in us. That's all I needed to know. Nothing else makes any difference now, because . . ."

His last words were puzzling. She was exultant with him, happy in his happiness. But how could they ever make it work? "Duke . . . we'll always be on opposite sides of the table."

"Not necessarily." He was smiling in a way that bewildered her. "But if we are, I can see you better." He laughed. Then he got serious and businesslike. "Look, Wynn Carson. I've got to talk fast. The guys'll be coming upstairs to get me any minute. There'll be reporters, TV cameras, a big *tumulto*. Bedlam. And I want you to stand right beside me. I want to introduce the future Mrs. Bellini."

He scrambled in his pants pocket and brought out a little plush box. He handed it to her and she opened it. A glorious diamond solitaire glittered against the dark blue velvet.

"I've been carrying this around," he said, "since the day after that . . . first night. I've been wanting to give it to you so bad I could taste it."

She was speechless, still confounded.

Duke slipped it on the fourth finger of her left hand. She knew then that she could never take it off, no matter what happened, no matter how impossible their situation was. It looked as if it had always belonged on her finger, its oval shape perfectly proportioned to her small hand.

"Oh, Duke." She drew his head down to hers and kissed him again and again. "But, darling, what's going to happen?" she pleaded when she could find words again. "We're still hauling dangerous cargo. We won't be allowed to pass through any highly populated city," she said wryly.

"Where've you been, boss-lady . . . out in Canarsie?" She had to laugh at his mention of the distant Brooklyn neighborhood, New Yorkese for left field, outer space. "I've kept up with *you* better than that. Don't you ever read the labor columns . . . the political updates? Duke Bellini's going into labor relations, and we're both off the hook."

"What do you mean?"

"I've got a lot of friends who believe in me, besides the guys downstairs. Take a look at those." He turned her around directing her attention to the law degree and other framed certificates above his desk.

"I still don't see," she confessed.

"I'm going to be a mediator, come September. I won't tell you it'll be easy, because my gut will always be on the unions' side, so I'll have to work hard to be impartial. But what the hell, all the guys come from one side or the other—management or labor. So there'll be other guys with the same problem. And I'll never be able to mediate for you, of course. But I've got a good guy lined up for president of 117 . . . and you'll enjoy being tough on him. And I'm going to practice law, too."

Wynn laughed, still dazzled, disbelieving. "But Duke, are you doing this . . . for me?"

"Not only for you, Wynn. For a few years now I've had it with the hassle, the rough-and-tumble. I've always wanted to go into another line of work that still had to do with labor relations. Who knows?

Someday when we're old and gray maybe I'll be the biggest arbitrator or labor lawyer around—most arbitrators don't even get the post until they're about fifty-five or so. Meanwhile . . ."

"I'm so glad," she said. "So glad it wasn't just for me."

"Listen, we've got to get married, lady, to save my good name," he teased her. "Any kids of ours are going to be Bellinis, wheeler-dealer."

"And the contract term is life," she said solemnly, meeting his bright, black gaze.

"At least . . . and in more ways than one." He took her by the shoulders, looking into her eyes with great earnestness. "I found out that life without you is no living at all." Then he cocked his head. "Uh-oh. They're coming."

He hugged her to him hard. "Let's wrap it up, boss-lady, before the guys find out I'm not asleep. One of the signatories is changing her name to Wynn Bellini. Agreed?" She nodded. He continued. "Now, change in contract language—*trouble* should now read *challenge*. We change *danger* to *excitement*. Management with me on this?"

She shook her head.

"Why not?"

"I'm not management in this contract," she retorted, and he kissed her hard and long.

"Before they come in . . ."

She could hear the men approaching down the hall. "The couch looks fine, but is there time?" she quipped.

He laughed. *"Dinner, baby."*

"Why bother? We won't have it."

The furor outside had become bedlam. Wynn didn't have time to say any more before the others burst in.

In the face of the shouting and shoulder-clapping and congratulations, Wynn stood in the circle of Duke's arm, thinking that she now had everything she'd ever dreamed of or wanted.

There'd still be problems. People wouldn't soon forget that Wynn Carson and Duke Bellini had been accused of double dealing. Their marriage would confirm some in that misconception. But, she reminded herself, It's a challenge, not trouble; excitement, not danger.

There was no problem too big for Wynn and Duke Bellini. Not anymore. Their love was strong enough to pull anything together. Whatever the game was, both sides would win.

# *Silhouette Intimate Moments*

## Available Now

### Serpent In Paradise by Stephanie James

At first Jase Lassiter had promised Amy paradise, offering her nights of love and days of sheer delight. But then she thought he'd betrayed her and she wondered if paradise would ever be found.

### A Season Of Rainbows by Jennifer West

Christopher Reynolds was a genius on the brink of realization—realization that beneath Lauren's cool exterior beat the heart of a woman waiting to be awakened by passion!

### Until The End Of Time by June Trevor

The private wilderness of Rafiki was Reed Kincaid's haven, until Elise brought the outside world to his door. He hadn't wanted to love again, but she was woman enough to change his mind.

### Tonight And Always by Nora Roberts

Kasey was an anthropologist, but her knowledge of men in general hadn't prepared her for one man in particular: Jordan. Together they did research for his novel, and found something even more precious than knowledge.

# _Silhouette_
## _Intimate_ 🖤 _Moments_
### more romance, more excitement
## Special Introductory Offer $1 75 each

# Get 6 new Silhouette Special Editions every month for a 15-day FREE trial!

**Free Home Delivery, Free Previews, Free Bonus Books.** Silhouette Special Editions are a new kind of romance novel. These are big, powerful stories that will capture your imagination. They're longer, with fully developed characters and intricate plots that will hold you spellbound from the first page to the very last.

Each month we will send you six exciting *new* Silhouette Special Editions, just as soon as they are published. If you enjoy them as much as we think you will, pay the invoice enclosed with your shipment. **They're delivered right to your door with never a charge for postage or handling, and there's no obligation to buy anything at any time.** To start receiving Silhouette Special Editions regularly, mail the coupon below today.

## Silhouette Special Edition

# Silhouette Desire
# 15-Day Trial Offer
## A new romance series
## that explores
## contemporary relationships
## in exciting detail

**Six Silhouette Desire romances, free for 15 days!**
We'll send you six new Silhouette Desire romances
to look over for 15 days, absolutely free! If you decide
not to keep the books, return them and owe nothing.

**Six books a month, free home delivery.** If you like
Silhouette Desire romances as much as we think you
will, keep them and return your payment with the
invoice. Then we will send you six new books every
month to preview, just as soon as they are published.
You pay only for the books you decide to keep, and
you never pay postage and handling.